MARGANA
2025

MAR
GA
NA
2024

a CRIMSON RIDGE CHRISTMAS

ALSO BY ELLIOTT ROSE

Crimson Ridge
Chasing the Wild
Braving the Storm
Taming the Heart
Saving the Rain

A Crimson Ridge Christmas
Bouquets & Buckles
Saddles & Snowfall

Mistwood Falls
Winter Wishlist

Port Macabre
Vengeful Gods
Macabre Gods

Nocturnal Hearts
Sweet Inferno
In Darkness Waits Desire
The Queen's Temptation
Vicious Cravings
Brutal Birthright

KENSINGTON
PUBLISHING CORP.

kensingtonbooks.com

KENSINGTON BOOKS are published by:

Kensington Publishing Corp.
900 Third Avenue
New York, NY 10022

kensingtonbooks.com

First Kensington deluxe trade paperback printing: November 2026

ISBN 978-1-4967-6065-4 (trade paperback)

10 9 8 7 6 5 4 3 2 1

Printed in China

eISBN: 978-1-4967-6643-4 (ebook)

Interior design by Kelsy Thompson

Character art by Marta García Navarro

Images courtesy of Adobe Stock, Noun Project, and Wikimedia Commons

The authorized representative in the EU for product safety and compliance
is eucomply OU, Parnu mnt 139b-14, Apt 123
Tallinn, Berlin 11317, hello@eucompliancepartner.com

For a full list of content warnings, scan below:

For those who don't want a lot for
Christmas . . . other than a hot cowboy,
and multiple orgasms.

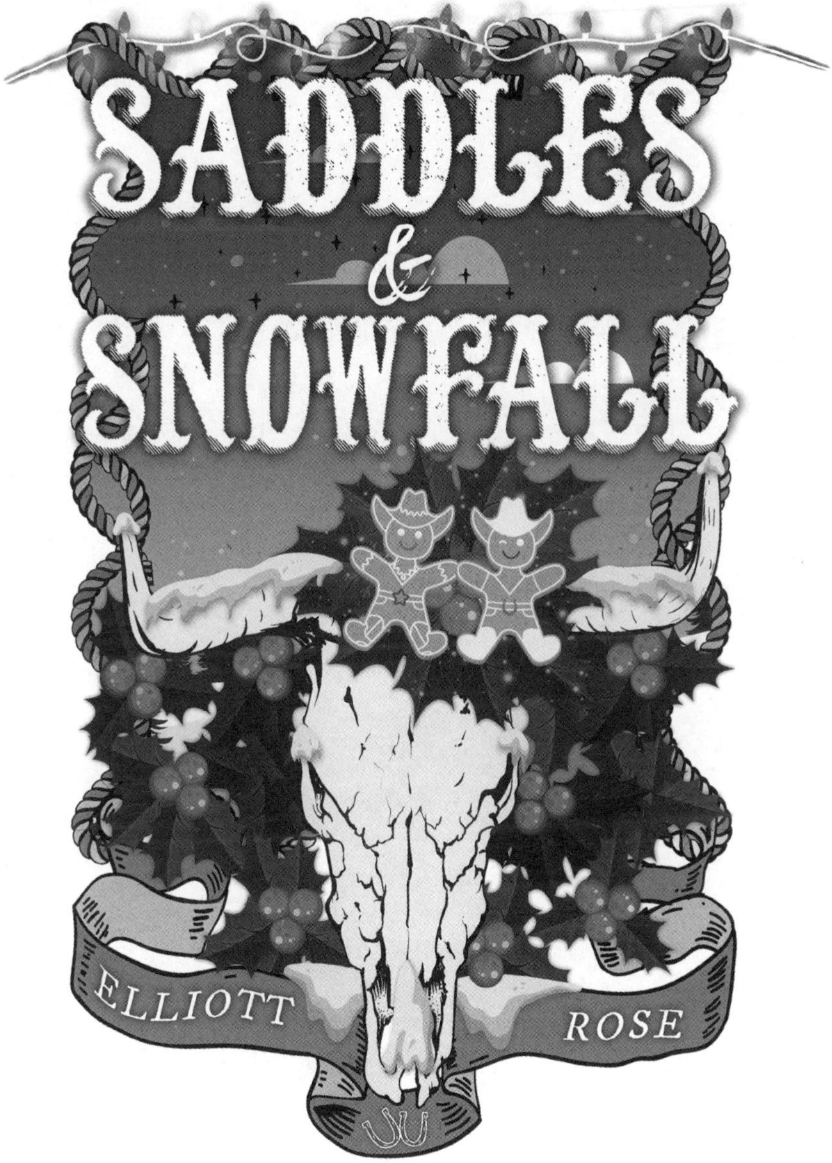
SADDLES
&
SNOWFALL
ELLIOTT
ROSE

CHAPTER 1

Brad

"I'm telling you, her donut has been glazed by him all year."

"*Noooo.* You can't be serious?"

Two blond freshmen in matching Santa hats giggle loudly from the kitchen, wearing not much more than a garland of flashing lights, red bikinis, and faux fur boots between them. They stumbled in here after me, already far too *merry* to even notice my presence or the December chill.

I'm hidden away, ransacking the pantry like a swaying Christmas racoon, hunting for the stash of solo cups I was assured would be in here. The first task in my quest to reign supreme at beer pong and enjoy a blow out, now that college is done and I'm officially graduated.

That's right, this cowboy has officially leveled up. *Art major, motherfuckers.*

Although, distinguishing my Monets from my Manets is worth fuck all at this particular moment. I squint and search through the chaos of this student kitchen, relying solely on the flashlight from my phone. Typical frat house vibes abound. The light bulb overhead has blown, everything is covered in crumbs, and nothing has a hope in hell of living where it should.

Doesn't matter—my buzz is starting to settle nicely in my

veins, and midway through my intrepid search, I discover a jar stuffed full of Christmas cookies. Not just any old cookies, either. These are all shaped like cocks, complete with jaunty little Santa hats made out of red and white icing. *Decorated dongs. Frosted frenulums. Sugared shafts.*

Why, yes, please and thank you. It's been far too long on a diet of pussy this year, and now that I'm single again, I'm not gonna lie . . . my horniness for getting with a guy has reached peak bisexual disaster mode.

Music thumps through the walls as I smirk and chomp down on a very well- endowed holiday johnson and his Jacob's Ladder, continuing in my quest for the elusive stack of cups.

Can anyone blame me? There's a cute guy out there with "fuck me" eyes who was interested in a party game where the point is getting sloppy drunk in record time. The shots I've already knocked back with him have set the tone just nicely for a night of being on Santa's naughty list. Or bouncing in his lap.

From just around the corner, the two girls are still gossiping and shrieking with laughter, their overly loud, drunk voices floating across the room easily.

"I swear on my Louboutins. Saw her getting out of his car and everything. No college student is in a professor's ride at five a.m. unless there's been wiener-in-bun action."

Snorting to myself, I take another chomp of my Frosty the Pierced Schlong and smirk. That is absolutely the truth. Everyone on campus knows the rules . . . Something about too many past scandals, professors being unable to keep it in their pants, *blah blah*. Academic policy gets damn near tattooed on the inside of your eyelids during freshman orientation. The staff are here for one thing and one thing only.

Sounds like whoever their friend is forgot to give her pussy the memo.

"Girl, that's so scandalous. You'd be kicked out for even

sniffing around one of the faculty members. The D must be premium if Izzie would risk her whole graduation."

I pause midway through shoving stacks of reused takeout containers to one side.

Did she just say Izzie?

As in the same name as my extremely recently *ex*-girlfriend? A person who I'd tolerated being in frankly the shittiest relationship I could have ended up stuck in with, for months on end. *Izzie*, who I should really have ended things with way earlier in the year but kept giving second chances to, because I'm a bleeding fucking heart . . . *That* Izzie?

Drunk girl number one hiccups and then drops the bomb. "Oh my god, and it gets worse. She's just outside, and I know I've had one too many Jell-O shots, but I swear I saw Brad here tonight. How's that gonna be for awkward if they run into each other . . . Bet he doesn't know Iz has been putting in *extra credit* all year, and that's why she broke things off with him . . . if you know what I'm saying."

Oh, hell no.

What the fuck?

The lying, cheating . . . *Ughhhhh.*

I shove the rest of the cookie in my mouth and can't even be fucked with coming up with a creative way to scathingly curse my ex out. She's old news, and any tiny lingering fragments of worry about whether I didn't make enough effort, about whether I was the problem, just shriveled up.

Tequila and recklessness have the reins when I spy the stack of red cups jammed in the furthest corner of the topmost shelf.

I've already made my decision.

Tonight, I'm gonna have myself a game of beer pong and secure a sweaty, X-rated night with someone who is down for the idea of no-strings-attached fucking merriment.

Happy Christmas orgasm cornucopia to me.

With all the swagger of a sailor at sea, including a brief bounce off the doorframe when my shoulder collides with solid wood, I reemerge into the kitchen. The gossip queens have disappeared—thank god.

Before I can go on the hunt for Blue Eyes, my phone pings in my hand.

Sky:
Don't miss me too much tonight!

Can't wait to be done with finals. I'm ready to never have to look at a textbook again.

I'm nowhere near drunk enough.

Apparently Izzie was cheating on me all year?

WHAT?

Just found out. So . . . happy holidays?!

My best friend since middle school is the lucky recipient of a blurry selfie. One where I'm biting down on another dick cookie, with the balls still clearly visible at the base.

Can't you come and save me from this clusterfuck?

First off . . . I hope she steps in dog shit daily for the rest of her life, that a terrible bleach job fries her hair so bad it falls out, and that her pillow is hot on both sides every night.

And I'm sorry, baby boy. You know I would be there to help you drown your sorrows in a heartbeat, but I gotta stay up late cramming for tomorrow.

I'm not even upset, just pissed off at myself. Why did I waste so much time on her?

Now I'm out here trying to get laid, and I'm in a stupid festive fucking costume and everything.

Of course you are. Brad Rhodes would never violate a party dress code.

Points for looking cute! Who would've thought an ugly Christmas sweater could look good on a cowboy?

I look ridiculous.

But green brings out the forest tones in your eyes . . .

Whatever. Pinky promise you're gonna get wasted with me at that stupid fancy Yule Ball.

Right now, I need an entire bowl of party punch and a cute guy's balls in my mouth to solve all my problems.

"Oh my god, you're taking forever, Rhodes." A girl's voice interrupts me before my best friend's reply rolls in. Blinking at her, I realize she was part of the group who wanted to play beer pong. *Shit.* Forgot about her.

"Did you miss me?" I flash a grin and wiggle the last piece

of cookie before chomping down on the last bite. Yeah, I'm definitely not gonna pump the brakes where my search for a hot guy and his *package* are concerned.

She gives me a coy little look in return and reaches out to lift the stack of cups from my hold. "I think more than one of us was missing your pretty face." Her thick lashes flutter, accentuating the glitter coating her cheekbones and eyelids. With a little swish of her head to one side, the Santa hat she's wearing bobs.

I know that look.

I'm in the mood for *that look*.

Reaching forward, I tug gently on the white tuft on the end of her hat. "More than one of you, huh?"

She runs her tongue over bright red lipstick and nods. "My friend thinks you're hot."

"And what do you think?" I'm still holding onto the end of her hat, and I roll the furry bobble beneath my fingertips.

Her cheeks flush a little as her lips twist. "I'd say if anyone can look as sexy as you while wearing a Christmas sweater . . . then I'm extremely invested in seeing what they look like *without* it."

I let my eyes drop down her body appreciatively, taking in the sight of a bright crimson corset and matching frilly skirt. She kinda looks like a figure skater who booked a taxi straight from the North Pole.

"And you'd want your friend to be there too? He'd be interested in seeing what's under both this slutty excuse for a skirt *and* my silly little sweater?"

"*Mmmhmm.*" She bites down on the swell of her bottom lip. Nodding slowly.

Right now, I don't give a shit that I can't remember her name. I don't even care if who she's talking about is the guy with blue eyes or not. I'm very much into the idea of whatever depravity this is, even if it's an unexpected proposition in the middle of a party in a random student house's kitchen.

I mean, threesomes don't turn up and flutter their eyelashes at you every day.

"Wanna play a game first?" I let my fingers drift down to the plastic cups and give them a flick.

"How about we go upstairs and play a private game?" she counters.

"Deal." I'm not even gonna pretend to be uninterested in that idea.

"I'll get my friend. You grab a bottle . . ." She jerks her head in the direction of a selection of liquor sitting out on the kitchen counter. "And meet us upstairs. Second room on the left." A wink and a cute little kiss blown my way are her last promises before she disappears.

Fuck yes.

I shove my phone in my back pocket and grab more tequila. Let me get obliterated and enjoy both a guy and a girl for a whole lot of no-strings-attached fun.

Thank you, Santa. I've obviously been a very good boy this year after all.

CHAPTER 2

Brad

Stick a bow on me and call me a GIFT.

Forget everything I said.

I'm about to have myself a very joyous threesome.

Sky:
What the hell, B? You're gonna give me whiplash.

Two minutes ago you were talking about cheating exes . . .

Now you're leaping into a game of naked Twister?

I smirk and take another sip of tequila straight from the bottle as I sway just inside the open doorway to the darkened bedroom. A bitter burn races down my throat, and I clench my teeth then let out a hiss while liquid fire tracks straight down to my stomach.

Second room on the left. Here I am.

Horny, tick. Festive, tick. Veins lit up with alcohol and anticipation like the Rockefeller tree, oh yeah. I'm more than ready to be extra nasty tonight.

The others aren't here yet, so I continue bugging Sky over text—and okay, maybe gloating just a little about this unexpected turn of events while I'm at it—since she's being *booooring* and studying and all.

And *boring* sounds a lot like *sensible.*

Squinting, I make an attempt to re-read her words written on the screen. As I do so and hover in place, a moment of far-too-sober clarity descends on me. Crap. Maybe this is too reckless? Am I seriously planning to jump into bed with a pair of total strangers just because I found out my ex-girlfriend is a cheat and a liar a few minutes ago?

I'm not that guy.

I'm a hopeless romantic.

I fucking love romance.

That's the way I'm wired and probably explains everything about why I stuck around in a relationship that was going nowhere.

I love the idea of love, okay? Sue me.

Wait . . . should I?

Or is this "diving headfirst out of a plane without a chute" level of dumbass?

Well, when have you ever turned down a party?

So, what I'm hearing is that you're enabling me to be a slut?

Yes. One hundred percent.

Do some shots.

Get a whole lot of slutty.

Suck some cock.

Who's the slutty one now?

God knows I haven't had the chance lately.

At least one of us should be getting some dick before the semester finishes.

A soft light flicks on, bathing this unfamiliar bedroom in a warm glow.

"*Uhh.* Hi—" From across the room, a deep voice is followed by a clearing of a throat.

I nearly drop my phone at the sight of the absolute smoke show filling the doorway. He has a beer in hand, a slight furrow on his brow, and I do a rapid-fire inhale of everything about him.

He's insanely hot. Stupidly so. The sort of solid build that screams football scholarship, except he's too old for college. Nor is he dressed like a typical jock. In fact, the Wranglers clinging to his muscled thighs and flannel shirt he's wearing scream country boy. He's even wearing scuffed boots that aren't too dissimilar to my own.

Add in the tousled blond hair and strong stubbled jaw presenting themselves and, well, there's no stopping my eyes from raking hungrily over him from head to toe. The prospect of *this* is goddamn mouthwatering.

Well, shit. All thoughts of that other dude from downstairs fly straight out my head.

Goodbye. See you never. Instant upgrade alert.

I'm gonna owe a massive thank-you to my brazen friend in the frilly skirt for finding a third member for this party who is exactly the type of man I go weak at the knees for.

It all happens in a blink.

One second, I'm eye-fucking him into next week, and the next I've successfully lost the tequila, tossed my phone on the bed, and launched myself at him . . . all before I could say, "Hey there, cowboy."

My fists curl into the front of his shirt, and oh my god, the warmth of him seeping through the worn fabric beneath my fingers is so damn magnetic. He smells like the night air . . . fresh . . . masculine . . . sending a coil winding tight and low in my stomach.

"Fuck, you're hot," I murmur, spellbound, eyes locked on his mouth, before I simply just *take*.

Sky's advice rings in my ears, giving me a surge of unbridled confidence to slam our mouths together as I drag him further into the room.

Get a whole lot of slutty.

He might be wider and broader and thicker set than me, but his powerful frame follows my lead all too easily. I continue tasting his lips, with glimpses of hops from his beer and mint lingering there, as I shove him backward against the wall.

Something rattles with the force of the two of us stumbling together. And it makes me let out a small growl of satisfaction that he's allowing me to immediately take the upper hand.

Lapping my tongue against his, I press forward, demanding entry into his mouth. To my horny delight, he fucking lets me, allowing me past the seam of his lips. The second I give that silent request, our tongues slide together.

Kissing him, a total stranger, somehow doesn't feel weird. In fact my entire body lights up at the feeling of his broad chest beneath my curled knuckles. I'm soaking in every tiny detail of the way his shirt feels softened from repeated wear, and the woodsy scent of him crawls into my brain.

He tastes so good and smells amazing, and my dick is absolutely *aching*. Blood rapidly flows south and I'm lengthening inside my jeans, eager as fuck.

The tequila is in control.

My hands have their own agenda.

Lust fuels me to go harder, to be entirely uninhibited, to be completely reckless.

I'm racing forward without pause, spurred on by how desperate I am. Fixated on wanting to know exactly what he's got going on beneath that tightly fitted denim.

Without wavering in the way I'm kissing him, I allow my hungry touch to delve lower between our bodies. Pushing beneath the hem of his shirt, blindly seeking out his waistband, I start working his belt buckle.

His stomach caves as I brush up against the scattering of hair dusting low on his stomach. My gorgeous stranger hisses into my mouth.

I chuckle and tear at his jeans. "Let's get this party fucking started. You seriously have no right walking around looking this sexy." He's not doing anything to stop me, and that turns everything even more feral.

When my palm snakes inside his boxer briefs and wraps around his hardening cock, he shudders, surrendering a delicious groan.

Oh, hell to the yes. He's smooth and velvety beneath my fingers and I wedge my hand as far down as possible to grasp the base of him. Tugging with a few forceful strokes, I jack him beneath the fabric and kiss him ruthlessly.

It's insanely hot, and I don't even fucking care that the girl isn't here yet.

This is a special type of Christmas package, one I'm in no mood for waiting to unwrap.

I need to taste him, right fucking now.

CHAPTER 3

Flinn

What the fuck. What the fuck. What the fuck.

All my brain cells are in my dick as a ridiculously hot stranger gives me a hand job and kisses me with the desperation of a sailor just returned from being stranded at sea.

It's . . . unexpected. Unexplainable. Unbelievable.

I knew campus parties were wild. Of course, I did. You don't need to go to college to understand that. So I didn't come here tonight expecting anything less than witnessing a whole lot of drunken foolishness. Especially with it being graduation and the holidays all sloshed together into one alcohol-soaked barrel.

But none of *those* reasons is why I'm here.

I didn't come here tonight for anything related to partying—I came here to look for *her*. That's the task I'm supposed to be focused on.

And yet, all of that has flown straight outta my head. I'm frozen in place, hypnotized by this guy and his confidence and the kind of roguish smirk that stalled my heart inside my chest the second he laid eyes on me. As if he took one glance and claimed me as his property.

I shouldn't like that feeling as much as I apparently do.

He pumps me a couple more times and it's almost impossible

to contain my groan when it's evident there's wetness there. I feel it at the same time he discovers it—precum smeared beneath his fingers. Those wicked lips of his smirk triumphantly against mine as his thumb swipes over my tip, giving me a dark noise of satisfaction. He's successfully reduced me to a horny mess within such a frantically short space of time, and he knows it too.

I'm leaking far too eagerly beneath his hold, simply turned upside down and inside out by the fact he's too much like my perfect sort of weakness.

"Goddamn, you're kinda slutty, too, huh?" Mystery Guy says, purring into my mouth, then proceeds to bite my bottom lip while shoving my jeans and briefs down. Relief floods my veins and heat pools low in my groin the second my dick springs free.

"You just kissed me?" I gasp for breath—this guy has somehow stolen all the air from my lungs. He's done a hell of a lot more than *kiss me*, but corralling my sensibilities to weakly protest is difficult enough as it is.

"Problem?"

"What the hell . . . You can't just go around doing shit like that . . . Kissing people if they don't want to be kissed." My words stammer out, the lies that they are. Because I do, in fact, want him to keep his mouth on mine. In a way I can't even begin to explain.

Another of those fucking smirks lights his face up. "Then why are you hard?"

"You shoved your hand in my pants . . ."

A self-satisfied grin takes over his expression, entirely unremorseful. "*Mmmm*, yeah, I did."

He leans forward to brush his lips over mine again. Thank fuck.

"Judging by the way you keep throbbing in my hand, I'm pretty sure you're enjoying it, too."

"Just. . ." This is nuts. I don't know what to say. It's insane and kinda overwhelming, but even though it's too much, I'm also finding myself unable to settle on a good enough reason to put a halt to this. Wherever this is racing toward, apparently I'm far too interested in discovering our destination to do anything about it.

He clocks my hesitation, winking at me.

"You never hooked up with a guy before, cowboy?"

With an arched eyebrow, those green eyes of his transform, pupils blowing out as he looks down at my cock standing thick and erect between us.

"*Umphfff.* I—" Any attempt to reply is cut off as his fist closes around me and goddamn *squeezes*. My eyes roll back in my head and words vacate my mind. This time when he strokes me, his grip is tighter than before. It's like he enjoys the fact I'm left panting, rendered unable to speak, with his closed palm tugging on me oh so fucking perfectly.

Hard. Fast. Ruthless.

Holy shit.

I can't get enough of this warm, tingling sensation building low in my stomach. This heady blend of doing something so wanton—with a complete stranger, no less—is unlocking a side of me I didn't know existed.

"*Aw*, you're shy. That's okay." He nips my bottom lip again, leaving a delicious sting blooming beneath the pinch of his teeth.

Everything turns hot and frantic. My hips lift involuntarily, chasing his touch. That subtle reaction must do something to cinch the rope tight, to have him going all in, because he moves with swift precision. His hand wrapped around me only half a second ago is now shoving the front of my jeans a little lower.

"Never done this before, huh?" As he hums out ravenous, urgent words, my mystery guy drops to his knees.

Jesus. Fuck.

What is even happening? He can't possibly be about to do this—cannot possibly *want* to do this?

My brain short-circuits. A thick haze crowds the edges of my vision. This all feels too good. I have nothing to offer up, except for a whole lot of overeager breathy noises and a stifled groan.

"Fuck, you've got a nice cock." His exhale gusts over the head of my dick, and I lose the battle to stop myself from making a choked noise. Desperation and foolishness collide in the back of my throat and I want this so fucking bad.

He doesn't give me enough time to catch up with the fucking game plan. Before I can register what's happening, he sinks forward.

His hot, wet mouth is on me, and I goddamn moan.

I. Moan.

"*Unghhh. Fffuckkk.*" My head collides with a thud against the wall at the first soul-stealing sensation of him closing his lips around my crown. His tongue presses and explores, running along the underside, tracing the veins there, sucking me eagerly . . . Jesus.

I've never had someone want me this openly, with so much hunger in their energy. I'm torn between the urge to stay just like this, with my eyes scrunched closed while I savor each second his mouth is on me, and the urge to simply stare at him in awe, to watch him suck me and not miss a moment.

Part of me is terrified that if I take a peek at him, it'll all be over. Like I'll scare this dream guy away and he'll vanish.

The other part of me is falling apart with the need to know what it looks like when he dips forward and, oh my god, when his tongue drags and swirls at the same time as he hollows his cheeks.

"Oh god. Holy fuck." I gasp and the near-empty beer I've been clinging onto hits the carpet. My hands fly to his hair, sinking into the soft, unruly mess of curls. A move far too intimate, far too desirous for a dirty blow job while a party rages downstairs, but I'm galloping recklessly into the night.

He hums in response to me touching him for the first time.

And that approving noise tumbles us into a place we can't come back from. The muffled grunt he lets out as I tighten my hold on his head is everything.

I want that. I want more. I want him to take me deep.

God, I just fucking *want.*

Those noises he keeps making send the most intense vibrations shooting along me, straight down to land with a heavy thud in my balls.

As if he can read my mind, he grips my thighs harder. Holds onto me just as firmly as I'm grasping him . . . and lets me hit the back of his throat.

He swallows around my tip, and I nearly goddamn buckle on the spot.

CHAPTER 4

Brad

This is wild.

The hottest guy I've ever fucking seen tastes like a Christmas miracle. Not to mention, he comes complete with a cock I would do very questionable things to ensure I get an opportunity to play with more than just this once.

Sweet Jesus. He's thick and veiny and makes my mouth water.

Thank fuck, because I'm drunk and horny and I haven't made out with a guy in a minute. This goddamn Adonis is seriously doing something for me, so it only makes sense to let myself have a little bit of private fun first.

He feels incredible, heavy on my tongue, feeding me bursts of precum like a reward for my service. Christ, I'm getting more and more turned on the longer I continue sucking him like this.

Partly, in the back of my mind, there's a hint of awareness that flashes brighter than a cherry-red festive light bulb. A very specific sort of arousal that comes with feeling like someone might walk through that open door any second. And yeah, that's a hot prospect and all, I won't deny it, but that's not the real reason I'm hard as steel inside my jeans.

It's the thought of making him lose it in a few short minutes.

To greedily take his climax all for myself.

To succeed in undoing him and having him in secret *before* this turns into a three-way.

That idea, right there, leaves my blood turning white hot.

As I swallow around the crown of him again and again, he keeps shuddering and making these raspy, groaning noises. Like he's trying really fucking hard to keep quiet and to act like he's not enjoying this as much as he is.

The drunker, hornier, brattier side of me comes out to play.

I come from rodeo stock.

I fucking love nothing more than a challenge.

He can be broody and silent and gorgeous all he likes. But he's no match for my mouth, and tongue.

"*Umphhff.* Oh . . . oh, god." His gasp is raw, unleashed into this quiet room, while bass thumps from downstairs. This time he doesn't catch those noises of pleasure before they escape, and I'm entirely focused on making him come. I've never been so determined to make someone lose their mind. There's just something about witnessing such a stocky, strong guy melt like this. As if no one has treated him so attentively before.

The musky scent of him fills my senses. Hints of his eagerness continue to leak and coat my tongue. Strong fingers tug on my hair to the point it stings, and it could be entirely the tequila's fault, but I'm more than a little obsessed.

I keep teasing him, ruthlessly pursuing every single one of those attempts not to straight up moan out loud.

That's it, you beautiful wall of muscle. Turn into a shaking, pleading mess for me.

With each suck and bob forward to take him deep, I can tell he's getting close.

He tightens his fingers in my hair and actively chases my mouth now. "Holy fuck. Holy fuck. *Holy fuck.*"

That's it. There he is. I swirl my tongue and hollow my cheeks and moan around him as he throbs on my tongue.

"Oh god. You . . . you have to stop. I'm gonna—" He tries to push against me in warning.

My muffled moan is louder in response. I suck him down as far as possible, and his hips stall. He swells, pulses, and unloads on my tastebuds. *Fuck yes.* The tangy saltiness of him fills my senses as he blows down my throat. I swallow his cum eagerly, enjoying every breathless, shuddering reaction as his dick twitches.

Taking my time, I lick him clean. With his softening cock still in my mouth, I seek out his eyes, and the expression on his face is one of complete awe and shock. Definitely the face of a guy who's never been sucked properly before.

Drawing back, I let him slip from my mouth and flash a knowing grin.

"*Mmmm.* Don't worry, there's plenty more where that came from. Once that girl walks in, I'm sure you'll find your rhythm again. We can start without you. I'm sure it won't take you much to get back in the game."

His face morphs, brows knitting together, and his muscles tense. "Girl? What girl?" He lets go of my hair and fumbles to tuck himself away. "Wait . . . Izzie?"

It's my turn to freeze. My already-racing pulse skyrockets, and I jerk back. "Why the fuck did you just say her name?" Scrambling to my feet, I drag the back of my hand across my mouth. "What the hell is going on?"

Mystery guy has an unreadable expression when he stares at me. "That's why I came up here. She told me she'd meet me upstairs . . ."

I don't let him finish. I don't even want to know what the rest of that sentence might be. "Are you the prick who's been fucking her?" I get in his face.

His lip curls and hazel eyes flare to a shade of liquid fire. "Gross. What the hell, man? That's my sister you're talking about."

A faint ringing consumes my hearing. I stumble back a step.

Tequila and horniness and the taste of his cum linger on my tastebuds.

Sister?

"Christ. No. What in the fuck . . ." Shoving one hand through my hair, I scrub the other over my mouth. Taking a few steps across the room, it feels like the room is spinning. "Oh my god." I turn to stare back at him with wide eyes, trying and failing to get my shit together.

He looks back at me, confusion and maybe a hint of dawning realization there on his features, too.

"Wait . . . you know my sister?"

CHAPTER 5

Flinn

Steaming water beats like a drum between my shoulder blades. Keeping my chin tucked, I press my palms harder against the tiny shower wall. Soap bubbles swirl around my feet as a procession of suds disappear down the drain.

There's a shipwreck of pink-packaged hair products, exfoliating scrubs, and bodywashes littering the floor. At least *one* brand was unscented; all the others brought an onslaught of feminine florals when I opened them one by one to conduct a sniff test.

My sister's roommate and her share this house on campus. I arrived, took one look around, and it was no wonder why she had begged me to come help her shift home once she's finished her last exam.

They've done exactly *zero* packing.

Apparently being the older brother with a horse trailer and a flexible schedule suddenly makes me a hot commodity. Or at least, when moving two hundred miles away is required, that is. Izzie didn't bother to text back for nearly the entire year, then she blew up my phone a week ago.

Of course, as much as I probably *should*, there was no way I could ignore her. I'm too much of the protective big brother to say no to either of my younger sisters. Don't even get me started on the baby of the family. Clara has me wrapped around her little bookworm finger.

As I linger under the pounding water, rivulets running down my chin and neck, this position brings back an overwhelming flood of memories from that night. I'd hardly been in town for five minutes—pulled up and attempted to find my sister at that damn party so I could get the house key off her—when my world was turned upside down.

My throat bobs as I stare at my thickening cock, and all I see is the way his lips wrapped around me. A ghost of intense pleasure shoots along my dick as I recall the way he hollowed his cheeks, sucking me deeper. His forest-green eyes are right fucking there, watching me with mischief and lust, determined to blow my brain apart in record time. Which he did, all too successfully, and now I'm horribly broken . . . because there's every possibility I can't get the thought of my sister's boyfriend out of my brain.

It's enough to have me losing my mind. Even though it's been a few days since the party, I've found myself doing a double take at any guy with scruffy dark hair and a cheeky, confident swagger.

The basest, greediest part of me wants to somehow see him again, and yet, I also know it would be the worst possible idea. Especially after how fast he bolted. As soon as the realization dawned on him—of who Izzie is in relation to me—he took off like a rocket.

I've got no business having a lingering obsession on the guy my sister has been banging all year.

Yeah, that thought leaves me squeezing my eyes closed and fumbling to turn the water off. I'm resolutely ignoring the fact that my cock demands I give in and get off to imagining what it might be like to do *more* with him.

"That's way too messed up," I mutter to myself as I step out of the shower and start to towel off. "Get a fucking grip."

I've just dropped the world's smallest, pinkest towel when the bathroom door flings open, slamming on its hinges—a door that, of course, doesn't have a lock.

"I'm not looking. I'm not looking. But I'm gonna pee myself if I gotta cross my legs any longer." Izzie's roommate stumbles in, holding both palms up as if I'm some sort of phallic eclipse she's trying to shield her eyes from. She's wearing only a baggy T-shirt, last night's makeup has formed racoon eyes, and her hair is a rat's nest.

"Oh my god, Lawson . . ." The blood drains from my face as I try to somehow swipe the towel up off the floor without putting my dick at half-mast on display. "What the actual fuck?" Even when I snatch the pink terry cloth up, it covers nothing. It's the size of an actual postage stamp.

She ignores me and carries on. Sitting on the toilet, peeing in front of me, while flapping a dismissive hand in my direction. "Don't be a prude. *That* is nothing I haven't seen before. Besides, you're into dudes, so what do you care?"

The tips of my ears burn. "It's called privacy." My fucking clothes are on the vanity on the other side of her, and there's no way I can get to them without giving her a full frontal.

"*Mmm*, pretty sure that word doesn't exist in college vocab—*ugh,* my head feels like it's gonna explode. Shoulda stopped chasing shots with . . . more shots. But I never learn. *Gross.*" She sticks her tongue out and makes a face.

I'm trapped in the world's tiniest bathroom, beside a hungover woman happily peeing in front of an audience, with a fluffy pink towel fisted in both hands as my only line of defense in covering my junk. Right about now is when I'd gladly be swallowed up by the floor.

And just at that moment, the doorbell goes off.

She locks bleary eyes with mine, looking green around the gills. "Please answer that. Tell them to go away . . . unless they have burgers and a crispy Diet Coke. Then they can come on in. But my brain can't handle this kind of torture."

I don't even have time to argue or at least ask her to hurry the fuck up and leave so I can get dressed in peace. The doorbell rings more insistently this time.

"*FLINN*," she squawks. "*Please.* Just get your ass out there and deal with it." The blaring chimes fill the house on repeat as she scrunches her face up and whines about how much vodka she soaked her liver in last night.

"Give me goddamn horses any day of the week. This is *not* how I planned to start my morning," I mutter while having to ever so carefully inch past her, and I end up awkwardly jumping from foot to foot while pulling my sweats on in the open doorway. Buck naked. Trying and definitely failing in my attempts not to give her an eyeful of balls or ass.

The doorbell screeches loudly again and she lets out a pained yelp. "I'm literally dying over here. Iz has gone to the library to study. You gotta take one for the team."

"*Fine.* Jesus." Tossing the towel over the hook, I fumble for my glasses and slip them on as I jog to the front door, wet hair and all.

Now there's knocking—actually more like an insistent hammering—which is completely unnecessary. What is this? The king's fucking debt collectors hounding villagers for their taxes?

"I'm coming. Jeez—" Wrenching the door open, I nearly butt foreheads with the guy standing there with his fist raised, mid-knock.

Messy dark hair beneath a cap.

Perfect cheekbones.

Forest-green eyes.

My dirty fantasy I've been lost in for days on end.

CHAPTER 6

Brad

"This is total bullshit," I mumble into the phone as I juggle the enormous bag of my ex-girlfriend's crap and make my way along the snowy sidewalk.

Sky hums distractedly on the other end of the call. "You're doing the *right* thing returning everything of hers. She might be a piece of shit and a cheating loser with a capital L, but you get to walk away from both college *and* this breakup knowing you were the bigger person. Fresh start, clear conscience, and all that."

"How did I end up with half of her fucking things at my place?"

A wry laugh tinkles down the line. "*Uhhh*, try because you were in a blissfully ignorant little relationship bubble, genius? That's what happens when you date someone, B. Things . . . *mingle*."

Snorting under my breath, I shake my head. Less than impressed with her early-morning sensibility. "I hear the innuendo all over that word, miss."

"Speaking of body parts and other things that mingle." Sky giggles and I roll my eyes. "Offload her shit, then get your ass over here to my place so we can plan what to wear this weekend. You and I both need to look hot as fuck, and that will require preplanning."

Yeah, there's one person I'd very much like to be reacquainted with in a way that involves horizontal intertwining and *mingling*, but that notion is entirely fucked up. I gotta forget that he even exists. Pretty sure I'll never see him again, anyway.

"Speak for yourself, ma'am," I tease. My best friend is too good to me. Forever putting up with my ribbing. "But consider me nothing but generous. I'll pour blood, sweat, and tears into giving *Skylar Addams* a Yule Ball–worthy glow-up. It'll take everything I've got, mind you."

"Oh, fuck you very much."

"Not everyone has this kind of naturally gifted, Rhodes-level genetic blessing."

The speaker rustles as she covers the receiver and splutters with a coughing fit in the background.

"Guess I've got a lot to thank my old man for, since he donated me the goods in the DNA department." As I get closer to the pathway leading to Izzie's house, I realize Sky has gone dead silent. "Hello? Are you still alive?"

"Yup," she says, popping the P sound. "Okay, just, whatever. Hurry up and remember to pick up a bagel and coffee for me on the way, or I'll throat punch you."

"Adore you, too. Bagels and coffee it is, but hold the throat punching, please. See you in about thirty." I hang up just as I reach the front steps.

While I'm tempted to dump all this shit outside and bail, I also very much do want to be the more mature one out of the two of us. I don't need to be accused of tossing her stuff in the trash if it gets stolen off her front porch—not when I've gone to all this fucking effort to bring it over here in the first place.

I jab the doorbell a couple of times in quick succession, a little aggressively for this time of the morning, but who gives a shit? Irritable is my middle name this week. Blame it on my overly horny state of mind. I've hardly slept since the night of the party, because there's one very off-limits slab of sex appeal I can't stop thinking about.

After a few attempts, I start knocking. It's not exactly early, but there's every chance either my ex or her roommate is still sleeping. Knowing Lawson, she'll be hungover as all hell and have some random guy in her bed.

I don't judge her for enthusiastically enjoying college, but the girl could learn to at least get a first name before leaping onto his dick.

As I lean forward, prepared to start pounding harder, I hear heavy footsteps and a deep voice on the other side. "I'm coming. Jeez—" The door swings open abruptly and I damn near fall through the entrance.

A whole expanse of bare chest greets me. My greedy eyes roam everywhere, from the bulge of naked shoulder muscles down to a scattering of golden hair dusted over firm pecs, then continuing on to take in the lowest-slung, sluttiest gray sweatpants I've ever been blessed to see from up this close. A trail of darker hair descends low, giving the runway to appreciate a prominent V just above the waistband. And that's when my attention flies up to the face of the mouthwatering specimen of virile masculinity filling the doorway.

He smells freshly showered, with blond hair looking slightly darker as it hangs damp and ruffled across his forehead.

My slow, distracted brain takes a minute to catch up. "You wear glasses?" My mouth goes dry. Fuck my life. He's gotta be fucking with me? No mere mortal should be allowed to be this hot. This must tip the balance of the universe off its axis or some shit? Too much hotness poured into one package must break some cosmic rule that exists somewhere.

"Normally, yeah." That way his voice stays gravely and slightly coarse, as if he's only just woken up, is stirring things in my body it has no business to.

Shut it down, Brad. This guy is your ex's brother. In no plane of reality is he someone you should continue to stare at open-mouthed.

Your ex's brother, who is half-naked . . . and still in town.

As I swallow rocks, I'm caught entirely off guard by colliding into him like this, in broad daylight and without warning. I ran off so damn fast at the party. In all honesty, not my finest moment, but who could blame me. It was all I could do to try and handle the reality of who he is, how we strangely connect and yet are simultaneously ill fitted within each other's worlds. Ultimately, the truth cannot be denied of how enormously fucked I am because I've been unable to stop dreaming about him ever since.

His brows do the frowning thing, and he looms there, immovable, blocking the doorway.

Okay. Whatever. I'm a cat on a hot tin roof and he looks lovingly hewn from marble. A Grecian God on a plinth in the Louvre. "It's barely thirty degrees out," I snap. "At least put a fucking shirt on."

"Why are you here? Following me around now?" He folds his arms, which only makes his biceps bulge and puffs his thick chest up more prominently.

Can't a guy catch a break?

I scoff, trying—and absolutely failing—to play it cool. Meanwhile, the back of my neck heats rapidly beneath my collar. "Please. Don't flatter yourself." That's the moment I remember to shove the bag toward him. "Look, I was packing up my place, and I found all this stuff belonging to your sister." Internally I cringe at the way that word tastes on my tongue. "Would've left it in the mailbox, but the bag is too big." The words rush out, narrowly avoiding getting tangled on my tongue.

As I gesture with the handle again, I catch sight of disheveled hair in my periphery. Lawson hovers near her bedroom, looking hungover as shit, wearing next to nothing.

"What's taking so long, Flinn?" she huffs.

My eyes pop wide, bouncing between the sight of him nearly naked and her . . . and the reason he took a hot minute to answer the door slams me sideways. The easiest of goddamn puzzle pieces slots into place. "Oh, well, don't let me interrupt you two." Bitter jealousy slithers a path down my throat.

He goes bright red, confirming that it's time for me to make a swift fucking exit. I don't care that he looks like he wants to climb out of his skin.

"Izzie isn't here." She scrunches her nose, like I'm some giant goddamn inconvenience, then spins on her heel and disappears into the bedroom. That girl is nothing but spoiled and bratty, so I don't give a crap if she likes me or not, but it makes my teeth grind that *this* is who he's getting his dick wet with.

"Go on. Don't let me stop whatever you two were getting up to," I hiss.

"It's not—it's not like that." He lifts one strong hand to rub his brow. All it does is put more of his thick-set, country-boy frame on display.

Isn't he cold standing here with hardly any clothes on? I have to work extra hard not to devour the sight of that V pointing toward his waistband.

"That's not . . . not anything." His throat dips.

Oh, right. Could this get any worse? He's midway through a meaningless quickie with the roommate. Nothing but a player. Just march me out back and put me outta my misery right now.

"It's nothing? Yeah, sure." I jut my chin in the direction of her room. "You literally let me put your dick in my mouth after like two seconds. I guess that tracks."

He makes a choked noise and quickly checks over his shoulder before hissing at me. "Sorry, but you were too busy undoing my jeans, drooling for my cock. I didn't exactly have time to explain anything to you." He reaches out, wrapping the handle of the bag in one fist.

"You could have said *no*." I don't release my hold on the bag.

He pulls it towards him. "You shouldn't have jumped me outta nowhere."

"Seems like you weren't interested in stopping anything." I refuse to give in, holding on tight, wrenching the handle back my way. "Guess I shouldn't be surprised. I sure know how to pick 'em, it seems."

"I . . . I just . . ." He's stammering, and it looks like his brain has stalled on the spot. The same hint of something unsure and endearing that I remember even through all the tequila haze from that night is front and center now, filling those hazel eyes. That part of him I couldn't quite put my finger on but seems almost . . . *naive.*

"Yeah. Too busy feeding me those little whimpers to put a stop to it, huh? I bet she hasn't sucked you properly."

"Screw you." He yanks on the bag once more and I tug right back.

"No. I bet you've *never* had your dick taken care of like that." As I lean forward, my voice stays low. "I bet you're still thinking about how hard you came down my throat. How I made you see stars and blow your load in all of a matter of seconds."

Color flushes high on his cheekbones, right below those sexy goddamn glasses framing his eyes. "*Don't.*" His Adam's apple bobs and goosebumps pepper his arms.

"It's alright." My smirk settles in place, satisfied that I've at least had some kind of effect on him. "Your secret is safe with me. You're just like all the men who think they're only interested in pussy but are sure eager as hell for a dude to suck them off."

Something flares in his eyes, not a feistiness, but a softness I wasn't quite expecting. "I promise, it's *nothing* like that."

Shaking my head, I let out a wry laugh and finally let go of the bag. Even though I don't want to walk away from him, I damn well have to, or I'm gonna do something irreversible and plain stupid, like try to kiss him again. "Sure, man," I call over my shoulder. "Keep your secrets. I'm outta here."

CHAPTER 7

Flinn

I don't know what I've done wrong this year to earn a pre-Christmas punishment of sleeping on my sister's couch while stalking her ex's social media . . . but here I am.

What I can confirm is that he's gorgeous, completely out of my league, and far too damn charming for his own good. It's not like I've got a vast amount of experience to use as a frame of reference here, but our run-in this morning left me feeling some kind of way.

Not even spending the afternoon biting my tongue while driving Izzie all over town—her being irritating as all hell while insisting on doing her Christmas shopping—was enough to erase how it felt to see him again. I mean, I'd been holding out for maybe a glimpse, with a flicker of hope in my little gay heart that I'd at least see some evidence of him before leaving town.

Kinda wanted to prove to myself he was actually real. Not some figment of my imagination.

Well, Brad Rhodes is, in fact, a walking, talking cowboy of my fantasies. And yet, I'm tossing and turning uncomfortably on the same couch where he's probably fucked my sister.

Oh my god. Just the thought of that makes my cheeks burn and my stomach clench.

On the phone screen in front of me is a whole intimate snapshot into his life. The tiniest crumbs of him that I'm inhaling as fast as possible, while being the most paranoid guy ever to lurk twelve months deep in an Instagram profile. For the love of rodeo, do not accidentally heart one of his posts from a year ago.

I'd have to change my name and flee the country.

Brad becomes more curious and captivating to me the more I scroll.

Art major. Rancher. Sushi lover.

When he's at home, apparently in a place called Crimson Ridge, he posts about horses nonstop. When he's at college, almost every second photo is of him and a petite ginger cat.

Other than all the animals he so obviously adores, there are a few taken with the same girl who sports pastel pink hair and tattoos. At first, I start to feel that curl of jealousy low in my stomach. Is she a hookup or another girlfriend? Then I scroll far enough to see that he captioned a selfie—two of them in his car pulling rockstar horns, with tongues sticking out—mentioning the fact that they've been besties for forever. Considering he's been dating my sister, I can't really be feeling any kind of way seeing photos of him with another girl.

One thing that becomes painfully clear to me is that I don't get how the fuck he ended up with my sister in the first place? It makes no sense. He and I . . . we've got so much more in common than she could ever possibly have with him. Aside from the most obvious—that I live and breathe horses and that he, from the looks of it, comes from ranching stock—Izzie literally hates the outdoors. She freaks out if even a smudge of dirt gets on her clothes. What the hell has she been playing at to be with a guy like him?

Scrolling dangerously deep in his profile history, I discover yet more photos of Brad with horses, and he's all smiles. Laughter and sun-kissed skin in abundant measure. His cowboy hat fixed in place while cuddling a glossy chestnut mare. God, he looks incredible. Wherever he is when he's not at college obviously suits him.

I swallow hard when I only have to swipe another couple of photos more and spot him wearing a branded Rhodes Ranch T-shirt. Am I a stalker if I look it up straight away? Probably. Definitely.

Wait, holy shit. *Rhodes* . . . As the search field populates, I already know that I've heard that name somewhere before.

A bounty of images pops up featuring rodeo riders, horse trainers, and stables. Leaving me quickly realizing that both Brad and his father Lucas Rhodes are, in fact, well known in the rodeo scene.

As I return to his Instagram, the image is set to stop my scroll, and my heart. A picture of Brad, only wearing the tightest of swimming trunks. He's deeply tanned—summer evidently loves his body—and I'm staring at his bare torso, the dusting of dark hair on his lower stomach and upper thighs, with mouth gone dry.

I glance furtively around the shadowy room, guilt filtering through my veins. As if I'm about to find either my sister or her roommate has crept up behind me and is snooping over my shoulder. Fortunately for my private moment of temptation, there's only me and the glow of my phone illuminating my chest and forearms.

Swallowing a lump in my throat, I realize something else isn't quite illuminated but is stirring to life. A very obvious physical response to seeing him dripping wet and practically naked on my phone screen and all those memories of his mouth and his eyes, and oh god, the inevitable happens. My dick leaps to attention.

This is so wrong on so many levels. Blood flows rapidly south and heat pools low in my stomach as an erection I should not be experiencing right now decides to override any rational thought. He's my sister's boyfriend. *Ex-boyfriend.* Jesus. The semantics don't exactly matter, because the fact that they were together means he's slept with her, and now here I am thinking about what his dick looks like.

Well, shit.

My cock jerks, flinching and filling rapidly until the fabric of my sweats is tented thanks to just how turned on I am at the memory of him. The way his tongue swirled, and his cheeks hollowed, and the goddamn overwhelming bliss of how incredible it felt. Nothing like a fumbling, cautious rub through layers of clothes. Nothing like lying alone in bed every night. Nothing like jerking myself off.

Brad knew exactly how to unravel me, and he went after my climax like it was something he wanted—no, had a right to. As if the act of me spilling down his throat was giving him as much pleasure as it was me . . . and oh hell, I'm in territory I can't possibly be entertaining thoughts of.

Everything aches, demanding relief. The throb of my rock-hard dick is an agony. Under no circumstances should I be moving my hand. Humiliation floods my cheeks with heat while I tentatively shift my grip on my phone, and my free hand drifts in the direction it really shouldn't. Shoving at the waistband, I push the material down, only to feel a rush of giddy, pulse-racing desire as the thickness of me bobs up. Hard and eager, my dick slaps against my lower stomach.

Jesus. I can't be considering doing *this* right here?

But as I internally debate the moral failings of touching myself with a certain cowboy front and center in my mind, I'm caught by the smirk on his face in the photo staring back at me. Like he's daring me through the phone screen. I can't stop thinking about how that same look transfixed me that night, and a shudder races through my limbs knowing that, for a brief moment in time, he gave me that same look.

For a frantic, breathtaking moment, I was the only person he stared at with that expression. He gave me that mischievous grin and sealed his mouth with mine, and fuck my life, what I would give to have him here right now.

How incredible would lying together on a couch like this be? A movie long forgotten in the background while we make out and I get to run my hands over him. Actually touching him was such a brief thing—I hardly remember consciously doing it, but he seemed to enjoy having my fingers tangled in his hair.

I liked the way that felt far too much. The intimacy of our bodies being connected. Of getting to push my fingers through his messy strands and feel the heat of him.

I'm done for. Officially lost to a dirty little scenario, where he climbs over my body right here on this couch. Our plans for whatever might have been playing on the TV screen in the background are entirely abandoned.

Brad hits me with a smirk that leaves my heart pounding, cock beginning to leak with anticipation of where this is headed. *Are we still watching?* Nope. The only thing I'm fixated on is the way he licks his lips, a man with pure hunger in his expression. The way he eyes me up exactly as he did that night—as if I'm someone worth savoring, worth going after, worth being with intimately.

He drops that smoking-hot gaze down to look at my straining cock and nudges at my hand still loosely gripped over the waistband now shoved down low on my groin. I give him what he wants. *Spit.*

Shame and a flood of tingling need are a potent mixture of emotions occupying my bloodstream right now. I lick a wet track of saliva across my palm and have to bite back a desperate noise as soon as I wrap my fist around the base of me.

My eyes want to flutter closed, but at the same time, the sight of Brad staring back at me in that photo, all bronzed and dripping wet and gorgeous, keeps me watching everything as it unfolds. There's no way I'm gonna last long. This is frantic, desperate, a driving need to satisfy the craving he's unleashed in me.

I start stroking, squeezing and pulling in a rhythm that mimics how his mouth bobbed back and forth to suck me down when he was on his knees. In my imagination, he watches me openly and enjoys the show I'm putting on for him all while bracing his weight over me.

It's written there in his roguish, sexy expression.

You're remembering everything, aren't you? The way my lips wrapped around you. How it felt when I swallowed around your tip. Just how slutty you were to have me suck you hard and deep.

I shuttle faster now, and the slick noise of wetness inside my fist sounds almost way too loud in this quiet, darkened room. A raw gasp escapes me as my movements speed up. With my mouth hanging open and those strokes turning frantic, those lewd, subtle noises are drowned out by the thumping heartbeat filling my ears. Tension surges straight down my spine. That coil winds tight, locking in ready for the moment this is going to end in something damn well explosive.

Brad sees it. Eats up every second I bite down on my bottom lip and struggle to contain the feral panting breaths I'm so close to accidentally letting out. I'm close, oh so fucking close, and he uses that moment to lean down.

My fist squeezes tight and tugs harder, just as my memory recalls how it felt for my dick to slip inside the heaven of his warm, wet mouth. The roar of my pulse takes over as I get swept up in a scenario where he adds his tongue and I fuck up into my fist and there's no stopping it. My balls draw up tight, throbbing with the need to come, and everything simply bursts with overeager need and want.

Thick ropes of cum paint my stomach and coat my fist. Beneath my grip, my dick pulses and pulses, shooting everywhere with so much force my release splashes up my chest. It's slick and filthy and made even more so by the knowledge that I just jacked off to a picture of my sister's ex-boyfriend.

They've had sex. Been dating all year. What am I doing thinking about him like this?

It's so completely and utterly messed up.

As my heart races and chest heaves, the glide of my fist slows. Stroking a few more times, I take in the sight of the mess I've made lit up by the soft glow from my phone screen. Everything about this is so wrong. I can't be fantasizing about him.

I've never been with a man, *properly*, so why is this now the fascination I can't rid myself of?

The thought of casual sex turns me off.

I've never wanted to randomly hook up with guys who weren't in it for something more meaningful, who weren't ready for an actual relationship. It's why I ended up in the stupid situation I did for way too long.

Looking down at the filthy evidence painting my overheated skin, I can't figure any of this out.

I've never been interested in something purely physical—or at least, I didn't think that was something I wanted—convinced I should find a guy who wanted to be with me for more than just sex.

So, why the hell did I let things go as far as they did with Brad?

More importantly, why did I do so without a second's hesitation . . . and enjoy it?

CHAPTER 8

Brad

"The hat's too much, isn't it?" As I take another look in the mirror, I straighten my cuffs and then readjust the wide brim.

"A cowboy in a suit ain't much of a cowboy without his hat." Sky slides up to my side, barely reaching my chest without her heels on, and presses a shot glass into my hand.

"You're sure?" Why am I overthinking this? It isn't usually my style to be concerned about other people's opinions, but I suppose there's been a whole lot of unsettled—and very much *unlike me*—energy swirling through my veins considering the events of the past week.

"No way." Her big smile lifts to meet mine as she clinks our glasses together. "You look fine as hell, Bradford Rhodes. A suit and a cowboy hat, goddamn. Watch out." She fans herself slowly with one hand before giggling and tipping the shot back.

I follow her lead, both of us scrunching our faces as the afterburn goes down. "What . . . the fuck . . . is that? Pure cinnamon poison?" Both of us double over immediately, lost to a coughing fit, eyes watering.

"It's some holiday special . . . flavored vodka." Sky recovers with a shudder before sticking her flattened tongue out. "*Blegh.* Gross. Never again."

"Until later, when you think it's a great idea to after-party with that shit." I pluck the glass out of her hand and point with my elbow at her boots lying beside the mirror. "Hurry the fuck up and get those on. We're gonna be fashionably late as it is."

As I deposit the empty shots in her tiny kitchen, I catch another shadowy reflection, this time of myself in the window. The world beyond the glass lies darkened with nightfall and promises of more snow tonight.

Thoughts of this hat, and home, and being on the precipice of leaving college life to return to Crimson Ridge all mingle with the alcohol warming my belly. That makes me start chatting away as I grab Sky's coat for her and check it over for any lint.

"I guess it makes sense to wear it, right? I always feel a little bit of home is with me when I wear this thing. Man, I miss the horses, and even though life with Dad at the ranch is nothing but stupidly hard work, I'm kinda excited about moving back." Watching Sky finish putting her heeled cowboy boots on, I hold the coat out, ready for her to slide her arms in. "Weirdly, I do miss my dad. Is that uncool to admit out loud? He won't tell me shit over the phone, and you know how that man is about as easy to convince to open up as a rusty trap . . . but I worry about him being lonely when I'm not around."

Sky splutters and squirms a little bit just as her arm slips inside the sleeve. When she turns back around to face me, there's a deeper flush high on her cheeks, and those blue eyes of hers look a little startled.

"You feeling okay?" Tipping my head to one side, I shrug into my own jacket.

With a quick fuss at her hair, she nods. "Yup. Perfect. How's my lipstick? Good? Okay, let's go."

And with that, Sky practically shoves me through the front

door, out into the chilly night air. Not even waiting for my response. Looks like we're on our way to tonight's Yule Ball.

Sky lives right in the heart of campus, which is a blessing and the reason we so often spend time at her apartment. After a few drinks, I've crashed here more often than not, since it's walking distance to almost everywhere at the center of college life. Unlike my place, which is a cabin out of town.

Cheap rent for the win. Even if it's a pain in the ass sometimes living further away than most students.

"Woah, they've really gone all out. The place looks amazing," Sky croons, and a giant white plume of frozen breath billows in front of us as we get close to the stone arch entrance illuminated by hundreds of fairy lights. The buildings on campus are all old as fuck and gothic inspired, very much giving off old-school *academia* vibes.

Tonight it basically looks like a snow globe and a castle just had a baby, producing this very festive scene we're climbing the worn stone steps up to. Sitting prominently at the entrance is a giant fuck-off Christmas tree, with groups posing for photos in front of it. The thing must be at least fifteen feet tall, commanding the space where coat check and tickets are being handled.

"Impressive." I smirk. "You know what they say about the bigger the tree . . ."

"It's all about the angle." Sky pokes me in my ribs. "Not to mention the girth and ability to decorate that spot *just right*."

A snort comes out of me as I hand both our coats over. "Let's see if we can find someone to polish your baubles tonight, huh?"

She gives a funny sort of look my way before scanning the crowd. I've hardly readjusted my hat as we step through into the thrum of music and noise when Sky drags me by the elbow, cutting a determined line across the crowd.

"Festive cocktails incoming . . ." she squeaks as the sight of a well-stocked bar greets us. "And your bitch-face ex at three o'clock." Her words morph into a whisper-shout in my direction, just loud enough for me to hear over the noise of the ballroom.

Oh, shit. Yup, drinks are gonna be required for this. At least there are more than enough people here to make it easy to stay well out of her orbit. Except, I already know, as I position myself at Sky's side and order a heavy-handed pour of the complimentary punch, that my skin has started prickling with anticipation.

Is he gonna be here with her?

It only takes one look. One moment as I turn and lift the glass to my lips. The split second when I allow my eyes to slowly tip up, that everything is confirmed. As I glance across the sea of students enjoying their final blowout before moving on from college, I see him.

He's already looking at me.

My lips curve a little, hidden behind the drink in my hand, and all I can think is, *Damn, he's so fine*. Of course, he's also wearing a cowboy hat. The way that makes my blood heat and goosebumps fly, because he couldn't look sexier if he tried in a midnight-blue suit and those glasses that highlight his features so damn well.

But our silent moment of connection is severed as quickly as it connected. Sky grabs my arm, pulling me toward friends we know from our art program, and I already know who he's gonna be over there talking with. Who he's got on his arm tonight.

Even though I do my best to ignore the fact he's here—by drinking my body weight in fruity, lethal punch in an effort to loosen up and try to forget about the guy I can't be thinking about—I'm failing spectacularly. There's no denying the pull, the magnetic goddamn force drawing my gaze in his direction. While I genuinely do make an effort to chat with other people, there's no escaping that feeling making the back of my neck glow and butterflies swirl in my stomach. I'm constantly aware that eyes are on me, and it's taking everything I've got not to give in and stride over there.

Just to prove to him that he's as strangely affected as I clearly am.

Because if he's not interested in guys, if he's screwing my ex's roommate, then why the hell is he spending so much time burning holes into the back of my head.

After an hour or so of talking shit, knocking back a couple more shots with our group of friends, and being dragged for photos in front of the enormous Christmas tree, I shout at Sky that I'm gonna meet her back inside. She hollers something back over the swell of noise about this being *her song*. Whatever, the alcohol is humming in my veins, and I'm definitely not interested in returning inside just yet.

There's been absolutely no one who I've been remotely interested in flirting with, and one particular person who I can't stop fixating on.

Happy goddamn holidays. I'm a slut and I want my ex's brother, who apparently isn't into guys. *Hooray.*

I lift my drink and sway a little, cheersing my merry little mishap of getting all kinds of twisted up in my newfound single life . . . when, of course, the object of my strange and unthinkable obsession is right there.

Seems like he's had the same idea.

Screw him and all his buff muscles.

Rich hazel eyes flicker to mine. He's leaning against one of those big-ass gothic archways that are everywhere in this place. I don't even stop this time, striding boldly up to him and getting right in his pretty goddamn face.

"What the fuck is your problem?" I hiss once I get up close and notice his eyes go a little wide behind those sexy glasses of his. "You can't keep staring like a creep all night."

"I'm not." He keeps his voice low, glancing to one side with just enough guilt in his expression to drag my attention with his. As I follow his line of sight, I can't help but laugh at the very obvious presence and proximity of the two girls he's here with—they're just around the corner waiting to use the restroom.

Smirking at him, I shake my head, leaning a little closer, because the punch has fundamentally obliterated my understanding of personal space. "Your sister is right there, cowboy. Quit eye-fucking me, or she's definitely gonna notice."

"Your *girlfriend*, don't you mean?" His upper lip pulls into a tiny snarl, and I want to catch it between my teeth.

"Ex." I stab his torso with a finger. Goddamn, he's so solid beneath that suit. "Heavy emphasis on the *ex*. Besides, your little fuck-buddy date is right there too." I touch my tongue to my front teeth, daring him to look at just how close the other two are and asking whether he's gonna do anything about it.

"She's not—"

"Yeah. Yeah. She's not anything more than a place to stick your dick. *Fine.* Merry Christmas, or Yule, or whatever." Rolling my eyes, I step back and get one final chance to look him up and down. One last moment to fully appreciate the sight of him, because I need another drink. Maybe the entire contents of the bar. "I bet she won't go down on you tonight like I would." With a smirk, I go to walk off, and that's when my world spins in a way that doesn't have anything to do with the liquor.

A strong hand grabs hold of the front of my suit jacket, tugging me forcefully. I collide with a broad slab of chest and all the air rushes from my lungs.

CHAPTER 9

Brad

"Stop being a brat."

The sexiest guy I've ever encountered stares at my lips, with a tortured expression, but I'm in no mood to give in and play nicely.

"Can't handle a little rough riding, cowboy?" My lips twitch. I feel the cocky smirk settling there and don't care. Let him see.

Our chests both rise and fall and his grip on me intensifies. "My name's Flinn. Not that you seem to care, even though you keep accusing me of being the one acting like a slut."

"Stare at me like that, and it's a dead giveaway."

"Brad . . ." His throat works, and there's a hint of desperation in his voice. Hearing him say my name—the fact that he knows that detail about me—is the thing that severs any restraint I had. Reaching up, I catch his hat, stealing it off his head in a fluid motion before slamming our mouths together. From the moment our lips connect, it's pure electricity.

Fuck, he tastes as delicious as he looks.

Flinn might be burlier than me but we're the same height, and what I don't have in bulk, I have in muscle. I can manhandle this cowboy with ease, and it leaves me smirking ruthlessly against his lips when I realize he's allowing me to get a little pushy with him.

The rocket fuel punch tag-teams with the shots from earlier to ignite a flame low in my stomach, sending a coil of heat further down to my groin.

"*Mmm*, I bet you've been thinking about my mouth nonstop, huh?"

"No." His grunt is deep and oh so sexy.

I chuckle and nip at the swell of his bottom lip. "Liar." While tugging on that tempting plump curve, I reach between us and cup the front of his pants. Oh, yeah, he's fucking hard, and a sizable bulge strains behind his fly.

"Don't flatter yourself." He hisses more than a little breathlessly when I squeeze.

Drawing back, I give him a little pout, then lean forward so that my exhale grazes his ear. "*Aw*, c'mon, baby. You liked my throat well enough once before. You gonna pretend you didn't beat yourself to the memory of fucking my mouth?"

A ragged noise comes out of him. *Guilty as charged.*

"Go on. Convince me that you didn't lie in bed fucking your fist, wishing it was me swallowing you down until your eyes roll back?"

With each word I whisper in his ear, he shudders, hips uncontrollably chasing after the firm glide of my palm. I fucking love that he can't help himself. That he knows this is all kinds of wrong, yet he's unable to stop the madness of being drawn together in the shadows.

"Well, aren't you a naughty thing . . . desperate enough to be your sister's sloppy seconds." I kiss his neck and a curve of satisfaction plays over my mouth when he bites back a string of curses.

"You're an asshole." Flinn's words are choppy, short of breath.

"Want me to stop?" I purr against his stubbled throat. "Want me to take my hand away . . . like this?"

The second I release my grip over his pants, he makes a feral noise and clutches my wrist. He prevents my hand from moving away, letting out a pained growl of frustration.

"Are you wanting something?" I *tsk* at him under my breath.

"I just—I don't know, okay?" He swallows hard. "This is fucked up. You've been drinking. We should never have done what we did."

"But you thought about it?" I push him. I push because I'm so fucking captivated by him and I hate that I can't have him.

"I haven't been able to stop . . . Haven't been able to get you out of my head."

"Makes two of us, cowboy," I groan, sliding my hand that's clutching his hat up to the back of his neck. With it, I hook him to pull his mouth against mine. All while continuing to rub him through his slacks with the other.

Our tongues slide as the kiss deepens, hot and wet and searching for the answers to why the fuck we can't seem to keep our hands off each other. Slanting our mouths, I'm so painfully aware we don't have long to remain hidden like this. We can only disappear for so long before others will come looking for us. And yet I can't keep from kissing him and fusing our mouths together, to inhale every single rumbling noise Flinn makes.

"Brad . . ." he moans softly into my mouth, and I nearly fall apart right then and there.

"God, I love hearing you say my name like that." No one has ever spoken those simple letters strung together with so much pure yearning and need.

It's how I always imagined it might sound when I finally met the person who completed me. A breathy, rich, warm feeling, as the letters of my name dance on his tongue.

As I rub the heel of my palm over him harder, his cock grows more and more rigid. He's so damn hot beneath me—every facet of this cowboy is entirely addictive. There's nothing but raw, greedy desire and lust in control as I taunt him through the material.

I'm floating five inches above the floor, I'm certain of it.

Flinn gasps, feeding me a stream of throaty noises, and clings to the front of my jacket. I'm spun out of my head at how gorgeous he is and how much I seem to crave having him melt for me.

"*Shhh.* You're being too loud." I pinch his bottom lip between my teeth and hold him there.

"We have to . . . we have to stop," he mumbles against my lips.

"Just a few more seconds."

Flinn shivers and his hips jerk. The weight of his erection throbs beneath my palm. "No—you need to—oh, god—"

"*Ffffuck.* It's like that, huh? Two minutes and you're ready to blow your load. I don't even have to touch you properly this time."

"*B-Brad*," he warns me. Voice hitching.

"Goddamn, I want you to make a mess inside these pants. I want to know I did that to you."

"You gotta stop," he pleads, all while continuing to chase my movements with his hips because he doesn't actually want to stop at all.

"Maybe I don't want to?"

"If you keep doing that, I'm gonna come." His chest heaves and I really, really wish that could be the end result here, but fate intervenes.

Hiccuping, drunken chatter, and the click-clack of high heels on polished flagstone draws closer, far too close for comfort. I haul myself off him, swallowing hastily and readjusting my tie. Flinn stares back at me, wide-eyed for a second, and my gaze ticks down to the extremely obvious outline of his cock bulging the front of his pants.

I have to scrub my hand over my mouth as he snatches his hat back and sets it in place. He looks every inch a man reduced to a terribly flushed, sexy mess.

"*Ugh.* There you are." The whiny voice of Izzie's drunk roommate echoes across the marble floor, and that seems to snap Flinn out of his daze. He wrenches off his suit jacket and holds it in front of his groin. A move straight off the pages of the "randy teenager with a boner" playbook.

The smug glee in my expression intensifies as I take the opportunity for one last deep inhale of how gorgeous he looks—ruffled, disarmed, kiss-bitten lips. Damn it all if he isn't an attractive sight.

Turning on my heel, I melt into the shadows before the others can notice my presence. Slipping my flask out of my jacket pocket, I take myself and my own raging hard-on outside to where I can suck in some lungfuls of the chilly night air. To put myself on ice for a few minutes until I've got the situation with my dick under control.

My best option for tonight? Get blind drunk.

It's snowing heavily outside now, so there's not a hope in hell of getting a taxi home. I'm too strung out by all this to think about staying at Sky's flat. Tonight's the type of night I just wanna be in my own bed.

I grew up on a ranch in the mountains. A little bit of snow doesn't bother me.

Fuck it, I'll hit the bar, and then I'll walk home.

CHAPTER 10

Flinn

My only concern is where he's gone.

Izzie and her roommate have friends they want to see and dance with, and that leaves me feeling a lot like a meaningless third wheel in the background.

I came here tonight as their sober driver, but if I'm daring to be truthful with myself—especially after that kiss—it's because I was *hoping* to see him here. A Yule ball on a campus where I don't even live, or a school I don't attend, is the last fucking thing I care about. The reality is I'm way too hung up on him to think straight.

To add to that, a part of me couldn't help but keep a watchful eye on him earlier, worrying about how much he's had to drink. Brad hugged that bar from the moment he strolled through those big ornate doors tonight, and it's not my place to tell him what to do, but all that alcohol is gonna slam him sideways as soon as he gets out in the cold. It's been snowing heavily since we arrived, and I shouldn't fixate on him, but he's acting reckless enough that it doesn't sit right to not pay close attention.

Great. So now I'm looking out for my sister, her wasted friend, and her ex-boyfriend, who I really want to disappear into a shadowy archway with so that he can shove his tongue down my throat again.

Yuletide greetings to my fucked-up conscience.

Hanging at the edge of the room over by the windows, I'm looking out on the white flakes pelting down when I see it. The very distinct outline of a cowboy hat trudging through the snow.

Jesus Christ.

I don't even bother to find my sister. There's a much more powerful sense of urgency pulling me from this crowded student party that I have no interest in being at if he's no longer here.

By the time I make it to the front steps, I'm shit out of luck. He's gone. Vanished into the night and swirling snowflakes. I can't see him, but I know the direction he was walking in at least. My truck is parked close and it only takes a few minutes to drive the short distance to catch up to where I last saw that cowboy hat of his tipped low, shoulders hunched against the cold.

He's on foot, in these conditions, with god knows how much liquor on board.

The idiot will be lucky if he hasn't fallen headfirst into a ditch already.

Crawling along the deserted road, the snow is sticking fast. It's not an issue right now for driving anywhere, especially not for my truck. But if it keeps up by morning, this sleepy little college town will undoubtedly be snowed in. Leaning forward, I scan the footpath for sight of the fool, with the heater turned on high to warm my cab up.

The gorgeous asshole is gonna be frozen to the bone.

Sure enough, I find him cutting a slightly wobbly path only a handful of blocks further along the street. Headed away from town.

Where the fuck does he think he's going?

As I pull up alongside him, he doesn't look over but keeps his chin tucked, arms folded in on himself. He's so stupidly underdressed for being out in snow like this. I don't know if I want to squeeze him tight or slap him senseless.

Winding down the window, I let out a long exhale when I see him stumble. Yeah. Drunk off his ass and walking to the middle of nowhere. That's about the worst idea he's probably ever had.

"Need a ride, cowboy?" I call out, and he lifts his head, blinking owlishly at me.

His lips are blue. The moron.

Slowing to a stop, I keep both hands on the wheel, but my heart hammers with hopefulness and an ache to be near him. I really fucking hope he gets in, but also, what the hell does this mean and what am I doing?

I just ditched my sister to chase after her ex.

Brad shivers on the sidewalk, staring at me with bleary eyes as if his brain is sluggishly trying to put things together. But then he moves. He climbs in my truck, fumbling a little, and there's fresh powder covering him everywhere. As he slams the door behind him, the seat and footwell resemble an exploded snow globe. Though I can't be mad. I'm just . . . relieved.

"M-my wh-white kn-knight, huh?" His teeth chatter.

"Something like that." I put the window back up and turn the heat as high as it'll go. "You got a death wish?"

He makes a whining noise and covers his face with his fingers. "I got a crush." Then he leans back and slides his hat over his face. "But *shhh*, don't tell him."

My heart flutters and a grin tugs at my lips.

"Okay, deal." Hiding my smile, I put the truck in drive. "Where am I taking you?"

Nerves race in upon asking, because obviously, our options are limited. I can't very well take him back to my sister's house. We have to go to his place, but I'm not so sure he'll want me hanging around. Even though I really fucking want to, I also know there are way too many complicating factors.

He slaps a hand against his suit jacket, numb fingers patting his chest in search of his phone until eventually he pulls it out. Squinting like a pirate at the facial recognition, he unlocks it and then hands it over. "There's the GPS pin thingy."

I shake my head, tapping with one thumb until I find the GPS and his home address. Christ, he was gonna try to walk all the way out there? He'd have ended up as headline news. *Cowboy Icicle Discovered Buried Beneath Three Feet of Snow.*

Brad slumps against the door, and after we've been driving for a while, I assume he's gone to sleep. Instead, he mutters in a voice that's a little slurred, "You're so hot." He pouts. "Why you gotta have those pretty eyes? You don't even look like her." His drunken sigh is adorable.

"Guess she takes after our mom. I got my dad's genes."

"I don't think your dad's jeans would look half as good on that ass." Brad flops his head to the side, cowboy hat tipped forward over his brow while he stares at me from beneath the brim. "You could bounce a quarter off that thing, y'know."

The tips of my ears glow red hot. I'm not used to having anyone talk to me like this. I'm not used to someone unreservedly wanting me . . . sexually.

My sloppy drunk passenger, and intense fascination, doesn't care that I'm stunned into silence. Now that he's warmed up a little, his mouth starts running. Of course, Brad is talkative, even when he's four sheets to the wind.

"Why did I waste my time, huh? I'm out here being the nice guy. The sucker being the best boyfriend I could be. I shoulda just manwhored my way through this year."

I glance at him. My fingers tighten around the wheel.

"This . . ." He jabs at his chest with a thumb. "Too much romantic bullshit in here. Shoulda known I'd be the side character, gettin' cheated on. No offense, since you're like womb spawn buddies." Waving a hand at me, he huffs in despair.

The GPS pings at me to make a turn, leading up a very long and narrow forested laneway. Eventually, we pull up to what looks more like a vacation cabin than student quarters. This far up the hillside, it wouldn't look out of place as a ski chalet.

"C'mon. Let's get you inside." I chuckle when he whimpers that he doesn't want to have to move as I cross the hood to his side.

"Are you a cuddler? Bet you give good cuddles." He prods and squeezes my biceps after I open his door for him.

"You betcha." I can't help continuing to grin. Even though I doubt he'll remember any of this tomorrow and he might never want to see me again, I get to have this cute side of Brad for a night. And I guess that will maybe have to do.

"Don't move, cuddle boy." He bends down and ransacks the base of a pot plant next to the front door, almost falling on his ass while turning over stones. Finally straightening up, while bumping into me, he triumphantly waves a key.

"Want me to do it?" I ask.

"I want you to do lots of things." He stumbles against my shoulder, and I pull him against my side as I take charge of the key and open the door. Not at all nervous that I'm going home with a guy for the very first time. "Want you to do things. That means *sex* things." The exaggerated whisper he hisses out leaves me biting my bottom lip to stifle a laugh.

The layout of his place is easy enough to navigate, even in the dark. One bedroom off an open-plan living and kitchen area. It's pretty simple, but the most noticeable thing is the handful of boxes stacked and packed. He's ready to leave college at any minute.

Why that has my stomach sinking makes little to no sense.

"Let's get you into bed, huh."

"*Oooooh.* Hottie cowboy is taking me to bed."

Brad is so floppy, he pretty much just barrel-rolls onto his mattress as soon as I help him to his room. He mutters something about shutting his eyes for only a minute but that he's definitely down to fuck.

It makes my neck heat. How he keeps talking about it and leaving me under no illusion of how he'd like things to go between us. Even though I'm all kinds of strung out by him, that's the last thing I'm interested in right now.

I help pull his boots off, then manage to get him out of his jacket and tie, popping the top two buttons at his collar. At least he's not gonna choke himself by getting tangled in his sleep. I suspect he's gonna pass out cold and not move until morning, judging by how heavy-limbed he is.

Setting his things over by the closet and hanging his hat up, I hear him wriggling around to get comfortable behind me. Crossing back to the bed, I pull the blankets up over him. "I'm just gonna get you some water, okay?"

"*Mmmhmm.* Then I'm gonna rock your world." His words are heavy on his tongue.

When I get back from the kitchen with water and some painkillers I found after a quick hunt around, I sit beside him on the bed.

Brad nuzzles into his pillow, all dark tousled hair. He might be half asleep but rambles away in a croaky, drunken voice, and I'm not sure if he's talking to me or himself. "Y'know, I'm probably just gonna be stuck eating dick cookies forever. Dick cookies aren't as good as the real you. Now I'm gonna have to eat a bag of dicks to get over this. To get over you. Because you're cute and hot. That's a *lethal* combo." He scrunches his nose and then blinks at me perched on the edge of the mattress.

"Dick cookies?"

He nods emphatically.

"Then you go putting glasses on and I'm one step from a heart attack with you getting even sexier. So I'm just gonna bury myself right here. RIP me. Slayed by your dick and stupid sexy reading glasses."

I chuckle and ruffle a hand through my hair. If there's anything I know right now, it's that I don't want to go anywhere else.

Sitting here listening to Brad drunkenly ramble sounds about the best plan for my evening.

"Stupid sexy reading glasses," he mutters darkly, then whines. "Oh god, you probably read books too, don't you? You're a *thinking* kinda guy, aren't you?"

"Well . . . my baby sister is a writer. We both like books, yeah. It's sorta our thing."

Brad moans into his forearm that is cuddled around his pillow. "I hate that I already know that. Because the reason I already know that is because of your *other* sister." Peeking at me over his shoulder, he whispers to me, "I am *such* a slut. I've done stuff with her . . . and you . . . and oh my god, I'm a slutty-slut-slut because I prefer you."

My heart pumps extra fucking hard as I listen to him say all those words, not knowing how much I want that with him too and yet feeling like there's no way in hell he'd want that with me if he knew any of the truth about my lack of experience in this particular arena.

With his eyes fluttering closed, finally giving in to the drugging pull of sleep hitting him, Brad sighs out of his nose and gives me another of those raspy little drunken whispers.

"I really wanna do stuff with you. I prefer *you*."

CHAPTER 11

Brad

Bleugh.

My mouth is so dry.

There's a hammer on an anvil somewhere inside my skull.

Am I still drunk?

Creaking my eyes open, I do a bleary-eyed scan of my surroundings. Okay, so I'm at home. *That's a positive.* Then, I scrunch my nose and cautiously peer at the space on the bed beside me to see what I might find. It's empty. *Another positive. Thank fuck for that.*

I definitely, absolutely did not want to roll over and find a one-night stand in my bed. God knows I didn't want to hook up with some random last night.

So why does it feel like a negative that my bed is empty?

Letting out a groan, my head sinks back into the pillow. Maybe I can just rot here until I leave for Crimson Ridge. Last night is a swirling drain of alcohol and thumping music and being twisted the fuck up by *him.*

I haven't been able to stop . . . Haven't been able to get you out of my head.

That much I do remember. Between the shots and the punch,

I remember kissing him and teasing him and being so pissed off I decided to start walking . . . oh, fuck.

My eyes squeeze shut. I walked home? What kind of jerk ditches his best friend and runs home pouting, all because he can't have what he wants. That's some petulant, tantrum-level shit my cock pulled on me. Sky is never gonna let me live that one down.

Twisting in a barrel roll like the world's most hungover gator, I turn onto my side and fumble for my phone. There's a half-empty glass of water and painkillers, but no phone in sight. Fuck yes. Thank you, drunk Brad, for the gift of hangover relief. I knock back the pills and gulp the water like I've just been stranded in the Sahara.

I better find my phone and text Sky. She's gonna have my balls.

It takes a moment to find my feet. The room tilts a little as I stand up. Looking down, I find myself still wearing last night's clothes. *Classy.*

With a yawn and scrubbing the sleep outta my eyes, I tug open my bedroom door. Weird fucking choice to close it, drunk Brad, but whatever. And as soon as I step through, I stop dead.

Gaping, I stare at the scene in front of me.

Broad shoulders fill the space by the stove. Sizzling fills the air, and the mouthwatering aroma of a cowboy's favorite hang-over antidote—fatty bacon and fried eggs—drifts my way. There is a man in my kitchen. *Cooking.*

My stomach swoops. Not just any guy. My guy.

Well . . . not my guy. *But the guy I want to be my guy who can never be my guy.* Jesus.

I'm instantly regretting not at least taking a look in the mirror before stumbling out here, and I quickly scrub my face, hoping I'm not all drool and creases imprinted from my pillow. Combing my fingers through my hair real quick, I take a few steps closer.

Is this some kind of drunk-ass dream? Am I dreaming right now?

Flinn whips around upon hearing my footsteps. That jaw and throat looking as bitable as ever. And he's here in my kitchen, still in his slacks and shirt from last night, with the sleeves rolled to the elbows—fuck him very much. He's here cooking breakfast looking like every book boyfriend Sky has ever introduced me to with her recommendations.

"You only have four potatoes," he grunts, brandishing a spatula at me, seeming personally offended by that fact. His eyes flicker over me real fast before he pushes his glasses high up his nose.

Not the fucking glasses.

I open and close my mouth. Still in a Flinn trance as my brain struggles to throw itself into first gear. Right now, I'm the living embodiment of a crunching shifter, stuck grinding the gearbox between neutral and reverse and what the fuck is going on.

"Half a pack of bacon, and not even a dozen eggs. They're the only things in this kitchen. Yet, you've got at least ten cans of cat food and twenty pounds of kibble in that cupboard." He shakes his head. "You grew up on a ranch. You know about being prepared for winter. What the hell were you planning on eating other than wet cat food and fish-flavored kibble?" Flinn scolds while turning his attention back to the source of greasy heaven cooking in that pan.

Swallowing hard, I sidle past him and pull the box of open cat kibble out of said bare cupboard. "I almost exclusively live on sushi while I'm at college. At this point, I'm pretty sure I'm ninety percent nori and ten percent teriyaki."

Flinn shakes his head, not looking at me.

With cheeks heating fast and questions starting to cartwheel as my brain wakes the fuck up, I wander out to the spot where I keep Lily's food bowls on the front porch.

It only takes a second to open the door and take stock of the situation. Holy fuck.

Thick snow blankets *everything* in easily a foot of fresh powder. It's one of those mornings that sparkles and glimmers, with the early sun casting a warm glow over the scene. If I wasn't feeling like the bottom of a tequila bottle rolling through a gutter right now, I'd be snapping a photo. Damn, I really need to find my phone.

Dragging my attention back to my morning cat-food routine, I top up the kibble and do a quick check for signs of paw prints. There's nothing to be seen, but my eyes do snag on a truck outlined in a puffy white coating outside my front door. But it certainly ain't my truck I'm looking at.

That realization leaps up and smacks me on the shoulder. *Do I see that?* Flinn drove me here. I'm suddenly freaking out a little bit about what actually happened after the part where I draw a blank on the events of last night. A shiver roams through me with the icy bite of the air, and I look down to reconfirm that I'm still dressed in what I wore to the ball. So clothes didn't come off at least—but in my experience that doesn't mean *nothing* happened, either.

Christ. *Focus.* I've got a cat that doesn't belong to me but that I feed every single day to be concentrating on here. *Not the man in my house.* Hopefully Lily is okay. I really fucking hope she wasn't stuck outside all night. But she's a wily fucking thing, a hussy with probably ten different homes all feeding her treats and letting her purr while curled on their lap. I'll bet she's more than okay, but I don't like the idea of her going hungry or being freezing cold either.

As I duck back inside, I blow out a breath. It's like that dose of fresh air and winter blast just woke me up properly, because I see things in fine detail now. Sharpened and drawn into focus. Fireplace roaring. Kitchen full of delicious breakfast smells. Coffee brewed.

Hot-as-fuck guy cooking for me?

Perhaps I've tripped and tumbled into cowboy heaven.

"Hey, so . . ." I put the box away, then turn and rest my ass on the counter. Using one hand, I ruffle my hair, then shoot a glance and a slightly apologetic wince at the man filling my kitchen. "Did we . . . ?" Making a circle with a finger and thumb, I use the other to poke my forefinger through.

Flinn's head jerks up, he immediately crosses his arms over his chest. He's all stern disapproval. "*No.*"

"Not even a little bit of . . ." I press my tongue against the inside of my cheek and push my fist toward my mouth in a pretend blow job.

With an exasperated exhale, his chin tilts toward the ceiling, eyes closing in a "so help me" prayer. But I don't miss the way he goes a tad redder in the cheeks. "No. I slept on the couch." He sighs, looking back down, giving me a once-over with an unreadable expression locked in place.

Oh. "Okay. Yeah. Cool." Wings flutter in my stomach. Why does that make it even more swoony . . . that he just kinda took care of making sure I got home and that he didn't try anything?

"I'm not in the habit of hitting on drunk guys," he adds.

"Did I . . . ?" Grimacing, I peek at him. I have some vague memories floating around, but I'm also not sure if I was dreaming or actually saying things out loud.

"Hit on me?" he finishes on my behalf, then narrows his eyes. Thumping me square in the chest with how gorgeous he is and how much I wish things were different between us.

"Yeah, *uhh* . . . that."

A twitch tugs at his upper lip, and he doesn't have to say a single word.

I drag my hands down my face. "Oh, well, fuck me sideways. Flinn, I'm so sorry. I don't know what I said, but I have a vivid enough imagination."

"It's okay." He pauses while sliding food onto two plates. "You remembered my name?"

I'm left gaping at him. Remember? God. Does this guy have any concept of how *unforgettable* he is?

I clear my throat and shrug it off. Be cool, Brad. "Lucky guess. Or was it Frank? Ford?" I follow it up with a wink to cover my tracks.

That earns me a scowl, and maybe it's the fact I'm still a teeny bit drunk, or maybe it's because I'm just goddamn pathetic, but I'm in so much shit because I officially fucking adore his frowns.

"Just eat, would ya?" He shoves the plate in my direction. Nodding at me to sit. At my own tiny kitchen island no less.

"Thanks, Floyd." I hit him with a smirk before fixing my eyes on the miracle appearing before me. Food cooked by someone else just hits different.

His sister refused to cook. *Ever.*

He's just gone and done all this, without even asking.

That has me inhaling my food until I've practically licked the plate clean, all in an attempt to stop fixating on the fact he's really, *reeeeally* looking like boyfriend material right about now.

"And by the way, it's *not* okay that I hit on you. You obviously saved my drunk ass to bring me all the way out here. And in return, I acted like a complete tool." My pulse starts to thud a little harder, now that I'm more awake and got some food in my belly to soak up the remnants of liquor lazing around in my blood. So I hop up off my stool and grab hold of his empty plate to clean up after ourselves.

Flinn makes a noise that sounds like he's about to protest, but I clear my throat. "*Uhh*, no way, cowboy." Jabbing a thumb against my chest, I tut at him. "Blackout drunks who embarrass themselves by hitting on their ride home do the dishes. Them's the rules."

He studies me. Again with that indecipherable expression, and I wish I wasn't feeling so fluttery around him.

"You don't happen to know where my phone is, do you?" I wet my lips. How the fuck am I this nervous all of a sudden? Is it the prospect that he's gonna leave any minute? His truck has off-road tires. The kind of ruggedly reliable vehicle that can easily handle the snow out there. All he needs is to scrape it off and I'm assuming he'll be on his way.

"Here." Flinn leans across the benchtop before extending his big hand. My cell is right there, wrapped in his palm and fully charged. "Plugged it in for you last night."

"Oh." Buzzing starts up in my ears. *Oh*, indeed. Why does something as simple as that feel like he just offered to fly me on a private jet to see the rodeo world champs in person? It's just charging my phone for me, for fuck's sake.

I quickly wipe my damp hands over my thighs and take it from him.

Messages from Sky fill my notifications, making me shrivel up inside at how shitty of a friend I was to her last night. Yeah, I'm gonna struggle to make up for that anytime this century.

But as I open our text thread, prepared to grovel, it's not what I expected. Not at all.

My eyes pop wide, and bounce between the messages on screen, up to Flinn, and then back down again. *Shit.*

This . . . is not how I imagined today would go.

Flinn clears his throat, obviously wanting to know what's got me standing still with my pulse kicking up a notch. I turn the phone to face him and show him Sky's text.

His eyes flick over what she's written, and much the same reaction as mine washes over his expression. That gaze flits to hold my own, and he scrubs one hand over his mouth.

"Well, shit."

CHAPTER 12

Flinn

We're cut off.

Trees came down blocking the road after last night's snow storm rolled through. Which means that even though the snow might not stick around for too much longer, the handful of properties out here are all isolated until further notice. The texts Brad shows me are from his friend with the pink hair. *Sky.* In them, she's forwarded the updates put out by the local sheriff's office.

Looks like there's not going to be any quick escape from my sister's ex-boyfriend after all.

"We can go take a look and do what we can to get started on clearing the road." I run a palm over the back of my neck. While it's tempting to fall into a trap of feeling like this is a cute little rom-com moment and we're snowbound together, the reality is Brad doesn't have any fucking food in this house . . . and I'm certainly not gonna share the mystery cat's goddamn dinner.

"Umm . . ." Brad's eyes bounce between me, our half-shed suits from last night, and the snow beyond the window.

"I've got a chainsaw in my truck."

"You . . . have a chainsaw . . . in your truck?" Brad repeats the words back to me slowly, his brows zipped together.

"Yeah." My shoulders lift in a shrug.

He shakes his head. "That's not what I was expecting a horse boy to be carrying around."

"Horse trainer." I offer in explanation, narrowing my eyes in his direction. "I work on ranches, remote properties. Sometimes I'm roughing it, camping out in the wilderness for a while rounding up the wild ones. You never fucking know what you'll need."

He swallows, runs a hand through his hair and types something onto his phone. "Yeah. Of course. Makes sense." The words sound a little distant. Like his head is somewhere else entirely. Not standing in this kitchen looking like the bottom of a whiskey barrel.

"Have you got anything . . . any clothes I can . . ." My throat tightens as I awkwardly gesture at myself. Heat races up the back of my neck to flame the tips of my ears. This is surprisingly intimate, needing to ask him for something to wear, and doesn't my stomach know it. Immediately doing somersaults at the prospect of getting to wear his clothes.

Brad clears his throat. "Yeah, of course." Then he chews on his bottom lip for a second, a flicker of something dashing across his eyes as he looks at my chest. "Might be, *uhh*, a little tight. But I'm sure we can make something fit."

Snow might be thick on the ground, and the temperature's already starting to drop as the evening approaches, but sweat beads across my brow and clings to my lower back.

The buzz and drone of the chainsaw vibrate through my arms as I slice off another branch from the hundred-year-old pine lying prone across the road. It's slow work, but methodical, making my way through the slash on this side—meanwhile down below at one of the bends further along the road, the sheriff's crew is busy clearing more pines that dropped from the other side.

As I step clear, machine idling in my hands, Brad reaches in to drag what he can off to the side of the road. Goddamn, he looks fine. There's not a lot I can do to keep my eyes from straying to him. Continuing to notice the sight of him looking in his element. This version of Brad isn't the art student on a college campus . . . no. Right now, he's the rancher, dressed much the same as I am. We're both in our chaps and boots and thermal work gear. The only difference right now is that there isn't a horse in sight.

I shouldn't be checking him out amongst the spit of sawdust flying up every time he bends over to haul freshly cut chunks of pine out of the way, and yet here I am. I'm no better than this tree, felled by the sight of his ass in a pair of Wranglers.

A sharp whistle catches my attention over the hum of the motor, and as I pull my earmuffs away, I'm greeted by the sight of one of the sheriff's crew waving in our direction from the other side of the massive tree trunk. It's easily six feet in diameter. A hell of a size. Considering how many other trees of similar stature must have come down, this isn't going to be a quick job to work through.

When I cut the motor, the sudden lack of noise brings a wave of silence to the forested slopes around us. I catch the tail end of what the guy is saying as he climbs nearer. ". . . brought you boys some essentials." He gets to a point where he can safely reach over and hand a carton in our direction. "There are some frozen meals in there. Dried goods. Enough to get you through the night, then we'll be able to reassess tomorrow."

"Thanks." Next to me, Brad climbs up to be able to take everything out of his hands.

"Anyone with medical concerns on the property?" He pulls out a radio from his belt clip.

"Nah, it's only the two of us. We're all good."

My stomach swoops at those words. *Only the two of us.*

The radio unit beeps. "All clear up here, boss. Over." Then he clips it back in place and gives us a nod. "Thanks for making progress from your side. Can't promise an ETA of when it'll be stable enough for y'all to get a vehicle in and out, but there's a contact number written down for you in case you need anything. Or if there's an emergency, don't hesitate to reach out."

"Sure thing. Keep up the good work." Brad flashes one of those smiles that makes him so damn effortless to talk to and be around people in general. "You've saved us from dining on cat kibble for supper."

The guy laughs and starts to clamber back down. "Sheriff's orders to call it a day, fellas. No need to be risking your neck after dark since it's getting late."

His hat disappears along with a retreating crunch of footsteps over snow, and I swallow hard. My eyes stay fixed on the box of food we've been handed as I try to make sense of how we've ended up in this scenario.

"C'mon. Let's go." Brad hoists the carton into his arms. "Dunno about you but I'm fucking starved after all that. There better be something in here heavy on the carbs."

"Sure." I feel like my chest is growing tighter by the second. Last night was . . . *different.* Brad was drunk and there wasn't anything more to it than doing a good deed. Of taking care of him and making sure he didn't pass out in the snow.

What does it look like when we walk into that house together, and there's nothing but a fireplace and a warm meal . . . and a choice between doing the right thing or the thing I really fucking want to do.

We walk the road back to his place in silence. Just the repetitive sound of our boots on snow accompanies the moment as daylight filters weakly through the trees. It's so quiet out here, like the world has descended into a hush now that the drone of multiple chainsaws working has dropped away.

I don't know what to say. *Sober* Brad hasn't exactly offered anything overly flirtatious or cheeky. In fact, since our brief chat in the kitchen this morning, we've not had much of a chance to talk about anything at all. Which leaves me wondering if this is all just gonna be awkward as hell. In the cold light of day, and now that I'm stuck here, it might all be a completely different story.

Brad might want me gone, and it's gonna be one hell of an uncomfortable night on the couch pretending that doesn't sting like a motherfucking hoof straight to the stomach.

We reach the house and I'm climbing out of my skin. I've not had sleepovers with guys I'm interested in. There's so much I haven't ever done before and that just adds to this jumble of guilt and confusion and frustration. It's much easier to allow Brad to keep walking while I put the chainsaw away with the rest of my tools and take a few moments to breathe. If I hang out here for a while, maybe I'll be able to settle myself the fuck down.

I don't want to check my phone. Other than texting my sister to say I decided to crash at a motel rather than put up with another night on her couch, I can't be bothered trying to invent more lies. Most likely she won't have texted back anyway.

I've only just secured the chainsaw safety guard when a cold thump smacks me in the back of the head. Snow showers all over my shoulders and some slips down the back of my collar.

Spinning around with a yelp on my lips, I take another snowball straight to the chest. This one is packed way harder and hits me with enough force that an "oof" puffs out of me.

Brushing my gloves over my front to dust the snow off, I look up and Brad's grin is pure mischief as he arches one eyebrow while packing another snowball in between his palms. Touching his tongue to the front of his teeth, he eyes me up from head to toe, then hurls it straight at me. This one I see coming and duck just in time. The projectile whistles by, narrowly missing me, but hits the side of my truck with a thump.

"Oh, you sneaky fuck. It's like that, huh?"

Brad lets out a maniacal chuckle and starts scooping snow. I'm down on my haunches, doing the same within a second. With heart pounding, something bright and hopeful races through my veins at the idea that maybe, just maybe, Brad does mean what he said last night after all.

We duck and weave and yell, racing to create snowballs and hurl them at each other. Breathlessly cursing anytime one or the other manages to land a blow. The awkwardness of earlier evaporates in the face of chasing him down as he skids to a hiding spot on the far side of my truck.

"Too fucking slow, horse boy," Brad hollers.

"Like hell I am," I grunt. Tossing one handful of snow across the other side of the truck, I watch as his head whips around to follow the spot where it landed. I strike.

I'm on him, tackling him to the ground, immediately smushing a glove full of soft snow in his face. He splutters and wriggles beneath me as our legs tangle and I brace myself over the top of him.

"Okay, okay. I yield. *Blegh.*" He coughs and sticks out a flattened tongue. Snow dusts his eyelashes and lips, rapidly starting to melt on his flushed cheeks.

Looking down between us, I see the way his hands fist the front of my jacket. He's holding me tight, not pushing me away, and my stare darts back to connect with his. We're both breathing heavily.

My throat dips, words feeling hoarse as I say the thing I probably shouldn't say, but my blood is fucking *rioting* being this close to him. "You said you had rules. That the *blackout drunk does the dishes*. Is that something you do often? Get wasted and have bed buddies stay around for breakfast on the regular?"

"Jealous?"

Maybe. Definitely. I haven't been able to stop thinking about it.

"I'm just figuring out what the lay of the land is," I grunt.

It's Brad's turn for his Adam's apple to work as he swallows hard. "Well . . . other than your sister . . ." The guilty flicker crossing his eyes matches my own. His fingers tighten their hold on me. "There's been no land to lay, or laying on anyone's land. So to speak."

And my world goes blank when he tugs me down, pressing our mouths together.

CHAPTER 13

Brad

I keep my mouth sealed to his the whole way inside, stealing kiss after kiss, inhaling this man like he's the only sustenance I need.

"You talk so sweet." I nip at his jaw, tracing along all that stubble. Loving every second of scratch and scrape against my lips. "I bet you're a cowboy who would say the sweetest words while doing bad, bad things. I bet you'd be the guy who could ruin a man because you'd say all the right words to make me melt and then ruin my life by being so wicked." We've made it inside, and I start shedding both our clothes for the two of us.

I mean, I'm nothing but helpful.

Flinn makes a noise, not exactly a protest . . . or at least, I don't think he's wanting to stop the direction this is hurtling toward.

"Talk to me," I coax gently, all while continuing to push his jacket off. Slowing the movements of my hands while his eyes search my own. Flinn could put a halt to this if he wanted—he could tell me no. "Do you like this?"

He nods. Swallows. The strong line of his throat dips. "I was in a shitty long-distance relationship." His tongue swipes a hesitant track across his bottom lip. "He said he wanted to wait. Wanted to take things slow. So, I respected that."

My hands keep moving, keep exploring, finally being allowed to map the way his torso feels. He's so damn solid, it makes my mouth water.

"Turns out he was more than happy to take things slow with several other guys at the same time," he says quietly.

"His loss," I murmur, dropping my hands to catch the hem of his shirt. Curling my fingers beneath the fabric lets me stroke the skin low on his stomach and we both shudder at the sensation.

Flinn catches my wrists, stilling my movements. "Once that trust was broken, I felt like I'd saved myself for something and someone that was a complete lie. Yeah, I could've gone out and fucked around. But that's not my style."

Those soulful eyes of his search my face with a thousand questions.

Are you like him?

Would you do that to me?

Can I trust you?

After a pause, he relaxes his hold. "I've somehow ended up never being with a guy . . . properly."

The way he says it makes my heart squeeze. He's so fucking gorgeous—inside and out—and yet he's been treated like shit.

"Girls?"

He shakes his head. "I love women. But only as friends."

"So just a jerk of an ex?"

Flinn's eyes search my own.

"You deserve so much better." I tug the fabric up, revealing all that expanse of broad chest I remember vividly from the day he answered the door in nothing but sweatpants. "You deserve someone who wants all of you. If that's what *you* want?"

Does Flinn even want to be with someone physically?

"One long-distance boyfriend didn't exactly build a relationship based on sex. When we did see each other, he wasn't into doing much. Claimed he didn't even really like oral." Flinn goes red and makes an anguished noise. "More fool me, huh? How stupid of me to believe that."

The shirt comes free over his head, and I toss it aside. Sliding my fingers down, down, down, I keep going until I hit his waistband. That trail of hair descending low, that V of muscle, everything about him is so damn sexy. His stomach caves as I start working the button on his waistband.

"The prick lied to you. He'd been cheating. Probably did you a favor." My voice drops into a rasp, appreciative of the sight of his cock bulging through his briefs as I lower the zipper.

"Guess I gave up trying to push it . . . since we only got to see each other infrequently. Seemed pointless to spend the whole time fighting or arguing over something silly like that." Flinn doesn't know what to do with his hands. I'm more determined than ever to blow his entire world off its foundations.

Dropping down to my knees in front of him, I pull and tug at what he's wearing, determined to rid him of every last stitch of clothing. As I drag his briefs down his thighs, that gorgeous rock-hard erection I'm salivating for bobs free, already glistening with precum.

"Have you ever had proper sex?" Finally, fucking finally, he's completely naked.

"What counts?" Flinn's words come out breathless.

"Well . . ." I lean forward and graze my palms up his thighs. Running across the hair coating his legs. Appreciating every slope of powerful, thick muscle. "Let's say, going beyond foreplay . . ."

As I look up at him from my knees, Flinn's eyes are wide, mouth parted, and that flush deepens high on his cheeks.

"Anything beyond a mouth or fingers?" My lips twitch with delight at the playground he's offering me.

That has him swallowing hard. His cock jerks in front of me.

"Toys?"

A shake of his head this time as his massive chest rises and falls faster.

"Okay, so is my guess correct that you've had sex in the definition of everything *but* the actual act?"

The way Flinn looks down at me with lust-blown pupils, there's so much goddamn yearning in his expression.

"Why is it you?" he breathes, then a ragged noise catches in his throat as I wrap my hand around the base of him. "Why does it feel right with you? I didn't care before. My life was perfectly fine, and now you're all I can think about."

This time, one of his hands drifts to my head. It's the last tether of my self-restraint, snapped in a blink by his fingers pushing into my hair.

"You don't even wanna know . . ." As I sink forward, I take a moment to run my mouth over his balls, testing how sensitive he is. Flinn shudders a fraction, sucks in a sharp breath, but holds me there. Lavishing attention over his sac with my tongue reduces him to shallow breaths as he watches me so intently I can practically hear his racing heartbeat. When I finally slide my way up to take his cock into my mouth, we both let out a feral groan of pleasure. The salty tang of him explodes across my tastebuds and, Christ, he's a fucking dream come true.

I swallow him down, sealing my lips around him and moaning loudly as he leaks all over my tongue. The way he responds, the shudders and shivers, the noises of desire he's making, all of it fuels my own. My dick is bursting to get in on the action, to treat him *right* for the very first time.

All I want to do is show Flinn the kind of attention he deserves. Even if it doesn't make any sense at all, considering our circumstances. With each time I take him deeper and sink further forward, my blood fucking sets alight. I want to keep him. I don't want this to be a random thing. I want so much more of Flinn, and I can't explain any of the reasons why.

He wasn't wrong. It just feels right being with him.

"Oh god. *Brad*," he gasps. Fingers curling tighter into my hair as the jerk of his hips takes over. "You gotta—you gotta slow down—*unghhh*."

My smile tips up wickedly, with him buried in the back of my throat. The sensation that crumbles him so rapidly. A needy moan escapes his attempts at restraint, filling the quiet of my cabin. I fucking love that all I can hear is my heartbeat, the sloppy, slick noises I'm making around his thick cock, and his frantic sounds of getting close to the edge.

Pulling back for a moment, I hold his eyes. He looks goddamn wrecked already. The stark contrast of his nakedness to me still being fully clothed is dizzying. Me on my knees, his powerful figure standing over me, it's enough to have me ready to fuck all night long.

I slide two fingers into my mouth, coating them in all that messy evidence of saliva and precum, then spit into my palm.

As I take his cock back into my mouth, I shove my hand beneath his legs. I force him to widen his stance for me and slide around to fondle his balls, to stroke the hot smooth skin of his taint, before pushing further to his ass.

Flinn watches me, transfixed, and it's the best goddamn feeling in the world when I hear his response. A rough, desperate noise chokes out of him, somewhere between a plea and a gasp.

He's so damn sexy.

I need lube to do this properly, but I let my saliva-coated fingers explore and tease and press. I'm gentle, coaxing, letting him get used to the feel of my hand there, while I keep sucking him. Hollowing my cheeks, I swirl my tongue, and at the same time rub my fingertip against his hole.

"Oh, *fffffuck*. Oh god."

Flinn's grip on my hair tightens. His cock throbs and the weight of him filling my mouth flips a switch in my synapses.

Every sense becomes heightened, his musky scent, the weight of his heavy balls, the bump of my nose against his hair. The rhythm of working him echoes in my brain with one word.

Mine. Mine. Mine.

I want this cowboy. Like nothing I've ever experienced before.

"Brad—I'm gonna come—I'm gonna come—*baby*—" His words dissolve into a series of moans and a deep grunt of release. The way his ass clenches as I keep rubbing him, how powerfully his cock unloads all over my tongue, it all leaves me floating. I'm lightheaded and so goddamn horny I'm about to lose my mind.

Keeping the mouthful of him and relishing the sensation of his dick still twitching through his release, I pull off his tip. Climbing to my feet, I fall against his lips and feed him the taste of his cum. I push everything into his mouth as I slam our lips together and slide my tongue to tangle with his.

I'm groaning, nothing more than a pathetic, feral creature who needs him to know exactly how perfect he is. With my hands in the back of his hair, I keep our mouths sealed once more. And the way he swallows down everything I give him leaves my dick throbbing, trapped inside my pants.

"That's how good you fucking taste." I pull back, catching his bottom lip between my teeth. "That's how goddamn perfect you are." Walking him backward, we cross the threshold into my room and I tumble us both down onto the bed.

Kneeling over him, I fall forward onto my hands on either side of his head. With panting breaths, I take in the sight beneath me, him splayed out with hooded eyes and dilated pupils. I let another track of spit fall from my mouth, past his open lips, giving another glimpse of his cum mixed with my saliva.

"That's how you should be adored every single day of your life."

CHAPTER 14

Flinn

"Say it again." Brad sinks forward and growls against my lips.

My brain is blank. I can't see straight. This cowboy is out to ruin me forever.

He nudges me with his nose, tracing my jaw until he finds my throat and uses that wicked mouth to nibble and kiss and suck on the sensitive spot just below my ear. The place where my blood thunders relentlessly. A stampede through my veins. *For him.*

"Please . . . say it again." As he brushes a kiss over the shell of my ear, this time his words are sweet, intoxicating, a little bit pleading.

My kryptonite, it would seem.

"*Baby.*" My voice is raspy. It lights a fire in Brad's eyes.

He's goddamn beautiful.

"I want to make you feel good, too." Fumbling a little—feeling out of my body—I hesitantly tug on his shirt. The weakest of attempts to suggest that he get naked alongside me.

Not knowing how to ask for what I want from him is torture, yet every single cell in my body screams with need. To have him inside me, to feel him, to finally experience the type of connection I've craved for so long.

Brad hits me with a quirk of his lips and sits back on his heels, straddling my hips. In the most pornographic move he could slay me with, he reaches behind his head and tugs his shirt off in one smooth fucking motion.

Goddamn, he's nothing but bunching and flexing stomach muscles, flattened nipples, smooth skin for days. Witnessing his body up close is enough to have my dick twitch, roaring back to life.

"You're sure about this? Just so you know, I'm on PrEP. I've been tested recently." He starts to work at his pants, and I nod.

With teeth sunk into my bottom lip, I'm unable to stop myself from obsessively watching the way his hands move.

Letting out a chuckle, he knows I'm staring with the hungriest of eyes. I'm caught. Hook. Line. Sinker. "Gotta give me words, cowboy." Brad levels me with a heated stare.

Reaching forward, I let my palms cautiously slide up his strong thighs. So unused to having the freedom to touch someone else intimately like this. When I reach his hips, I pause, then roam a little higher to take hold of his forearms for just a moment. My eyes flick to meet his, and my throat works a heavy swallow.

"Consider this my permission for whatever you want. Anything. I want that. And I want it with you . . ." I guide his hands to keep going. To keep moving. To get us to the next part where he's naked and I get to finally appreciate every glorious inch of him. "And I want it *because* it's you."

Brad's face lights up. He has to climb off me—much to my annoyance—and off the bed to get properly undressed. But at least when he comes back, it's with lube in hand. And no condom.

Thank god. I want him to take me raw.

"Eager, *hmm*?" he teases.

I swear my entire body flushes with embarrassment that I obviously said those words out loud. My post-climax brain is a hazy, heart-eyed, incredibly slutty place.

"Feels like I've been waiting for you for a long time." There's no place for hiding now. Might as well let him know the truth.

In all honesty, I'm just as taken aback, not sure what the fuck is even happening. Not because it doesn't feel right with Brad, but because it does. I'm not into casual hookups. I don't fool around with strangers. And on paper, Brad is very much both of those things. Yet, I don't hate this.

I'm infatuated with the idea of him and how absolutely perfect this moment feels.

Brad has such a good-looking cock. My mouth waters and my eyes lock on the place where he strokes himself. The veiny length of him flinches and fills more and more with each stroke, revealing a perfect slight curve and swollen head.

I fucking love the fact he's leaking from the tip.

I like knowing that I've had such a clear and obvious effect on him.

"Goddamn, I need to be inside you." He shudders on the next firm stroke of himself. "I thought I could be patient . . . but . . ."

"That's not your style. *I like your style.*" My tongue runs a line to wet my lips, and I hope, thanks to the way I beg with my eyes, that he'll put me out of this misery of waiting.

"Careful, cowboy. Talk like that, you're gonna make me want to keep you," Brad purrs, and he takes hold of my legs, pushing my knees toward my chest. "And promise you'll tell me if anything feels like it's too much."

Words have upped and left me. I feel so exposed, with the act of opening me up to him like this. It's intensely vulnerable, and yet he soothes the part of me that could never imagine being like this with someone I didn't have a connection with. That I couldn't fully trust.

"Breathe. That's all you gotta do." There's a click of a cap, a drizzle of cool gel right down my seam. I feel like I'm shuddering and shivering and he's barely touched me. And then his fingers are right there. All focus ends up on him, watching him as he watches me. This might be my first time doing this, but that notion hardly registers with how right this feels in my bones.

Brad couldn't be more wrong for me, and yet more perfect all in the same breath. The way his roguish hair falls across his eyes, the hungriest of expressions ignites his hooded gaze. With each stroke and press of his fingers, he keeps reminding me to breathe and to relax and it's like he's drugging me in the best possible way.

My body sinks back into the bed with how incredible it feels.

"Oh my god." I let out a shaky gasp when he gently presses forward, breaching me with a single finger and gradually working deeper.

"Jesus. Fuck." His eyes squeeze shut. "You're the tightest fucking thing, baby. Goddamn."

We lose track of time as he takes care, being so attentive to my every flinch and response to the way he's working me. I could melt beneath his velvety, deep voice. The fact that he adds more lube, builds up to two fingers. It's so overwhelming and full feeling already.

I have no fucking idea how he's going to make this work. But I trust him.

My lips buzz and limbs tingle as any discomfort eases and melts and turns me into even more of a puddle for him.

"*Please.* Please, Brad. Oh fuck." I'm mumbling. Begging. Fists clenched in the sheets as I writhe with pleasure. Trying to encourage him deeper becomes my only goal as he scissors his fingers until I'm seeing stars.

Finally, with a groan, he relents. He carefully removes his hand and strokes a thorough coating of lube over himself before shifting his weight forward. I can't help the needy sound that bursts out of me when I feel the plush head of his cock slide through my seam—oh god, the size of his swollen tip feels like it's gonna be impossible to take—and he nudges forward.

"Give me your eyes. Stay with me, okay?" His words reach into my chest, warming my blood further, soothing my racing pulse. "Christ, you're so fucking perfect." Brad looks down, eyes drifting over where I'm almost fully hard again between us, and my knees pushed against my chest.

"I need you—I need you inside." There's nothing holding me back from outright begging.

"Just relax . . . We're moving slow . . . Keep breathing . . . All you gotta do is bear down on me . . . Let me take care of you." He talks me through every step. Inching forward. The moment the crown of him slips inside, we both gasp. This is absolute ecstasy, the smooth glide of him, the heat of our bodies. Who would even fucking know there was snow on the ground outside? My blood is a raging wildfire.

His hips work, ever so gradually. Pushing forward slowly, drawing back slightly, before slipping a little deeper. Methodically dragging me to the brink with every torturous inch he glides further inside.

"*Fffffuck.* You're gripping me like a fist. Holy fuck," Brad pants, dampness coating his forehead and hair. He's never looked sexier. "Baby, you feel incredible. Christ, you take every inch like a goddamn dream."

As he says it, his hips sink forward, driving that final, unbelievably pleasurable distance. Fitting our bodies together, we both let out dark grunts of relief.

My head tips back. I can feel him *everywhere*. It's so full. So hot. I'm just entirely consumed by everything about this cowboy and his perfect, pretty cock.

"The goodest fucking boy," he murmurs. "My good boy."

He eases back, then sinks forward, testing a thrust, and my body lights up with fireworks. A guttural noise escapes me.

"More. Holy fuck. *More.*"

It's the last word I can coherently form. Brad lets out a string of curses, reverentially giving me every sweet and sinfully wicked word of praise as he fucks me into the mattress. He's the perfect balance of rough and tender, sending me spiraling on wave after wave of pleasure.

His cock bumps a spot inside me that leaves me gasping for air. My length throbs, lightning shoots right through to the base of my spine.

"*Oh god. Oh god*," I mumble, struggling to focus on him, trying not to simply explode at the first hint of his steady thrusts grazing my prostate.

"That's it . . . Come for me, you beautiful fucking thing. Show me how good you can be. Show me just how perfect this ass is when you're filled with me." His words turn me upside down and inside out. "Show me." *Thrust.* "How much." *Thrust.* "You love." *Thrust.* "Taking my cock." *Thrust.*

I'm done for.

The surging wave claims me. My cock jerks and explodes all over my stomach, splashing up my chest and onto Brad, as our bodies slap together. I've completely flown out of my head as he buries himself deep and grunts.

I feel him. I feel everything. Everything turns searing hot as his load shoots inside my ass. As he marks me and claims me and throbs in the act of filling me.

It's perfect. He's perfect.

And I think I've fallen head first, tumbling straight into this man.

CHAPTER 15

Brad

Someone alert the sheriff, because I've found myself in deep peril.

I'm currently digging out clothes to loan my ex's brother and contemplating ways to ask him to never leave me.

Yeah. Totally normal behavior.

I'm fundamentally incompatible with *keeping things casual*, I fear.

Flinn has to borrow yet more of my clothes—not that I'm complaining—since the only thing he has with him is that sexy-as-hell suit he arrived in. After being all *cowboy god with a chainsaw* today, and after the best sex of my life, the least I could do was offer him a shower and some clean clothes to wear.

And of course, because he's built like a superhero, everything is kinda tight on him and just makes those muscles I'm not supposed to be drooling over even more prominent.

He walks out of the bathroom, emerging from a cloud of steam wrapped only in a towel slung low on his hips, and I'm trying really fucking hard to be decent and to keep my hands to myself. Seeing him like this? Flinn makes it damn near impossible not to jump his bones again immediately.

I want to rip that towel off him, suck his cock until he's

bricked up, eat his tight little hole, and then fuck like we never need to come up for air.

"What's that look for?" He reaches for the side table and slides his glasses onto his face. Nothing but pecs, chest hair, a towel, and slutty little frames highlighting his perfect cheekbones? Is he trying to kill me?

Those glasses should be illegal.

What the fuck am I supposed to do with that? He's so hot with them. Fuck my life.

I cough and hand over the sweats and hoodie. "Nothing." It's barely a croak. This cowboy has rendered me speechless more than once, and it's churning me up.

Now, seeing him in my clothes again? Goddamn, that is definitely doing something for me. His sister would never. She always wore her own stuff, would turn her nose up like mine weren't good enough. I don't know why it sent such a pang straight to my chest, all because of something entirely silly and meaningless, but my romantic heart would shrivel a little.

Is it a crime to want to see the person you're into curled up on the couch, wearing your hoodie?

Hooking my thumb over one shoulder, I make a hasty exit before I tackle him to the bed and indulge all my depraved fantasies. Fucking Flinn while he's wearing my clothes? Peeling those sweats down and licking every inch of him from rim to taint to tip? Fisting a T-shirt of mine against the small of his back while I drive into him from behind and listen to him moan into the pillow?

Well, there's no limit to just how badly I want this guy, it would seem.

"I'll make sure that fire is heating up properly." Muttering to myself and cursing my luck that of course it's *him* I'm already pining over and he hasn't even left yet, I fuss around, stacking up more wood inside and poking at the flames while he gets dressed.

"*Uhh*, what's the deal with your cat?" His voice sounds a little raspy as he walks into the kitchen.

"I don't have a cat," I say on reflex. But my head whips up, and of course, Lily is perched on the window ledge outside, eyeing up my houseguest as if she has a fortune teller's insight into all my sins. "There you are, baby girl." I cross over and pop the window open enough that she can slink through. A little *chirrrp* of greeting is followed by a shake of her ginger fur to flick off the dusting of snow she accumulated on her way over.

"She's been out there in the snow this whole time?" Flinn's brows zip together.

Lily pads straight across the counter and firmly bunts her cheek against his hand with a very ungraceful headbutt. Her only setting is to force affection upon people.

We have way too much in common.

"She's not mine, but turns up pretty much every day. So I let her stay whenever she wants," I say, offering a shrug.

Flinn scratches behind her ears, and the ginger hussy starts purring loudly. Am I a little jealous of a cat getting to enjoy having his hands running all over her fur, stroking absently? I discreetly readjust myself.

"Are you gonna take her with you?" He raises one eyebrow at me, then at the boxes I've got stacked ready to go.

"Nah. I don't want to take her away if her actual owners are somewhere nearby." With a heavy swallow, I rest my ass against the table, shove one hand in my pocket, and rub the other back and forth over my nape.

"You have more cat food here than human food," he scoffs. "Are you sure you aren't her owner and you didn't realize it?"

"I dunno, man. Lily just comes and goes whenever she wants. She's well looked after by *someone*." As I say the words, she lets out another little *chirp* and hops down, then comes over to forcefully throw herself against my legs, weaving around my ankles. For a tiny thing, she's like a fifty-pound weight when she wants to be.

Reaching down, I scoop her up, and she curls into the crook of my elbow.

"Yeah. *Someone.* It's a total mystery who that could be." Flinn rolls his eyes, then starts moving around my kitchen as if he damn well owns the place. I like it. I like it way too much, and I have to ignore just how incredible he looks standing only a few feet away.

Because this is all going to be over as soon as that road is passable.

The facts are plain and simple. I cannot go getting attached to my ex-girlfriend's brother.

As I cradle the cat in my arms and watch this man mountain, it all hits me with the force of a whip cracking across my chest. The reality is that I'm leaving here, without either of them. I'm on the precipice of establishing my life back at Rhodes Ranch . . . solo.

That has me pacing up and down the room, indulging Lily in scratches while she vibrates like a goddamn motor against my chest. "We can get up early tomorrow to keep working on the tree blocking the road. You'll want to be getting back to town, I know. And I'm sorry you got stuck here, all because of me and my stupid, drunk decision to walk. In case you haven't noticed, I'm a disaster of a human—"

Flinn's bulk magically appears in front of me as I turn around. He's right there, holding out a bowl filled with steaming hot lasagna, and one of those big palms reaches for the cat, lifting her out of my grasp.

"For the love of god, boy. Let me feed you," he mutters, pressing the meal into my empty hands.

"See? I didn't even help," I weakly protest. "This is how much of a screw-up I am, and here you are having to figure out simple things like *food*, because apparently I can't even do that right."

"Stop talking and eat." He points in the direction of the seat at the kitchen table. All gruff and no nonsense.

As I follow behind his broad frame, Lily's tiny head and ears poke up over his shoulder to watch me. Pure superiority fills her green eyes as she lets Flinn carry her around like a ginger princess. The only thing missing right now is a crown on her head.

Why does it feel even worse that she likes him, too?

Sitting down to eat, I sneak little glances at how he naturally puts out a bowl of biscuits for the cat, who isn't my cat, but I've somehow ended up looking after as if she's my cat. Then he finally sits down to join me.

The only sounds are the crunching noise of Lily gobbling biscuits, the pop of the fireplace, and my heartbeat as we both fill up on much-needed carbs. For someone the size of Flinn, I feel like he probably needs about triple the portion he's got in front of him.

Just as I'm about to start scaling the walls, not knowing what to say, but feeling like I'm about to burst if I don't say *something* . . . Flinn clears his throat.

"I don't share. I don't do noncommittal, and after what I've been through, I can't deny that I'll probably get jealous too easily." His big hands come up to drag through his hair, ruffling it until it stands on end. There's a muscle pulsing in the side of his jaw as the words grind out. "Just gotta lay my faults all out there."

"Well, if it makes you feel any better, I'm needy. I hate the idea of not spending time together." I blow out a breath, hardly daring to look at him.

Flinn gives me a long look, trapping me in a steadfast gaze. "I'm not interested in something halfway."

My pulse feels like it's about to sail through the roof. "Well then, considering that I'm a clingy mess . . . I'm definitely not a good idea for you, am I?"

His exhale is heavy, eyes hooded with something that undoubtedly mirrors my skyrocketing desire. "A terrible idea."

"The worst." My cock stirs, taking in the sight of him, and it happens without really registering the decision to go to him. I'm already on my feet, crossing to where he's sitting. Flinn widens his knees and sinks back in his seat so that I can step between his strong legs. Sliding one hand into the back of his hair, I tug gently until his focus tilts up to meet mine. "How about you let me remind you just how bad of a decision I am? Don't want to let you forget before you leave tomorrow."

Flinn's strong throat dips, and all it takes is a nod. All it takes is that tiny moment of relenting, of giving in for one more night.

One. More. Night.

Then I'll have to deal with the fallout of saying goodbye.

CHAPTER 16

Flinn

"*Mmm*. I thought you said you wanted to sleep in," Brad mumbles against my ear. His rough touch splays possessively over my front, sliding down the front of my stomach, tracing the dusting of hair below my navel until he reaches my rock-hard cock.

A shudder runs through me as he swipes a thumb over the precum beading at the tip. Everything inside me lights up in anticipation of *more*.

We fooled around last night. Brad could hardly keep his mouth off me, and I was way too much of a boneless mess, nothing but gasping need by the time he finished edging me into oblivion. He didn't even need to fuck me; all it took was his tongue rimming me to have my eyes rolling back in my head. It only took my cock being in his hot mouth to end up lost to the way he eagerly sucked me down and tortured me until I couldn't see straight.

Only once I'd outright begged for his dick did he finally fuck my face and give me permission to stroke myself until I made a mess all over my stomach. The euphoric sensation of swallowing him down as he knelt over me holding the headboard, how he whispered how perfect I looked stuffed full of him, yeah, that had me unloading cum *everywhere*.

Brad's attention and wicked playfulness is beyond anything I could ever have imagined. There's so much more to *sex* than just having him inside me, although that's definitely something I really, really need from him right now.

"You're cute when you wake up all horny." His teeth nip at my shoulder, firm grasp stroking me, coaxing my hips to chase after his touch. Behind me, the weight of his cock settles between my cheeks, his own hardness sliding back and forth as we rock together. The kind of lazy early-morning moment I really shouldn't be enjoying as much as I am, our circumstances considered.

"Gonna do something about it?" I grit my teeth to stifle a moan when he squeezes and twists more forcefully. Just how he knows I like him to.

"Maybe I need to hear a little more of that begging . . . You were oh so very good at that last night, cowboy." His mischievous grin curves against the back of my neck, and goosebumps scatter down my arms at the rough edge to his sexy morning voice. Brad is gorgeous at any given time of the day, but here, tangled in his sheets when his words are a little gravelly and coarse with sleep, is maybe my favorite. That and having him wrapped around me from behind.

Of course, Brad likes being the big spoon.

He lets go of my cock, brings that palm up to my mouth, and chuckles. "Spit for me, baby."

A deep groan rumbles out of me. The way those words immediately send heat pooling low in my stomach, my balls aching within seconds. It's like everything this man does is sent to drive me out of my mind with the type of intense pleasure I didn't even know I wanted before now.

I do as he asks, warmth glowing on my face and back of my neck as I let my saliva fall into his palm.

"Good boy." Brad's lips are hungry, working the side of my throat, as he wraps that slickness around my cock. His strokes reduce me to a panting mess within minutes. Reaching out, my fists clench in the sheets, and there's no stopping the way I'm unashamedly thrusting in and out of his firm hold. Vaguely, I'm aware of the desperate, mewling sort of noises I'm making. Somewhere in the back of my mind, an alarm goes off, warning me that this is too much, too fast, and that I can't possibly be feeling this way about someone I've barely spent a day with. I can't hope to find *my person* under circumstances like these.

Last night, we joked about both wanting *all or nothing*. But that was all it was. A joke. Teasing. Followed by a mind-blowing orgasm.

Who the hell finds the love of their life in their sister's ex? No one. That's who.

"Goddamn. This ass," Brad grunts, pushing himself tight against me with a desperate sort of noise rolling through from his chest to mine. He feels so impossibly hard, demanding, even bigger than I remember. "Are you gonna let me take care of you, just like this?"

I nod. Turn my head to the side. Our mouths connect in a sloppy kiss. The kind of need for one another that dissolves into licks and teasing bites and sucking on each other's tongues as he shoves his hips harder against me, grinding until I feel the smeared, slick evidence of his precum against my seam.

"*Please.*" Another full body shudder rolls through my limbs. With our legs tangled and his fist gripping me until I can't think clearly, I'm pinned down by him, and it's the best kind of feeling. He makes me feel safe to let go and be taken care of, and in turn I get to take care of him in other ways . . . and if that isn't just the worst realization in this murky, predawn moment.

There isn't any more time for talking. This is nothing but pure *need* and indulging in how fiercely we both want this. Brad has to let me go while reaching for the lube, drizzling the cool gel all over my ass. Slick noises come from behind me as he does the same for himself. Then his clever fingers are there, slowly stroking and circling and easing into me.

Everything dissolves into a place where time has no meaning. All I feel is him, and the slight stretch and momentary sting before it melts into intense pleasure. As he slowly works me, eases forward past a knuckle, then builds to eventually having two fingers scissoring inside me, I'm trembling with how goddamn incredible it feels. Shivers coat my lips, and I don't know what kind of noises I make, but it seems to please him.

Brad murmurs in my ear how good I am. How perfectly I let him in. Reminds me to breathe when I simply forget to.

And then his fingers are gone, and the flared head of him is hot and demanding at my hole.

"Oh god. I need you. *I fucking need you.*" The words gasp out of me as I press back. I don't want him to go slow, or be gentle, or treat me like I'm something precious just because I'm inexperienced. If this is our final moment together, without knowing where things go once we leave this bed, I'm more eager than ever to be fucked until I'm boneless.

"Jesus. *Fffuuuuck*," Brad groans as the tip of him slips inside me. We're both panting now, our chests rising and falling, damp with a sheen of sweat. "You're so fucking tight. This ass was made to take my dick like a dream."

His knuckles brush against my cheeks as he fists himself and slowly, carefully fights to work his way inside. Cursing softly, lowering his head to brush seeking lips over my spine and shoulder every now and then, pausing to squeeze and knead the globes of my ass. It's heaven. Right here in this bed, with him, feels like we fit together in the most perfect of ways.

Finally . . . fucking finally . . . he sinks that last inch, and we both groan at the feeling of him sliding to the hilt.

"Is that okay?" Brad sounds strained; his teeth graze my skin this time. "Oh, Jesus. You're squeezing me so fucking tight." He gasps as my body fucking lights up at the thought of him biting down on me while pounding me hard.

"Were you this big before?" I can't help the moan that drops out. He throbs inside me, feeling like he's *everywhere*.

That draws a ragged, breathy sort of grunt from him as he gently eases back, then slides home. "*Flinn.* Baby. My god."

I'm seeing stars.

"Brad—" I bite down on my bottom lip.

"I know. I fucking know." He draws back, then thrusts into me again. "*I fucking know*," he whispers.

And it's over. I'm his. I'm nothing but raw, greedy noises as he reaches around and takes my cock inside his fist. I try to chase his dick sunk deep inside me and his hand. Bucking into his touch while pushing back against his groin, until my teeth are buried in the pillow with how badly I want to come, but I also don't want this to stop.

That's when Brad fucks me like he owns me, and I completely melt for him.

My fingers twist into the blankets. Drool coats my pillow as I goddamn lose my mind. "Please . . . please . . . I need . . ."

Behind me, Brad makes a roughened noise in the back of his throat. Each pump of his hips against mine punctuates his words.

"What." *Thrust.* "Do." *Thrust.* "You." *Thrust.* "Need?"

His words are dark, gritted out, as he punches his hips, flesh slapping against flesh.

"Mark me, baby." It's a confession I shouldn't be letting slip, but I'm too far gone to care. *Mark me. Prove this was real.* Give me something to take when I leave and have to wake up tomorrow without this man.

"Holy fuck." It's a surprised gasp that rushes out of him, and Brad sinks deep. Tingling rushes to that spot in my lower back. He keeps hitting that perfect goddamn angle, the one that leaves me crying out. *There. Yes. More.* As he drives me into the mattress, his teeth pinch the fleshy part of my shoulder, and we both detonate.

My balls draw up tight. Heat flashes down my spine. As my cock swells, pulses, my stomach clenches. I'm a moaning, jerking mess of cum as he jacks me hard and my release bursts everywhere. At the same time, I feel his rhythm stutter. He buries himself to the hilt and the warm flood of his release bursts forward. I feel every throb and swell, every powerful shot of him unloading to fill me.

I don't even notice the sting of his bite. Hardly register the way he tenderly sucks on the spot afterward to ease the pain. It's just agony knowing that it's so good with him, and yet it can't be *him*.

Brad drops kisses all over my neck and shoulder as if he can't stop roaming his lips across my blazing hot, sweat-slicked skin. With a hiss, he eases out of me, then crawls over my body. I'm rolled onto my back, my brain still flung somewhere into outer space, as he licks up all that filthy evidence of cum off my cock and stomach. He murmurs words against my dick that I can't even tell what he's saying, but I sink my fingers into his curls, tangling my grip in his hair. Slowly, reverently, he climbs up my body until our mouths connect and the weight of him pins me down, blanketing me perfectly.

I cocoon him in my arms, hook my ankles over the backs of his thighs, drag him as tight as possible against my front. We stay entwined, kissing like goddamn horny teenagers with the taste of me on his tongue.

My heart is surely going to explode; it's galloping like the wind.

"How am I supposed to let you go?" Brad leans his damp forehead against mine.

"When you find the answer to how I'm supposed to walk away . . . maybe I'll be able to tell you," I mumble in reply.

The feeling of his lips curving into a smirk against my own

is way too addictive. I growl and kiss him again fiercely. We're in way too deep. In too much trouble, because the way this is going, the way we're making out, things are absolutely going to get hot and heavy again real fucking fast.

Brad starts biting a trail down my jaw, scraping his teeth over my Adam's apple. Nipping at that slope of skin, he roams his tongue all over my stubble, seeking out my pulse point. I'm fucking lost to the way he licks and nibbles and makes sultry little noises just below my ear.

A door bangs.

We both jerk.

"Was that the wind?" Brad sounds a little dreamy, hardly getting the words out, before we hear footsteps.

"Brad? Oh my god, I'm so sorry it took me so long to get here." A feminine voice draws closer and closer, and oh shit, is that his friend Skylar about three seconds from bursting into his bedroom? "I came to check that you are okay. They've finally cleared enough of the road. What a fucking mess out there. So I knew I had to bring you coffee and a bagel, because I'm guessing you probably have zero food in this place . . ."

The door bursts open on its hinges, just as we both fling ourselves out of the bed. Brad stuffs a pillow in front of his cock, and I nearly crash through the door of the bathroom. In my periphery I catch sight of a tiny woman with pink hair carrying a coffee and giant takeout bag, mouth gaping at the sight of two naked cowboys scrambling for cover.

Her voice carries as I kick the door shut behind my naked ass.

"Oh, well . . . hello, sailor . . . Who is that hunk of a specimen?"

CHAPTER 17

"Oh, well . . . hello, sailor . . . Who is that hunk of a specimen?"

Sky's face contorts into the wickedest grin possible. Her blue eyes startle wide, focus bouncing down to my hands covering my dick and then to the buck-naked globes of Flinn's ass disappearing into the bathroom.

"*Out.*" Clearing my throat forcefully, I carefully readjust the pillow. Keeping it clutched carefully in one fist, I spin a forefinger in the air, gesturing in the direction she came from. "About face. Outta here. Right now."

The shower starts running, and Flinn remains hidden as I follow behind my best friend. Knowing that I definitely smell of sex, I have cum on my tongue, my hair is a mess, and in all honestly I've barely reconnected with my body after that orgasm . . . yeah . . . she's gonna have a million and one questions for me.

None of which I'm entertaining. Certainly not right now.

"Well, aren't you just full of surprises . . ." Sky's voice is all lilting singsong over her shoulder. "Here I am, worried you've starved to death all alone under ten feet of snow in your little hillside shack. When the truth is you've been eating just *fiiiiine*."

Fuck. I readjust the pillow, keeping my groin covered, and

drag my fingers through my hair. We really are just sneaking around, indulging in something kinda insane. I've gotta snap the fuck outta this and get back to life as normal.

"Who's Buns of Steel in there?" She sets the coffee down and spins around to face me, arms crossed. A smirk a mile wide occupies her lips.

"Okay, I adore you forever. Thank you for the provisions . . . but you need to leave right now," I hiss.

"Why? Can't I meet *boy toy*?" She tilts her head, not so subtly peering around me. God, I hope Flinn isn't hovering in that doorway.

"No." I snap my fingers repeatedly in front of her face, getting her focus back on me.

"Why are you going red?" She narrows her eyes on me. "You, of all people, don't get flustered about a hookup. What's going on?"

"Nothing."

"Bradford Rhodes." Sky props her hands on hips.

"*Shhhhh*. Just . . . I can't tell you. And you cannot say anything to anyone about what you saw here."

Her brow furrows, then those baby blues grow wide. "What have you done?" She peers around me again.

"Nothing."

Just fucked my ex's brother. And if you hadn't walked in, I probably would have wanted to propose to him if I wasn't so obsessed with having his cock in my mouth.

"This whole lot of nakedness doesn't *look* like nothing." She shakes her head, fluttering both hands in the direction of the pillow shielding my groin.

"Well, consider yourself blinded in both eyes, rendered incapable of sight at this present moment. Now run your pretty backside off to campus and I'll call you when I get home for the holidays." I jerk my chin at the door, having to quickly grab the pillow with my other hand again when I feel it starting to slip.

"You're telling me everything, and I mean every last detail, at Christmas." She rolls her eyes, blowing me an air kiss as she walks toward the door.

"No, I'm not," I call after her.

"Text me later. You can tell me all about how good that D is."

"My lips are sealed."

"Your lips are blow-job messy, is what they are." She cackles and shuts the door, leaving me damn near slumping to the floor in a heap.

Grabbing my phone from where it was plugged in at the kitchen counter, I see a trail of messages from Sky informing me that she was coming to "save the day" with bagels and caffeine. God, I owe her one.

There's also a text from my dad. I quickly send one back to him confirming that I'm packed up and gonna be heading back to the ranch tomorrow.

Tomorrow.

Ugh. The worst sort of sinking feeling occupies my stomach.

I can only assume this is where everything comes crashing to a halt. The road is obviously passable, and Flinn will be gone the moment he emerges from the shower. In fact, he's probably having an existential crisis in there right this very second.

Tossing the pillow aside, I drag my sweats and a hoodie on. Every second longer that shower runs, I'm beginning to imagine the worst. By the time the water cuts off, I've convinced myself the length of time Flinn has spent hidden in the bathroom is cowboy code for "I'm having regrets about everything and can't wait to run as far away from you as possible".

Whatever, I suppose I can understand. Fuck, do I wish we were two different people, that our situation was anything but this. And yet I can also fully appreciate there's no fucking way. Even though his sister screwed me over, ultimately, what the hell does it look like to have family gatherings—how do you in good conscience meet the parents and shake hands—when you've slept with both of their darling children?

God, I'm an idiot with no hope.

The bathroom door opens, and Flinn emerges. This time he's wearing the clothes he originally turned up in. A slightly rumpled suit, collar left hanging open to accentuate that strong throat, and those glasses framing his face. He looks like some sort of cover model for horse trainers.

"Don't worry, Sky's gone." My exhale is heavy with unspoken declarations and regret that I have to swallow them all down. "I guess this is the bittersweet goodbye part, huh?" I swallow, drinking in a last look at him. Maybe this will be the only time I ever get to fully appreciate the sight of him, without having to catch myself . . . you know . . . if we ever cross paths again in the future.

Flinn gives me a crooked smile, one that doesn't quite touch his eyes.

I hate everything about this.

"C'mon. Walk me out?" He tilts his head in the direction of the door.

"Sure," I grumble. Stupid goddamn tree-clearing people doing their job too well.

"Don't let me catch you sharing food with the cat for supper," he playfully scolds, and I know he's joking, but I also love the fact that he cares enough to think about a detail of that insignificance.

He shoves into his boots, then straightens up, reaching for the door. But it's all happening too fast. This man is slipping through my fingers, and I can't fucking stand it. Before he can touch the handle, before he can walk away, I catch his elbow and tug him back toward me.

I pull him in for one last kiss.

It's slow, unhurried. His stubble rasps against my own. He's rough beneath my lips, and also so warm. The taste of mint toothpaste and scent of my own bodywash swirls around me, nearly knocking me on my ass.

This feels like the sort of kiss I'd want to share with him every morning.

When he pulls back, I'm breathless and regretting everything about how we have to go our separate ways. And yet, for someone who always feels like they've got words, right now, I'm tongue-tied and simply staring at him.

Flinn looks back at me with an unreadable expression, his eyes flickering between mine, before he finally lets out a heavy breath. Running a thumb over my bottom lip, wet from his own, he leans in close, pressing his mouth against my forehead. The gentlest kiss is placed there before he speaks in a hushed tone.

"I'll see you around, my sunshine boy."

And with that, he's gone.

CHAPTER 18

Flinn

"Can you two hurry up and get home for Christmas already?" my baby sister grumbles at me over the phone, making sure to lay the guilt on extra thick. "Mom and Dad are breathing down my neck nonstop about why I'm not seeing anyone."

"You could just invent a girlfriend. Pick one from your book collection. They'd be none the wiser," I say, rubbing a palm over the back of my neck.

She snorts in disapproval. "Like you can talk. You know they're gonna be all over you like a rash about that moron you were seeing. At some point you're gonna actually have to tell them they're never meeting the guy."

I shove one hand in my pocket, looking out for any sight of Izzie, who told me to wait here while she did some last-minute Christmas shopping. Considering I'd rather punch myself in the face than listen to any more festive carols, I'll happily hang out in front of this café in the cold.

"Well, I think by the time I get there, our sister will succeed in taking all the heat. I don't know what she's gotten herself into, but it's a hot mess."

My baby sister makes an intrigued noise. "Gossip straight

from the horse trainer's mouth. I knew you were my favorite brother."

"I'm your *only* brother," I deadpan.

"Semantics." She brushes me off with her prim and proper scholarly voice. "Now give me the dirt so I can be ready with the popcorn when you two arrive."

Should I be getting into this? Should I be talking about things concerning Izzie and her relationship status . . . ? Especially because it skirts mighty close to my own tremendously poor decisions where sneaking around with Brad is concerned.

Although, there is no *Brad*, because I left and we've parted ways.

I hate it.

"She cheated on her boyfriend, and I don't know what else happened, but she's been acting all sort of weird since I got here. Even more so than normal," I add.

"Well, that tracks. You know she loves to trample everyone and everything to get what she wants. Our sister's big three is officially *bitch sun, narcissist moon, and self-absorbed rising*. Look at the fact you've driven all the way there, generously offering to move her shit, and I bet she hasn't said thank you either."

A laugh belts out of me.

"See? She might be our blood, but to be honest she's got a lot of work to do in order to actually start showing up as a *sister*."

Truer words have never been spoken.

"Okay, wise one, so we let Izzie be the family train wreck at Christmas, and you and I can sneak off somewhere. Maybe go ice skating and get tipsy on that peach schnapps poison you love."

"*Ew.* That was one time when I was sixteen, and I think I'd hurl if I ever smelt it again. But I'm down for escaping the family interrogation by candlelight and drinking spiked hot chocolate."

"Done."

"*Annnnd* you have to promise me you'll tell me about whoever this boy is you're seeing."

That has me coughing up a lung. "There isn't—"

"*Pfft*. Don't try denying it, Flinn." She tuts, and I can imagine her eyebrows arched behind her reading glasses. "You haven't sounded this happy in forever. Not even after seeing your favorite ponies are you this . . . chipper."

My silence stretches out.

Clara huffs. "Besides, Izzie texted me some list of super specific groceries she wants to make sure we have at the house ready for her—you know, because the world revolves around her, and her alone—but she mentioned you were being a squirmy little bitch about where you disappeared off to for a couple of nights."

"I booked myself somewhere to stay that *wasn't* her shitty couch," I protest weakly.

"*Mmhmm*. More like you booked yourself a cute guy with a nice big cowboy hat. I know the kind of Wrangler butt thirst traps you enjoy on repeat."

"Well, I know what kind of books you read. Cowgirls with more skills than just fast fingers and licking ice cream cones."

She splutters and admonishes me. "I'm literally never giving you access to my Kindle ever again."

"Okay, I gotta go . . . Pretty sure I see Izzie. God, she looks like she's on a warpath. So much for Christmas cheer." Rolling my eyes, I take a few steps toward my sister, who stomps along the sidewalk, seriously looking like she's got a stick shoved up her ass today. "I'll text you when we're getting close to Mom and Dad's." Can't wait to be stuck in a vehicle with her thundercloud mood.

"Drive safe. Love ya."

I've barely hung up when Izzie barges into my personal space, thrusting her shopping bags at me to carry, like I'm some woefully inadequate personal assistant.

"I told you to order me a decaf with extra caramel," she snaps.

Shaking my head, I grit my teeth and push open the door to the café. "*No*, you said you didn't trust me to get your order correct, so I needed to wait here for you."

"*Ugh.*" She throws her hands up, as if this is the biggest inconvenience of her life. According to the world of Izzie, it probably is.

I still don't truly understand how Brad ended up dating her. I mean, I know my sister can be capable of being charming and sweet, but it's usually short lived, and it's usually only to get what she wants.

What do I know? I train horses and much prefer them to people. I've also slept with her ex, so I'm hardly a pillar of society exuding moral standing right now.

Following after my sister, her shitty attitude, and self-absorbed ego, I check the time. We really need to be hitting the road soon. If there's one thing I don't want, it's to be running into icy conditions while driving after dark with my horse trailer full of her crap.

We join the short queue, and just as we do so, the door behind us opens, a tiny bell tinkling as it swings to let in a gust of chilled air.

The space damn near crackles around my back and shoulders.

My nape prickles.

I immediately know it's *him* without needing to turn around.

And yet I swivel to take in the sight waiting for me. To inhale another glimpse of Brad, because it might have been less than twenty-four hours since I walked out that door, but it feels like every minute has dragged into eternity.

I'm fighting to keep my reactions in check, especially since my body warms all over seeing him in his backward cap and disheveled hair sticking out, wearing the same forest-green hoodie I borrowed from him.

Does it still smell like me?

Is that why he's wearing it?

"Oh. *You.*" Izzie sounds like she just stepped in something unpleasant. "Hey, Brad. This is my brother, Flinn." She huffs and waves a hand between the two of us before turning back to her phone.

Brad's eyes crease at the corners. He seems a little taken aback at seeing the two of us, mixed with a mischievous smile somewhere in there too.

"Hey," I mumble, palms damn well itching to cup his jaw and hold him steady while I brush our lips together.

Brad goes to open his mouth, but my sister beats him to it. Her head jerks up from scrolling her phone, eyes popping wide, and for a moment—a stomach flipping, everything falling through the floor second—I think she's somehow seen the way we just looked at each other. Like we've both got big neon signs flashing above our heads saying, "Guilty."

Everything shifts at lightning speed. "*Move.*" She shoves Brad out the way, face going pale, holding a hand over her mouth, and rushes past out onto the sidewalk.

And right there, in the middle of town, she hurls into the trash, heaving her guts out as we look on awkwardly and watch it happen, dumbfounded.

"Izzie?" I shoot Brad a sideways glance. As much as she's been a raging bitch, I do the big-brother thing and push through the door to go after her.

Brad follows on my heels, and when we get to her, she's already dabbing at her mouth with a wet wipe from her handbag and sipping on her bottle of water.

"Gross. That's like the fourth time today," she groans.

When I look over at Brad, he's turned white as chalk and stands rigid. "*No.* No. No fucking way." He stumbles over the words a little. "You and I—we haven't actually—not for months—"

Now it's my turn to feel the blood drain from my face as I look on in horror. "Izzie . . . are you . . ." God, I can't even say the word. What if it's Brad's? What if this whole situation is about to go south faster than a sinking ship blown to pieces by cannon fire?

I'm gonna be hurling my guts into that trash can alongside her if that's the case.

"*Urghhh.* Quit looking at me like that." She presses a wrist to her forehead. "It's not yours. You can quit freaking out over there, Rhodes."

It doesn't make me feel much better.

"Start talking," I grunt. Not liking the way she just spoke to him at all.

"Fine. Yes, I'm pregnant. But I'm not supposed to be telling anyone, not until we've got a few things sorted out."

"The professor?" Brad snorts. "Yeah, I bet you've got a few things to sort out if it's *his*."

That's when my sister does something I didn't actually think would be possible. Big fat tears well up in her eyes, and she sniffs. "Brad, I'm a terrible person for lying to you. I'm sorry I dragged you into this, but he told me it would seem less suspicious if I had a 'boyfriend' . . . especially if I was seeing someone . . . another student."

A gruff noise bursts out of me. I don't give a shit that she's crying and apologizing. "What the fuck? You can't be serious. You *used* him?"

She starts crying more freely now and has to wipe her cheeks on her sleeve. "Okay, okay. I messed up, alright? Is that what you wanna hear? I was scared Karl would dump me if I didn't. And you're a good guy. You're smart and good looking. It wasn't hard to . . . You know, it wasn't like I had to *fake* being into you or anything. We had fun, right? I'm sorry, I really am."

Her hiccupped apologies just feel so damn hollow to my ears.

I fucking hate that she manipulated him.

All my own experiences being duped and taken for granted, the anguish of finding out the truth about someone who I'd wasted time and trust on, that all simmers just below the surface.

"And the worst part is, now that I'm knocked up, I don't even think he wants to know me anymore. He won't text me back."

Well, Merry fucking Christmas to one and all of us.

Fuck.

CHAPTER 19

Brad

Sky:
Looks like I'll be blessing you with my presence at your New Year's Eve party after all, bitch.

???

My folks decided to do a loop back to Crimson Ridge in their RV. So they'll be home for the whole holidays.

But they've decided to put the house on the market, so they're permanent gray nomads now. It's gonna be our last Christmas together at the house.

Wow. Look at them, living the dream.

Wait . . . so does that mean you won't be staying in Crimson Ridge after all?

You're abandoning me all alone in the land of zero sushi?

Undecided. There's a cute shop coming up for rent.

Come with me to check it out in the New Year? I gotta make sure it's not a total roach fest.

Deal. Although you're gonna have to promise me that when you're a rich and famous florist to the stars, you'll still come hang out with me on the ranch. I'll need someone to watch stupid movies with and eat ice cream.

Spending the rest of my days hanging out with my old man isn't exactly going to do my dating life any favors.

Jesus Christ . . . looking at how long he's been single, I don't exactly have a good track record to follow, do I?

It takes her ages to reply, and meanwhile I keep one eye on my phone and the other on the chestnut mare, Maple, I'm grooming. Life back at Rhodes Ranch is ninety-nine percent horses, one percent having a social life.

It's not THAT far away. Don't be dramatic.

Besides, don't you go pretending like the *naked man in your bed* incident didn't happen.

Have you started planning the "his and his" embroidered towels yet?

Don't know what you're talking about.

I swallow heavily and shove my phone away. Feeling the raft of incoming text vibrations,They will no doubt be from Sky, with her hollering at me for sidestepping questions about Flinn . . . yet again.

The girl has spent every possible opportunity trying to pull details out of me, and there's only so long I can hold her tiny, but mighty, self at arm's length about him.

Maybe I'll just get drunk on New Year's Eve, sob on her shoulder, and confess all my sins, while ruing the fact I should have been kissing Flinn senseless beneath mistletoe for Christmas.

But that's not gonna be happening, so I guess I'm just destined to be single and miserable forever.

"Can you check in on Grizz for me once you're done here? Need to give his legs and hooves a thorough looking-over." The rough voice of my dad cuts into my thoughts.

"Yeah, of course." Lifting my eyes over the back of the horse, I see him readjusting his hat over hair that definitely is a little long overdue for a cut. That white curl that's been there long before he ever started showing signs of a little salt and pepper hangs over his forehead.

My dad, Lucas Rhodes, gives everything he's got to this place. And as much as I love to give him shit about being a grumpy old hermit, I'm proud of what he's achieved. Although, from the looks of it, I might need to work on roping him to a chair and attacking him with the clippers.

Aside from now needing to groom *him* as well as these horses, I know I've got my work cut out for me with a few *modernizations* that are long overdue. Namely, bringing Rhodes Ranch into the modern era . . . y'know, *social media* and a *website* just to start with.

The faded notebook full of scribbled names and phone

numbers sitting in the tack room gives me hives just to look at it. That's been the system he's relied on for years, and while I guess it isn't all bad, I know from talking to plenty of our clients that they'd be over the goddamn moon if we got ourselves online. They want to be able to book boarding more easily, have cameras installed so that we can live stream the stables, and make appointments for arena time.

Lucas Rhodes would rather eat a duck, feathers and all, than have to handle things like marketing this ranch. It was part of our deal: He wanted me to get out of this place and go to college first. He didn't want me settling for life here in Crimson Ridge before I had a chance to spread my wings a little.

So, art school and a few years away came and went . . . and I've never felt more sure of my choice to come back and work alongside my dad running this ranch.

I mean, he's done it alone ever since my mom decided she wasn't actually interested in the whole *parenting thing*. So, surely I can handle it, too?

"You know . . . you don't have to be out here working on your first day back at home." Dad comes over and gives Maple a rub along her nose before scratching beneath her chin. Murmuring something quietly in the way he always does to talk to every horse here as if they're lifelong friends.

I shrug. "Might as well. I've missed this."

There's another massive thing I'm missing from my life, and this is proving to be the perfect kind of distraction rather than stalking Flinn online for the hundredth time.

"Need any help with stuff for tomorrow? All that Christmassy shit?" This man has given me his gruff cowboy routine about my annual holiday season parties ever since I turned sixteen and informed him that Rhodes Ranch needed to start being *cool*. I thrust a hand-drawn invitation into his muddy paws and told him to take a shower and be ready by six because we had folks coming over for a BBQ.

I swear to god he nearly choked to death in the middle of the barn, yet he did everything I asked—even manned the grill—and has done so religiously without a single grumble every year since.

That's where we're fundamentally wired differently, he and I.

For my dad, a good time is falling asleep on the couch with his book splayed across his chest and hockey on in the background. For me . . . well . . . it's not that I wouldn't be perfectly happy to fall asleep on the couch—I just like the idea of having friends over and a house humming with people.

"That *Christmassy shit* is actually a party for New Year's Eve. Ya know . . . the event that without fail gets you new clients each time spring rolls around." I shake my head. "And you can leave it to me. Besides, I've got Sky helping me out."

"The one with the . . . pink?" He gestures in the direction of his head, brows knitted together.

"*Yes.* The pink hair. You know who she is. My best friend, Skylar Addams. Sky's been hanging out here with me for years."

"Okay, keep your hat on." He clicks his tongue. "Wondered whether you'd be bringing anyone from college to this party . . . maybe the mysterious girlfriend I heard a few whispers about?"

A rock wedges itself in the back of my throat. "Uhh, no. She wasn't the right one, ya know."

"Sorry to hear that, son."

"I dodged a bad situation, trust me." I let out a wry laugh, feeling every inch of that moment on the sidewalk when my stomach just about fell out of my ass when I realized that Izzie was pregnant and had my entire life flash before my eyes.

And then the look of anguish on Flinn's face when I hightailed it out of there without really saying a proper goodbye. What else was I supposed to fucking do, all things considered?

Dad moves to grab the broom leaning against the side of Maple's stall. But he's not racing away, so I decide to poke at him about his own love life, since deflecting attention off my own misfortune sounds like a much better plan.

"What about you?" I clear my throat, guiding the grooming brush along Maple's flank.

"What do you mean?" He pushes the broom with enough force it might snap.

"You don't need someone?" I smirk.

"No." That broom must be made of steel.

"Sure about that?"

"You betcha."

A smirk plays on my lips. Oh, so maybe the old man isn't quite as dead inside as I thought after all. There might be hope for him yet. "Maybe you'll find someone this New Year's Eve?"

"Unlikely," he mutters, more to himself than to me.

Giving Maple a final pat and a kiss on her forehead, I toss the brush into the bucket and fold my arms, watching him sweep out the center aisle. "They might be right under your nose and you never opened your eyes." It shouldn't give me as much joy as it does to push his buttons.

"Well, open *your* eyes and turn that fucking trough water off before you flood the place," he barks at me before stalking off in the direction of the tack room.

Ahh, yes. Back home . . . Rhodes Ranch, where the cowboys are hopelessly *single.*

CHAPTER 20

Brad

I miss my cat, who isn't my cat. And I miss my cowboy, who isn't my cowboy.

How much more pathetic can a guy be, two days out from Christmas?

I've just watched Hans Gruber fall thirty floors off the top of Nakatomi Plaza—in the ultimate holiday movie, if there ever was one—yet, there's only so much *action* a marathon of shoot-'em-up flicks can be useful for providing a distraction. Iconic catch phrases only go so far toward temporarily numbing my brain to the reality . . . that I'm lying alone with an aching empty space occupying my chest and my bed.

Apparently Flinn switched my hopeless romantic setting to expert level, and now I'm stranded here, flying solo, with no idea how to play the game anymore.

So maybe that's why I'm staring at his Instagram profile, hoping he'll post something . . . anything . . .

Not desperate behavior. At all.

I can't help it. All I keep seeing in my head is that final moment on the sidewalk, with him and his sister side by side, and the fallout of her bombshell reveal about being pregnant with the guy she's been screwing behind my back.

Jesus. What a mess.

It's eating away at me not knowing how he is or what happened after I walked away. In all of this, it's Flinn I'm thinking about nonstop. As it turns out, the guy I was supposed to move on from is impossible to forget.

Taking a big gulp of whiskey, I groan and press send on the message I've written and deleted fifty times while lying here. I shoot my shot.

Hey. Got any suggestions for what a guy should make to eat tonight?

I'm all out of cat kibble.

"Sent" appears below the little bubble of text.

Immediately followed by "Seen."

My stomach flops in dramatic fashion.

Seconds crawl by.

Is he gonna ignore me? What's taking so long? Is he chiseling his response into stone? Am I going to be relegated to waiting for a response during business hours of Monday through Friday, nine to five?

Dots start to flurry and I feel like my heart is about to explode. He's replying. Or at least . . . I think he is. The ordeal of waiting while fixated on tiny bouncing pixels on my phone screen—which stop and then start up again—drags on and on.

After damn near climbing the walls, I see the most Flinn of replies. Frustratingly simple and no fluff. This is a cowboy who obviously shuns emojis.

Flinn:
Hey. Sorry, I'm out with people at the moment.

It's okay. I get it.

Don't wanna interrupt.

How goddamn pathetic? The guy I'm obsessing over doesn't even want to text back? Message received. Loud and fucking clear.

I drain the last of my drink, feeling like I want to sock myself in the jaw for even reaching out in the first place.

A request to video chat fills the screen.

Oh my fucking god.

I nearly drop my phone in my haste to jab the green button, spluttering on a mouth full of whiskey. It burns like hellfire going down my throat in a rush as I cough and choke and my eyes water. This is peak unsexy. A great look for me. Nothing says, "Hey, wanna reconsider your stance on hooking up with your sister's ex?" like coughing up a lung.

"Well . . . if I'd known you'd be this pleased to see me . . ." Flinn covers his mouth with a big palm, stifling laughter. "Are you losing your touch? Thought you could swallow?"

"Sh-shut up," I croak, blinking away the wetness coating my lashes. God, he looks so good. "Why are you whispering?" As a ragged noise comes out of me as I clear my throat, I realize he's got earphones in.

His eyes flicker off to the side, and he shifts his weight before looking back at me. "I'm at a Christmas tree farm with my sisters."

My giant grin is a problem. Absolutely impossible to hide the way it stretches across my face. "Sneaking off to talk to me, huh?"

"You started it."

"You called *me*."

"I missed you." Flinn says the words hushed, but he doesn't miss a beat. The sentiment rolls off his tongue like we've exchanged moments like this thousands of times before. Not like we're two cowboys who *shouldn't* know each other so intimately.

He doesn't waver in saying those three little words, but my heart certainly stutters and trips over itself hearing him say them nonetheless.

"I-I really wish you were here." The confession blurts out. Heat scrambles up the back of my neck and chest. "This whole situation has got me twisted upside down, Flinn. You gotta know, I can't stop thinking about you." My fingers dig into my hair as I readjust the phone and lean back.

His eyes bore into me. We might be a thousand miles away from each other, but I feel everything in that stare. I'm lying on my couch, holding him in front of my face, and the urge to kiss him is damn near blinding.

"Glad I'm not the only one." Flinn exhales heavily, his features softening a touch. Like a weight has been lifted upon hearing me say it out loud. "Kinda assumed you wouldn't wanna . . ."

"Flinn. I only bolted the other day because shit was already too hard to keep under wraps around your sister. It was crappy of me, but I figured you would rather I disappear than accidentally slip up and say something stupid like 'I'll call you tomorrow.'"

His lips twitch. "Borderline planning to casually stalk me were you, *hmm*?"

"Oh, there's nothing casual here. Certainly nothing *casual* about what your voice does to me, cowboy." I dart my tongue out to wet my bottom lip.

Through the screen I see his nostrils flare, then his gaze drifts to whatever is in the background, out of view. He pulls the phone a little closer and my heart starts zooming around behind my ribcage.

"Brad . . ." My name is almost a soft groan. One of those big hands comes up to run through his hair.

I'm already rock hard.

"Say my name like that again." My pulse kicks in the side of my neck, matching the heavy throb in my balls. Every memory of our time together collides, my cock twitching as I subtly lift my hips. It's like I can feel his heat and bulk even though he's not here. Goddamn, all the ways it felt so incredible to sink inside his mouth . . . his ass . . . *Fuck.*

"*Brad.*" This time when it says it, there's a whole lot more desperation there. Unspoken need and secretive wants behind the tone of his voice.

"Can anyone see you right now?" Fuck it. I'm not passing up this opportunity. I fucking crave Flinn in a way that defies any sort of logic, and he's gotta know that.

He shakes his head. Eyes going wide as he sees me start panning the phone down my body.

"Gonna keep quiet for me?" As I say it, I lift the hem of my T-shirt.

"Fuck." His strong throat dips. "I want that to be my hand, right there." Through the phone, the sound of his breathing intensifies.

"What would you do to me, baby?" I cup myself through my sweats, showing off the bulge tenting the material. "If I was right there with you . . . would you help me feel better? Would you sneak around with me and get me off in secret?"

Flinn makes a rough noise in the back of his throat. "I wouldn't want you to be a secret. I *don't* want you to be a secret," he's quick to add.

"Well, we can't exactly go fucking out in the open without getting arrested." My lips curve into a grimace of pleasure as I squeeze and rub. "Let's pretend. Just pretend with me, Flinn. In this little fantasy, we're not sneaking around about being together . . . but if you want to be a good boy for me, you're gonna have to be sneaky about fooling around in a public place."

He swallows, then pinches his bottom lip between his teeth. "Here? Like . . . right here?"

I hook my thumb beneath the waistband and pull the elastic

away just enough to tease. To taunt him with the hidden evidence that he can't see on camera but that he *knows* is there all the same. "Gonna prove how much you missed me? "

In the dim lighting of the festoon bulbs overhead and starry night sky, Flinn's pupils bloom.

Daring him to do this is reckless. Yet, it lights a fire, the amber in his hazel gaze catching alight in a way I'm fucking addicted to.

"I bet you wouldn't dare."

CHAPTER 21

Flinn

"*I bet you wouldn't dare.*"

My blood sizzles with such a heady proposition.

Risky phone sex? Being exposed with nowhere to hide if someone were to come back here deeper into this crop of trees? Even considering for one *second* to play this game with Brad?

All I can think is . . . I don't know what the hell I'm doing and I absolutely need to be able to do this with him again.

I've never had anyone so unreservedly and openly desire me. Brad makes me feel fucking invincible, like I could sprout wings and soar among the clouds. He leaves my heart beating stronger, rather than in tatters.

He's the kind of man I could all too easily fall into.

The cowboy I've already tumbled head over heels for.

"Would you put your hand right here?" Brad's voice is husky. The view on screen of his lower stomach and dusting of dark hair below his belly button makes my mouth water.

I gulp down the nerves. This is something I want to do for him. I want to be brave and show him that he's special to me, even if that doesn't make any sense. Being with him in this way is just as potent as touching him.

I've done long distance. It was never like this. Not once.

"I would." My eyes fixate on the dark shadow below his waistband, where he keeps teasing by tugging on it. "I'd pull that down. Your briefs too."

"Where would you like your mouth to be? Would you be kissing me right now if you could, cowboy?"

My dick leaps at the husk in his voice.

"Goddamn, you better believe I would be. I love how your lips feel when they're on mine."

"I miss how good your stubble feels," Brad hums, obliging me by pushing his sweats out of the way.

"Fuck." A deep grunt escapes me. "You're messy already, sunshine." There's a glistening bead of precum at his tip when his cock bobs up against his stomach.

"Show me." Brad pans the phone lower, giving me a better angle to appreciate *everything*. His thickness, that smooth skin, the vein I want to map with my tongue. "Let me see you."

My brain stalls. My heart too.

"Here? Right now?" I shoot a furtive look at my surroundings. My ass rests on the edge of a stack of wooden pallets. This is beyond a terrible idea. Yet my hand is already moving south.

Brad hums, swiping his thumb over that wetness to smear it around the swollen head of him. "Since you're busy undressing me, it's only fair I get to see how sloppy you are."

"Jesus," I mutter, and before I can successfully overthink it, I adjust my weight and fumble one-handed with my belt.

"Fuck, you're so sexy." Brad wraps himself in his fist and starts to leisurely stroke. It's hypnotic the way his fist shuttles up and down, casting shadows over the screen that add to the tease of it all. "I wanna fuck you wearing just the glasses. You goddamn kill me with how good you look with them on."

Heat intensifies on my cheeks. "Want me to leave them on while I suck you?" I can't quite believe I'm playing this game so eagerly.

Brad makes a desperate sort of sound. "*Fffuuuck*. Put me in your mouth."

My breathing shallows, growing choppy with the effort to stay quiet. "I love feeling how heavy you are on my tongue. When I feel you push inside my mouth, it drives me crazy."

"I need to see," Brad whines. "You look so hot with those sexy glasses and your lips wrapped around the base of me. Fuck yes, I can feel you taking me all the way."

He says the words and I feel it. I feel him. That musky masculine scent is so visceral in my mind's eye, filling my nostrils with all the recollections of him—it's as if he truly is sliding hot and heavy across my tongue. Those potent memories of being with him swirl through my senses, grabbing hold of my every brain cell. "Wrap your palm around my throat. Put your hand there. Feel how I swallow you," I murmur, fixated on the place where he juts up inside his fist.

"*Ummmppphhf*. Fuck." Brad gets caught off guard by that visual I just painted for him. The camera shakes and his dick jerks.

"Hold your hand out. Let me spit," Brad commands, voice more than a little ragged now. "If you're gonna deep-throat me, you can at least play with yourself properly while you're on your knees."

I quickly spit in my palm, just as he would if he were here and I were actually on my knees for him.

All it takes is that first moment I touch myself, slick and desperate, to have me biting down on my bottom lip. The noise that threatens to escape is worthy of a porn star, and I'm in agony at how good this feels but how wrong it is that I'm sitting here with my cock in my hand. Something about that combination trips a wire in my brain. Heat zaps down my spine and I know this is gonna be fast and terribly messy.

"Oh, baby. Look at you." Brad hits me with that dose of praise I shouldn't like as much as I do. "You look like a fucking dream."

"I-I'm already close," I gasp. Tugging on myself near frantically. Have I ever been this turned inside out? Nothing compares to how it feels to do this with him. To watch him fuck his fist. To see his stomach muscles bunching and flexing with that V more prominently outlined by shadows. To hear his heavy breathing and quiet groans and soft curses delivered so intimately in my ear buds.

This is sensory overload.

Everything about this has me primed and ready to burst.

Right here, surrounded by pine trees and shoveled snow, I'm seconds away from rocketing cum.

"*Ffffuuuck.* Your mouth." Brad squeezes, tugs harder, thrusts his hips to chase the sensation. "Use your tongue, just like that. Goddamn, the way you suck dick is too good."

My heart thunders, and I'm battling for my life not to start making pathetic fucking noises out loud. "Brad. *Fuck.* Sunshine, I'm gonna . . ." Gritting my teeth to get the words out, I'm right on edge. Tingling gathers low in my balls, everything tightens, and my grip is brutal as I race for the point of no return.

"That's it. Sweet fuck, suck me deep." Through the screen, his cock throbs. "I'm there. God. Swallow me. Swallow every fucking drop."

"*Unghhhh.* Fuck." A feral noise bursts past my lips. My dick fills and surges and fucking explodes all over my palm. I think I go blank. As my vision blurs at the edges, I watch cum pump out of Brad's dick on my phone screen at the same time as my own. White ribbons streak out to coat his fist, his knuckles, and the camera wobbles as he moves it closer. He gives me the kind of lewd, carnal view I would have if my mouth was right there.

I can taste the salty tanginess of him. I can feel the heat of him. I can smell his musky, masculine scent of sex and sweat.

Something moves and catches the corner of my eye, and I

damn well have a heart attack, scrambling to shove myself away. I'm a fucking mess, cum all over my hand, the sticky evidence of what I just did smears over the hem of my shirt and soaks the cotton of my boxer briefs.

"Holy shit." At the rate my heart is furiously pumping, I feel like I'm out of my body right now. Shoving my hand beneath my top, I wipe the slickness over my stomach, doing my best to hide the fact I just jacked off out in the open.

"You okay?" Brad pulls the camera up so that I can see his gorgeous face again. He looks dreamy as hell, but his brows tug together ever so slightly when he notices my wild-eyed expression.

Letting out a chuckle of relief, I finish wiping my hand as clean as it can possibly be for now. "Yeah, *uhhhhh*, I thought someone was about to walk this way and get a whole eyeful. False alarm."

Brad grins, unremorseful. "Your dick looks pretty fucking incredible on camera by the way."

The back of my neck glows hotter.

"Send me a photo tonight?" His energy is so damn addictive, so playful.

I find myself nodding.

"This is where the thing I'm supposed to say goes along the lines of 'Have a nice life . . .'" he murmurs, eyes sparkling at me through the phone. "But I don't think I'm strong enough to say the words, cowboy."

Chewing my bottom lip for a long moment I simply stare at him. I stare, because it's all I ever want to do where Brad is concerned. He makes me want to be in his orbit. He's got this gravitational pull I feel deep in the marrow of my bones. I want to cook him breakfast, lunch, and dinner . . . and I want to spend so many more nights with his arms wrapped around me.

"In everything else I would say I'll gladly be strong enough for the two of us." I blow out a long exhale, a white plume gusting past my lips. "But in this? When it comes to trying to walk away from you, my sunshine boy? I'm so goddamn weak, you have no idea."

CHAPTER 22

Brad

Christmas Eve party mode is here, and in all the years I've insisted on Rhodes Ranch being the hub of holiday spirit—much to old man Rhodes's chagrin—I've never once felt like I wanted to run away. Yet, here I am, knee bouncing, eyes glued to my phone, battling the urge to sprint out into the snow. Anxious little thoughts nip at my heels as I wonder why I haven't heard back from Flinn tonight.

Rationally, I keep telling myself he'll be at his local Christmas market. He told me he's spending the evening with his family. No doubt he'll be occupied, probably catching up with old friends, running into the usual small-town round of fifty questions about his life and what he's been up to since this time last year.

But I'm itchy with all the unknowns, the damn spinning chaos of wondering if my guy is entertaining conversations of a different kind.

Wanna grab a coffee sometime?

Shall we exchange numbers?

How about you come back to my place?

I can't stand this feeling. We've been texting and calling virtually nonstop since the other night—after we flew straight past the undisputable boundary of whether or not we were going to forget about each other and move on with our lives. And it's more than just hot-as-fuck phone sex, too. I've given him a tour of the stables, introduced him to the horses, and confessed that I worry about Lily something chronic. For a cat that didn't even belong to me, I somehow ended up awfully attached.

Story of my life.

My last message sent to him earlier sits forlornly unread.

Wish you'd meet me under the mistletoe.

Flinn hasn't opened the text or responded, and my silly little heart drags its bottom lip along the floor with every passing hour I don't hear from him. Oh god, I think—well, I know—I slipped and let myself get hopelessly swept up in him. How could this possibly be a good idea? We're not even in the same state . . . I don't really know where he is for most of the year or what his regular life looks like, other than the fact that he travels around for work as a horse trainer.

I've been a coward and have been too afraid to ask. My skills at deflecting to different topics are ninja level. The reality I'm all too familiar with is that men like him who operate as freelancers in the equine industry end up being on the road *a lot*. He hasn't mentioned working with one particular ranch or stable, and I'm honestly just too shit scared to poke a hole in the flimsy gift wrapping of all that encompasses *Flinn*. This is a truth I don't want to discover: that even with all our other problems aside, he might *want* to carry on his life of travel and freedom.

How the hell did I wake up one day and become ball-and-chain Brad? I'd never do that to him.

Scrolling back through some of our messages from when we chatted briefly early this morning, I find a photo he sent me. It shows his big, strong hand holding a chipped mug with a cartoon sun giving a cheesy thumbs-up on it.

He'd sent it along with a text . . .

Flinn:
Even at five a.m., I can't escape you, my sunshine boy.

"Christ. Do I even wanna know what caused a smile that wide? Hope it's not one of those dick pics you kids seem to think is a good idea to splash all over the internet?" My dad narrows his eyes at my phone, looking at it with all his forty-plus years of distrust in modern technology. His expression is wary, as if the thing was about to leap out and transform into a real-life trouser snake, forcing him to see unsolicited cock.

I quickly lock my phone screen and scrub a palm over my mouth, a poor effort to hide the enormous, goofy smile occupying my face. "No sneak attack dicks. Officially a dick pic–free zone."

I mean, that's not exactly true. Those are safely stored in a private album. An ode to Flinn's perfect cock.

My dad claps me on the shoulder, half dragging me to my feet. "Step outside with me for a minute, would ya?"

"Need a hand with the grill?" I glance around at the group of friends and neighbors filling the house. On New Year's Eve, we throw a big party each year, but tonight—on the cusp of Christmas—this is much more of a low-key gathering. Lucas Rhodes cuts a relatively relaxed figure and doesn't spend the entire time hiding behind the grill on nights like this, but come the party to ring in the New Year, he'll be nothing but a cowboy shadow. The kind of stand-up guy my old man is, he's already offered to be a designated driver for anyone who needs it on the night.

"There's something I need to show you." He shrugs, noncommittal, and I follow behind his broad shoulders as he moves in the direction of the front door.

"Is this about setting up an extra Christmas tree on the front porch? I know you probably think it's way overboard, and I know, I know . . . 'Who needs more than one Christmas tree?' But it's not gonna kill you to have a little extra Yuletide spirit around the place—" Anything I was planning on saying next in defense of my overeager decorating escapades this year flies from my lungs like a punch to the gut. He holds the front door open, and an "oomph" wheezes out of me as I stop dead in my tracks on the threshold.

My dad's firm hand plants between my shoulder blades and gives me a subtle nudge, encouraging me to step outside. "I found a stray hanging around out here in the cold. Pretty sure this one might belong to you?" With a knowing look, he pulls the door shut, leaving me standing outside with my heart in my throat.

Flinn.

He's here.

What is happening?

"Hoping like hell I wasn't too late to meet you under the mistletoe?" Flinn pushes his glasses up his nose.

All I'm capable of is gaping at him. Flinn. My dream guy is standing on my front porch, and I'm frozen to the spot, freaking the fuck out. Is he here to end things in person? Oh my god, I want to kiss him, but do we do that?

"You . . . you're in Crimson Ridge?" I say hoarsely.

Flinn swallows and clears his throat. In his big palm is a present . . . Well, at least it's a brown box with red twine tied in a bow. "Umm . . . Merry Christmas." He extends the gift my way. "They're cookies. Well, actually, they're dick cookies . . . and when I bought them, it seemed cute and funny, like it's our little inside joke, but now I feel like I'm the lamest person you've ever met. Who turns up with a box of dicks?" He grimaces. "I've been staring at your front door, too nervous to knock, until your dad spotted me. And well, fuck, Brad, I'm basically just all clammy palms and nerves right now, so it's okay for you to tell me this was a disaster of an idea. This was a terrible decision, wasn't it?"

Stunned silence fills my brain. Fluttering wings of hope swarm my belly. "Wh-what are you doing here?" My software malfunctions. My hard drive freezes. I'm trying to reboot, but it's taking too fucking long and now I'm worried he's gonna vanish just as suddenly as crystallizing into solid form.

"I just dropped off my sister . . . not Izzie, but the youngest one . . ." he hastens to clarify. "I dropped her at some cute bed-and-breakfast that had a vacancy, then came straight over here. Basically, I was miserable, and Clara could see right through me. Earlier, I was standing there with that sunshine mug, almost losing my damn mind, because I've hated every second not being with you. So we decided Crimson Ridge sounded like a great idea for a spontaneous Christmas road trip, considering the mess back at my folks' place." Flinn steps into me, pressing the box of cookies into my hands. "That professor Izzie was with? Yeah, he turned up. It seems like Iz went and blabbed to someone who told someone . . . Well . . . long story short, he doesn't have a job any more, and they're moving back to his home in Germany for him to start a new job. I don't know how else to explain that, or to apologize for my sister being a person who will only ever be interested in herself. They're moving away, and I don't know how often Iz will ever be in touch because she's kind of a jerk like that, and I just couldn't imagine moving on with my life without telling you to your face that I would rather put up with a thousand potentially awkward family dinners than never see you again." Everything rushes out in a long breath. Is this the most I've ever heard Flinn speak all in one go?

I open my mouth, but Flinn holds up his hand to interrupt. He's not done yet.

"Just let me get this all out, before I explode . . . I've never felt this way about *anyone* before. You are there in every single thought I have, everywhere I turn. A hundred times a day, I'm resisting the urge to text you and send a photo of whatever I'm looking at because it reminds me of you. And that's crazy behavior, right? Love-bombing, don't they call it? Or some weird, unhealthy shit. I know nothing about how to do this, but I'm pretty sure you're not supposed to crave talking to someone nonstop, twenty-four seven. That goes against all the dating rules. Except, I guess I blew that off and went one step further, since we're not even dating, I just drove for hours, then turned up without warning like a creep. Which makes me sound delusional and more desperate than I should admit out loud, but this is all I've got. The honest truth of it is me, standing here, begging for you to pretend . . . I dunno, maybe just imagine I'm an orphan or some kind of stray animal with no family, and forget that I have siblings, if that's what it takes."

I'm clinging to the box like I'd really rather be clinging to him, and my brain is an out-of-control Ferris wheel, spiraling, spinning lights and no hope of finding my balance, other than by simply grabbing his face and yelling at him that I want all of that too.

Just as I wet my lips and finally think I can croak something out that isn't completely unhinged, like "Will you marry me?" a bulge inside Flinn's coat squirms of its own accord, and I jolt.

"What the fuck is that?" Is this where I discover Flinn's beautiful declaration is actually because he's been body snatched?

"Oh, umm . . . I bought you another gift." Flinn glances down sheepishly and undoes the front of his jacket a little.

A tiny head covered in orange fur pops up with a *chirp*, bleary-eyed and drowsy.

"Lily?" My voice catches. I reach for the front of Flinn's jacket, and my gaze bounces rapidly between the cat tucked against him and those gorgeous eyes of his. "You brought Lily with you?" I'm blinking fast.

Flinn gives me a hesitant smile, covering my hand with his.

"I went back to find her. She was waiting at your old place, so I took her to get checked for a microchip, and they confirmed that the owner had been an old lady. We did some calling around and discovered that she'd passed away. The family didn't know where the cat had gone when they sold the house and assumed she had run off. Little did they know she'd been living with you all year."

This man. I'm gonna husband him up one day.

"You went to all that effort . . ."

"It's nothing."

"It's definitely NOT nothing."

Flinn squeezes my hand. "Told you that you're my sunshine boy . . . and somehow in among all the snow, in the darkest part of winter, I managed to find the brightest ray of hope I could ever wish for."

CHAPTER 23

Flinn

I've turned into a fountain of words. A burst water main. The equivalent of a verbal geyser unable to be contained.

"I don't know why I didn't tell you before turning up unannounced. Brad . . . believe me when I say, I needed to see you more than I needed air, and I'm sorry if—"

Brad chuckles, a wheezing sound of delight and relief, before leaning close. The nearness of him soothes my frayed nerves and brings my incessant ramblings slamming to a halt. His lips meet mine, both of us numb with cold from lingering out here, though our kiss is anything but. Beneath the surface, we're fevered in our connection. The calming, masculine scent of him washes through my brain, and the only thing stopping me from dragging our bodies flush together is the cat contentedly purring against my chest.

"We're ditching." *Kiss*. "This party." *Nip*. "Right." *Lick*. "Fucking now." Brad tangles his tongue with mine, sinking deeper while groaning into my mouth. As if the concept of pulling back and separating for even a single moment is physically paining him.

I feel the exact same way.

He weaves his fingers with mine, determinedly dragging me—and the snoozing Lily, who seems utterly oblivious to our intense make-out session—down the steps, leading me along a shoveled path in the direction of other buildings on the ranch. I'm struggling to know where to look, heart pounding. This is his place . . . *his home*.

And he wants me here.

We pass the stables, scents of hay and leather and horses drifting on the frozen night air, faint but familiar. The setup they run looks incredible, and it has me hesitating, my steps slowing with curiosity and eagerness to explore. "Holy shit, the photos on your website do *not* do all of this justice, you know that, right?" I say.

Brad squeezes my hand and lets out a frustrated whine from the back of his throat. "Seriously? You're gonna go all weak at the knees for the horses and some stables, when I'm literally out here begging to suck your dick?"

My teeth catch my bottom lip, and I give him a pleading look. The way I must look ridiculous right now, but I don't even care.

He shakes his head in exasperation. "After." Damn near crushing my hand, he tugs me with him. "I promise you can have the world's longest horse-cuddling session *after*."

"Oh my god. I've fucking missed you." My fingers sink into Brad's hair as his throat closes around my tip. "I've missed you so much, baby." I'm panting, damn near levitating off the floor at the sight of my cowboy on his knees, his thick, leaking cock in one fist and those flushed, kiss-bitten lips I want everywhere all at once wrapped around the base of me.

We hardly made it through the door. His small cabin is warm and cozy, but it isn't much more than two connected rooms. We've been wild creatures, bouncing off every surface in our need to touch and kiss and paw at each other's winter layers.

Brad raced like lightning to ensure Lily had a warm blanket to curl under and a saucer of cream—her forever weakness apparently—and settled her in the bathroom, amid crooning and kisses, so that she wouldn't attempt to sneak off exploring without us.

Now we're naked and allowing ourselves to simply indulge in rediscovering each other's bodies. I've seen Brad from every angle possible on my phone, been gifted the chance to share his most intimate and vulnerable moments. I've watched his eyes roll back as he pumps his cock and cum spurts all over his fingers. I've watched him tease his hole and show me exactly what he likes. I've also watched his entire face light up when walking around the ranch, showing me the side of himself I've only glimpsed in those tiny squares on his Instagram before now.

I'm so in love with him.

It's reckless. Far too soon.

But my heart is his, and I can't wrap that notion up and present it in any way that appears logical. The longer I've spent time with him, the more we've connected, and it keeps solidifying the way I feel. I wasn't lying when I said it scares me to hell and back to feel this intensely about someone, especially within such a short space of time. I've tripped and fallen harder than I could ever imagine possible.

Loving Brad is easy.

Losing him would be a crushing blow, the kind of trampling into the dirt I don't know I'd ever recover from.

As if he can tell I'm falling apart in more ways than one, Brad hollows his cheeks while firmly grabbing my hips. He stuffs my dick into the back of his throat until I'm certain my knees will buckle.

"Br-Brad. *Baby.* I'm close. I'm so close. *Unghhhhh.*" My lips shiver, each word punctuated by moans and gasps. With each pulse of my hips, chasing that glorious sensation of his throat swallowing my tip again and again, the grip I have on his hair tightens.

Thank fuck we aren't anywhere near that house or the party going on inside. I'm fundamentally incapable of containing the slew of wanton noises bubbling up.

Brad's beautiful eyes seek out my own, and they're *burning*.

He gives one last torturous suck, a flick of his tongue, and then lets me pop from his abused mouth. A long line of spit hangs between his bottom lip and my dick, covered in a sheen of saliva and precum.

"Holy fuck," I pant. Barely able to see straight.

"I need to be inside you." Brad is breathing hard as he kisses his way up my body, following the trail of hair on my lower stomach, licking my chest, before pausing to swirl his hot mouth over my nipples.

My cock throbs.

My heart is ready to burst.

My entire world has tipped upside down in the space of a couple of weeks.

"Please, baby. Let me be so good to you." Brad's tone is smooth and so achingly sexy. Promises of more than just *sex* lie behind each of those words.

"I want you . . . Been going crazy without you." I pull him to my mouth, grinding our leaking cocks together. Now, this is the perfect *climb inside your skin, let's merge souls* type of contact I was so desperate for earlier.

"You already have me," Brad mumbles against my lips, walking me backward until we reach his bedroom. "Gotta . . . get you . . . ready."

His hand stays firmly planted over my hip, holding me in place. Those dreamy lips don't ever leave my flesh, trailing along my jaw, biting my Adam's apple, before roaming down my shoulder as he fumbles in the bedside drawer for lube.

The messy, rumpled sheets make my blood run hot. I've seen

him rest his head there, watched him lie back with one arm behind his head in that very spot. His king bed is pushed close to the wall on one side, following the length of a big window overlooking snowy pastures beyond his cabin and the barn. A scene I've peeked at through a phone screen, but now being here in person, it truly drives home that this is Brad's life. Those pristine acres of white powder glowing under the moonlight blind me with the reality that I never want to leave this place if I'm not with him.

"Put one knee on the corner of the bed." He scrapes his teeth across my pec, gently catching my sensitive nipple to tease for a brief second. "Use the wall to hold yourself steady, baby."

I do exactly as he asks, and a flash of my arm moving to place a flattened palm beside the window catches in a mirrored surface. Goosebumps race across my skin as I stare at myself: rock-hard erection jutting out, flushed cheeks, standing with one leg bent to rest on the edge of Brad's bed.

Brad at my back, drizzling lube into his palm.

His eyes, glittering with want and need, meet mine in the reflection.

Oh, fuck.

He wants to screw me senseless in front of a mirror.

My throat dips, heart pumping faster than ever.

It's only then that I realize I'm stark naked, but I've still got my glasses on. My fingers feel clumsy—so worked up and horny after almost blowing down his throat a moment ago—and I go to slide them off, ready to toss them aside.

Brad catches my wrist. That gaze of his drills into mine in the reflection, and the ravenous look on his face is enough to make me whimper.

"Nope." He sucks my earlobe past his lips, continuing to melt me with every second of foreplay. "Leave 'em on, cowboy."

Christ. I'm done for. All I can do is stare as he gets down on his knees and pushes his tongue against my hole. He swirls and pushes against that tight ring of muscle until I melt for him. It's too much, not enough—I want everything all at once.

Brad adds his hand, beginning to fondle between my cheeks, rubbing lube up and down my seam, reaching under to stroke that hot, smooth patch of skin behind my balls before gliding back up to gently press at my hole. Over and over, his clever fingers work to unspool me until I'm damn near babbling.

"Watch me take care of you," he instructs.

Of course, I obey.

I lose track of time, struggling to keep my eyes open when the pleasure hits so intensely I just want to tip my head back and cry out. Brad works me, easing into me gradually, all while murmuring the filthiest things about what he's imagined doing to me since we've been apart.

I want you on your knees in the shower, being a good boy, swallowing my dick.

Would you let me fuck you into a puddle of cum on the floor at any time of day?

I need to lick you until your balls are tight, then sit on your face while you make a mess of yourself.

"Jesus. *Ffffuck.*" My breathing stalls as he works two fingers past the second knuckle.

Brad hums, nips my earlobe between his teeth. "Christ, you're so tight. Remember to breathe for me, baby."

"*Please.*" I'm beyond caring how goddamn needy I sound.

At my back, Brad shifts, easing his fingers away and replacing them with the plush head of his dick.

"Watch us together." He kisses my neck. Easing the tip inside. Giving me the most incredible feeling of stretch and deliciousness, a fleeting moment of slight burn as I adjust to having him there again. "I want you to see everything, and see how much I goddamn need you." Those demands of his are everything, spoken against my overheated skin, accompanied by kisses and the scratch of his stubble.

I do exactly that. I don't just watch everything—I devour.

I fixate on the way his fingers sink into my hip and the sight of his fist reaching around to stroke me from root to tip. My gaze locks on the sides of his ass, flexing and indenting with each thrust. The sensation overwhelms me, submerges me in the deepest pool of bliss, as I chase his hand and back up against his thick cock pumping deep inside me.

I beg. I moan. I gasp for air.

My dick swells, and Brad's grunts intensify. Our sweat-slicked bodies slap together as we dissolve into a fevered mess of him rutting into me—or maybe I'm fucking myself back on him—the only thing I know for certain is that everything feels so insanely right and perfect.

Pressure coils at the base of my spine, and when I feel the way Brad jerks into me with less rhythm, how he's thick and throbbing inside me, that's the moment I let go.

I sob out unintelligible words, curses, his name. Cum spurts out of me in thick, pearly ribbons all over his fist, streaking up my lower stomach, seeming to keep going with no end. Brad makes the sexiest damn gasping groan, buries himself deep, and stills. Pulse after warm pulse jets inside me, painting me with his cum, renewing the truth . . . that I'm wholly *his.*

And as we both struggle for air after tumbling over the edge, the three little words I so desperately need to say to him thunder in my mind in time with my racing pulse.

I love you. I love you. I fucking love you.

CHAPTER 24

Brad

As I stretch out, limbs heavy with sleep, a sweet little purr greets me. Lily bumps my hand forcefully like the tiny ginger menace that she is.

"Hey, sweetie." With a yawn, I groggily scratch behind her ears, my eyelids still half closed.

How is this real life? How is this my Christmas?

Flinn's arm drapes heavy across my stomach, his hair disheveled and achingly sexy as he lies face-down on the pillow beside mine. His face is officially adorable when he sleeps, all relaxed and crumpled while he lingers in dreamland.

"Looks like you've got yourself a new home."

Lily chirps and tucks her paws beneath her steadily vibrating chest, turning herself into a mini gingerbread loaf.

"Hope you like horses, because they kinda run the show around here. Although you can make yourself useful and earn your keep by catching mice for us. Just don't bring us presents dropped on our doorstep, okay?"

Us.

Ours.

Him and me. Me and him.

I'm already talking about our life as a couple as if it's a foregone conclusion. Here I am, with Flinn in my bed, fantasizing that he'll want this. *God.* My clingy ass is mentally already moving him in here, unpacking his stuff into the drawers beside mine, without truly knowing if Flinn will wake up and see things differently in the cold light of day.

He said a lot of things last night—uncharacteristically so for him—but I wouldn't hold it against him if that was maybe a concoction of adrenaline and infatuation talking. We were both giddy, drunk on the heightened emotion of the situation and our unexpected reunion—it's easy to get swept up in the way we've had a whirlwind romantic fling, a few days spent texting and furtively calling at any opportunity. But Flinn is Mr. Practical. He's got a job and a life, and what am I? I'm just the college grad, the guy who sucked his dick at a party, the eager fuck buddy who has given him a chance to learn a few things about himself.

But then, would he have made the effort to come here, to surprise me, to bring Lily . . . ? Are those the actions of a cowboy who sees this as a casual, meaningless chance to screw and nothing more?

"I think I'm in love with him," I whisper to Lily. Her eyes stay closed, despite my outrageous announcement; her tiny motor runs loudly enough to drown my confession out.

My phone vibrates on the bedside table, fortunately within arm's reach, because I'm cat-trapped until further notice. When I lift the screen to squint at the text, it's from my dad.

Dad:
Awake?

You know me.

Bright-eyed and bushy-tailed.

Merry Christmas, old man.

Yeah. Bah humbug. Or whatever they say.

Are you texting me to let me know you've played Santa Rhodes and delivered a trailer load of gifts to my front porch?

Well, it involves a trailer, but the only gift is probably going to be of the horse shit variety.

Oh goody . . .

My dad's texting is slower than a Galapagos tortoise, and the next message seems to take an eternity to arrive.

Your friend gonna be sticking around for a while? I promise not to cramp your style, but the two of you are welcome up here at the house for breakfast.

I know for a fact you ain't got any real food down there.

Sure we won't be cramping YOUR style?

Jesus. You know the answer to that.

"Merry Christmas, my sunshine boy." Flinn's morning voice is sexy as hell. Scratchy and deep, the best kind of present to wake up beside.

"Sorry, did I wake you up?" I ditch my phone and mentally apologize to my dad for abandoning our conversation. "Blame old man Rhodes for texting me at the crack of dawn." I reach across to push his hair back off his forehead.

Did he hear what I said just before?

"No . . . but in all honesty, Lily's purring is enough to wake the dead."

"She loves to fire up all cylinders in the morning." I have to bite back the grin rising to the surface when I think about how much effort Flinn went to in finding her and bringing her with him. "Merry Christmas, baby," I whisper, heart pumping extra hard at the risk of saying those words out loud.

Flinn's stubbled mouth tips up a little at the corners.

He's still groggy with sleep when he leans over to place a soft kiss on my lips before tucking against my shoulder. Even though I can't move, thanks to the feline weight bearing down on my chest, he hooks a leg over mine beneath the covers and keeps his arm over my stomach.

This is it. Right here is heaven.

Cute morning cuddles in bed with my dream guy. Christmas morning or not, this is exactly how I want to wake up every day.

With him.

Only him.

Flashes of us in the future, with sweet morning snuggles and Merry Christmas kisses, occupy my mind. Both of us with more smile lines, more gray hairs. Flinn will, of course, look even more dashing, with his blond beard disguising those traces of grays—he'll absolutely age to become a silver fox—and I see us having coffee together on endless lazy Sunday mornings in a house of our own. Something like the place I grew up in, with a big wraparound wooden porch and a huge living area to fill with friends and laughter. Our kids. Our grandkids.

My heart skitters around inside my chest. Talk about putting the cart before the horse.

"What do you normally do? Any Rhodes family traditions

I should mentally prepare myself for?" His question pulls me from our imaginary future scrapbook of playing happy families.

I chuckle, stroking his hair. "Nothing in particular. My dad is a certified grinch." There's just something about feeling his warm skin pressed against mine, the comfort of having him wrapped around me, this gentle giant filling the hole in not just my bed but my heart. "You? What does family *Flinn* partake in? Don't tell me you're a horde of Christmas carolers, because that might be where I draw the line."

He turns into me, lightly biting my skin. "So cheeky. You would seriously kick me out over carols? What if I'm a perfect baritone?"

"One hundred percent. Apologies to that fine ass of yours, but I couldn't live with the knowledge you might spontaneously erupt into festive singsong. *Terrifying.*"

Flinn huffs out a laugh, then yawns.

I gnaw on my bottom lip. A thousand questions pounding on the door to be set free.

"You're not . . . you're not going anywhere, are you?" I whisper.

His hold on me tightens. "Are you okay with me sticking around?"

Air rushes from my lungs with relief.

"More than okay." *Please stay. Forever.* "I've gotta find a creative excuse for some jobs my dad wants a hand with today, mind you."

Flinn squints at me. "C'mon, I wanna have the official Rhodes Ranch tour you so selfishly denied me anyway . . ." His lips quirk when I attempt to protest that it wasn't my fault we spent the entire night fucking and cuddling and talking. "Let's get dressed. Whatever it is, we can do it together."

CHAPTER 25

Flinn

The moment to ring in the New Year has arrived, and I've got a decision to make.

Tonight is the big party at Rhodes Ranch that Brad organizes every year. It's been the most natural thing ever to remain here since Christmas Eve, to be with Brad, to help work with him around the ranch. But there's a big question mark hanging over us about whether I'm gonna find that I've overstayed my welcome and need to disappear out of Brad's life after all.

We have to talk about it, and I'm fundamentally not good at *talking.*

A tiny part of me feels awful that my whirlwind holiday romance has left my youngest sister somewhat abandoned in Crimson Ridge.

Mind you, Clara keeps texting me to say she's fine at the bed-and-breakfast on her own. I've asked if she wants to come visit Rhodes Ranch or bunk in with us here at the cabin, but she's insisted that she has never been happier to have a cozy fire and a choice of two king-size beds to sleep in. Of course, the fact that my credit card is paying for her room and all expenses has nothing to do with it, I'm sure.

I suppose it's the least I could do since she offered to come along with me.

In my head, I can't even call this a vacation . . . because I truly don't want to consider the prospect of leaving. There was a very real possibility when I punched the details for Crimson Ridge into my GPS that I was making a one-way voyage.

A notion that should feel more terrifying than it does.

In fact, nothing about this feels awkward or wrong. There's only a warm, glowing sensation filling my chest to bursting, like all of that radiance and sunshine Brad exudes have filled me up from the inside and brought me to life.

However, one thing hangs over us like an ominous storm front approaching. Thoughts of my *other* sister, and the fact that I haven't told her the truth, occupy my mind. Do I want to be sneaking around with Brad? Hell no. There are times when you just gotta take the risk and make the right move. Here and now is one of those moments.

Before I can successfully overthink it, my phone is in my hand, and I've brought Izzie's name up on the screen.

Here goes nothing.

My grip tightens as I bring the ringing phone to my ear, a complete scramble of words ricocheting through my mind in anticipation of my sister answering.

"Flinn. Hey," she says flatly.

"Hi, Iz."

"Are you with Clara?"

"No, it's just me."

She blows out a breath. "Good. I kinda can't be bothered dealing with another family pile-on. I don't need the two of you ganging up on me."

"That's not why I'm calling." I scuff my boot in the snow.

"Well, me and Karl are headed out shortly, so I don't have long for whatever this is."

"Okay . . ." I clear my throat. Goddamn, it feels like an

elephant is sitting on my chest. "You know how Clara and I decided to take a road trip together . . ."

"Yeah." She sounds bored.

"We're in Crimson Ridge."

"I'm supposed to know where that is? Sounds like *Hicksville*."

"That name doesn't ring any bells?"

"No? Why should it?"

My teeth clench at how little she ever cared about Brad or his life.

"Crimson Ridge. It's where Rhodes Ranch is." I guess I'm diving into the deep end.

Silence.

"Izzie, I'm at Brad's place."

"Brad?" She says his name like she's attempting to place the face of an acquaintance she just bumped her cart into by accident at the grocery store.

"Jesus, Iz. I'm here with Brad . . . because I'm seeing him." I spit it out, angrier than I have a right to be, yet I'm hot and prickly beneath my jacket, feeling a territorial surge of protectiveness over my guy.

"You're there with him? As in *with* him?"

"Yes. I wanted to tell you the truth so that you're hearing it from me, and—"

"Ew," Izzie interrupts. "Are you kidding me right now? Were you two sneaking around behind my back or something? That's so messed up."

I'm either going to crack this phone or a molar.

"Izzie, be real." I dig my hand into my hair and tilt my head to the sky. Wanting to yell and rant at her so fucking badly. "Don't you dare accuse me of anything like that. In case I gotta refresh your memory . . . you were the one cheating on *him*. We only met for the first time the night I arrived at your stupid college party. You admitted to using him. If I remember correctly, you said it yourself—it was never a real relationship to you."

"Brad is nice. Like I said, it wasn't so hard to be with him. I could have really been into it. You don't know shit," she says so offhandedly, it makes my blood boil.

"Izzie, this isn't like collecting toys or favorite shades of fucking lipstick. You were screwing around behind his back!" All my heated instincts to defend rise to the surface.

"Are you seriously gonna be mad at me?" Ahh, the classic Izzie pout.

"Yes!" My wry laugh burst out of me. "I'm hella mad at you! I'm furious, because you didn't deserve his kindness. You didn't even care about him. You never once—"

Izzie cuts over the top of me once again. "Don't yell at a pregnant woman."

"Iz, just listen to me . . ." I'm blurting it out before I can catch myself. "I'm in love with him. I'm going to be with Brad. Maybe that will be too much of a burden to bear . . . Maybe that will make it too strained for our relationship to continue. And while I genuinely hope that's not the case, you have to know, I'm sorry if that's how it plays out for us. But I'm choosing to follow my heart."

There's a pause. Blood pounds in my ears. I'm honestly not sure if she's going to start screaming at me or hang up the phone and never speak to me again.

Her voice goes quieter. "You love him?"

My eyes lift to watch Brad through the open door to the barn. His messy hair sticks out beneath his cowboy hat, hoodie flecked with bits of horse hay and shavings. He's grinning to himself, talking to one of the horses that has swung their long neck over the stall door and nibbles at his shoulder.

"Yeah. I love him. Like nothing I've ever known." I swallow hard. "This is the real deal."

Izzie takes a beat before saying anything. "Sounds like a case of insta-lust if you ask me." Her words harden. "You always did fall for the first guy who bothered to look your way for more than two seconds." She sniffs. It's harsh, but I sense something a little deeper that she's not saying. As close as Izzie will probably ever get to saying anything approaching, *I'm happy for you, Flinn.*

"Maybe it's too fast. Or maybe we're just meant to be. All I know is that I don't want to waste more of my life waiting around and not finding out."

As she scoffs, I can just picture her examining her nails with the phone tucked against her ear. "Well, good luck to you, I guess."

I lift my hat and rake my fingers back and forth through my hair. "Izzie?"

"Mmm?"

"I hope you find happiness. Wherever you head next and whatever life brings your way, I'll still be your brother, and I'll still be on the other end of the phone if you ever want to talk."

My sister might not deserve that much of an olive branch, but my bleeding fucking heart doesn't have it in me to be callous.

"I'll think about it."

"Don't sound so enthusiastic." I shake my head, letting out a humorless laugh and shove my hat back down.

"The baby is gonna be a big adjustment for the two of us. We're gonna need some time away . . . some distance so we can focus on us feels like the right decision." She huffs, and I can hear an eye roll in her voice, though her words have a little more levity to them by the time we say our goodbyes.

The rest of the conversation is brief, functional; Izzie promises she'll contact Mom and Dad regularly once they reach Germany—even though I know she probably won't, and they'll worry—and the silence of our call disconnecting feels oddly freeing.

I know without a doubt what I've gotta do, right this second.

My long strides eat up the distance between me and Brad. Hearing me approach, he turns around, that wide smile faltering for a second when he takes in the serious expression plastered on my face.

But I don't pause. Before I know it, I'm standing in front of him, slipping my hands inside his hoodie pocket, threading our fingers together.

The brims of our hats bump for the briefest second.

"Brad—" My mouth is dry, nerves suddenly hitting me hard. The realization that I want to get this right and to say everything perfectly.

"I don't want you to leave." He beats me to it. "Please don't tell me this is the big 'Goodbye, see ya round, I'm leaving in the morning' moment I've been dreading. Please don't make me fall in love with you and then you walk outta here saying you'll call sometime. I want you to stay. I don't want to do long distance. Quit working on the road; there's always more work than hours in the day here. I can give you the cabin. I'll move up to the big house with my dad if it's too much, too soon for you . . . If it's too intense, I get it. I'm a lot. I'm pretty sure I have no sense of personal space where you're concerned."

I shake my head, try to open my mouth to say something, to alleviate that anxious look cartwheeling in my beautiful guy's stare.

Brad tightens his hold on me. Blurting out his next words before I can find my own. "Please don't go anywhere. Be with me? Even though I'm clingy and too much and want to adopt every animal we'll ever come across . . . and oh my god, I haven't even told you about my stupid obsession with cheesy car-racing movies yet. Crap, I really hope that isn't a deal-breaker. I'll change my ways. I'll never watch a dumb action flick again if you hate them."

My lips curve, the smile there growing wider the longer his impassioned plea goes on.

"Breathe, baby." I grudgingly slide one hand out from his pocket to take my hat off, nudging the brim of his up so that I can rest my lips against his forehead.

"You're my sunshine boy. You're the bright glow I forever

want to tilt my head to and follow wherever you might lead. When I'm with you, it's like being in the saddle and letting your horse fly. This is 'wind in your hair, cheeks hurting from laughing so hard, warm sun-kissed skin' kind of love, baby. I'm so deeply in love with you, Brad."

He exhales shakily. "Do you think you might want to start a life here . . . with me?"

"Do you think you could stop me? I'm all in. Boots and all. I want this, more than anything."

"*Thank fuck*," Brad curses under his breath with relief. "I loved you from the moment you first tucked me into bed, you know."

"I've been head over heels for you since the night of the ball."

That brings a glint of mischief back to his gaze. "Truth be told . . . I'm pretty sure you loved me from the moment you first laid eyes on me in that hideous Christmas sweater." His eyes sparkle. "Or was it my killer blow job?"

I choke out a laugh, grinning wider. "Well, I'm pretty sure you fell for me the minute I first wore your hoodie."

"Guilty. One hundred percent. You're lucky you didn't find me down on one knee as soon as you'd pulled it over your head."

My heart feels like it's got wings. We're really doing this.

"Lucky for me, you're clingy and needy." I drop my mouth to his, sinking into a deep, promise-filled kiss.

We pull back, slightly breathless, definitely giddy or whatever punch-drunk feeling this is taking hold of us. Brad chuckles. "Fortunately for me, you're stubborn and don't do *halfway*."

"Damn right I don't. All in," I murmur against his lips.

Brad's smile against my mouth feels like pure joy filtering through my veins. "All in. Always."

"My sunshine boy. I love you." My fingers tighten, threaded with his.

"I'm hopelessly besotted with you." Brad chuckles. "I love you, cowboy."

EPILOGUE

Brad

ONE YEAR LATER

I slam the tailgate of our truck closed, just as the sound of hooves on snowy gravel approaches. My dad leads one of our quarter horses toward me, saddled up and just returned from a ride through the fresh powder covering the pasture.

"Finished packing?" he grunts, giving the horse a pat on her long neck as she reaches forward, her whiskery muzzle sniffing my pockets.

Horse logic. Always gotta check the pockets.

"Yeah, we're almost ready to hit the road. Flinn's calling the owner of one of the fillies we're boarding. They wanted to check how that new feed supplement was working out before they left on vacation."

I fiddle with the brim of my cap. It's been a whirlwind year, but Flinn has taken to this place like a duck to fucking water. If anything, I think Lucas Rhodes prefers my boyfriend to me. Not that I'm complaining in the slightest—I truly love that they get on so well.

Just remind me never to give the two of them a bottle of whiskey and allow them to exchange horse-training techniques. They literally cannot shut up once they start swapping stories.

"You sure you're going to manage around here without us?" I hit him with a smirk.

Gotta find some way to ignore the butterflies filling my stomach at the thought of officially spending our first Christmas with Flinn's family. We've visited plenty of times before—turns out they live only a three-hour drive from here—but this will be our first time staying under their roof.

I'm more nervous than I should be.

"Yeah. I'll be fine." Dad shakes his head at me.

"I feel kinda bad you've gotta do everything without us for the next couple of days. Don't want you putting your back out or breaking a hip or something."

"Jesus. I'm not ninety, y'know." He scrubs a palm over his stubble. "Brad, I managed perfectly well by myself all that time you were away studying, in case you've forgotten."

"Right . . ." I roll my eyes, loving how prickly he's getting. "And you had zero social life as a result."

He gives me a classic Rhodes shrug. "People are overrated."

"You're gonna have to get back on the proverbial horse one of these days." If there's anything that can successfully distract me from being nervous about extended time with Flinn's parents and making a stellar impression—I know I don't need their permission, but I can't help feeling the pressure to lock down their support of me eventually marrying their only son—it's teasing my dad about his hermit lifestyle.

Dad narrows his eyes at me.

"Did you ever even use that dating app I downloaded for you?" I poke my tongue against my cheek, waggling my eyebrows at him.

That leaves him pinching his brow and tipping his head skyward as he mutters beneath his breath. "So fucking help me." As he looks back down, he scratches at his jaw, then jerks his chin in the direction of our loaded-up vehicle. "Don't you two need to be getting on the road?"

"Oh, I see right through your classic Rhodes tactic of deflecting the conversation." My laugh bursts out. "We'll be back in time for New Year's Eve. Don't even worry about that."

"Do I look like I'm worried?"

"You look like you're hoping Crimson Ridge will get hit by a snowpocalypse and that the party will be canceled."

I don't miss the way that makes his lips twitch as he leads the horse in the direction of the barn. "Hey, if it snows, it snows." He holds out a flat palm toward the sky. "In fact, feel that? The air's already thick with 'Get outta here and take your shit-stirring somewhere else for Christmas.'"

My grin widens as I watch his shoulders and the rump of the horse walking away. "Love you too, Dad. Merry Christmas."

"Yeah, happy holidays, or whatever. Text me when you get there," he hollers without looking back.

Flinn emerges from our cabin—our cozy but perfect home together—carrying Lily in his massive arm like the ginger queen she is. "I packed extra kibble and added more of those pouches of the chicken meals she likes so we don't accidentally run out . . ." he mumbles, scrolling his phone to tick off the list of jobs I know he's got written down. "Her bed and toys are already packed . . ."

"For a cat who survived winter pretending she didn't live with me but totally did . . . I think our tiny troublemaker will be *fine*." This cat gets the royal treatment from Flinn every damn day of her life. There's enough cat food in the back of the truck for a month. We're going away for a couple of nights.

It's adorable the way he dotes on her.

It makes me forever swoon off kilter over how good he'll be as a dad . . . *one day*.

We're definitely *not* at that place in our lives yet—both of us agree on that front. But someday, we know we'll have kids.

"C'mon, bring your crown, and you can have a nice nap while we drive, m'lady." I open the door to the back seat and hold open the front of her cat carrier. She gives a little purr and bunts her head against Flinn's chin when he lifts her into the waiting truck.

"I feel like I'm forgetting something." Flinn's brows furrow as he secures her inside, then shuts the door.

"Pretty sure you've actually thought of everything. I'm the one totally winging it without much attention to detail, as always." I scrunch my nose apologetically. "Although I plan to make up for my lack of *lists* and *planning* with a knockout road trip playlist, snacks, and personality."

"Can't forget the presents." Flinn chuckles.

"Look . . . don't blame a guy for attempting to buy his future in-laws' affections."

My cowboy goes a little pink in the cheeks. He turns from this strong-as-a-mountain figure into a mushy little puddle of bashfulness whenever we talk about those sorts of milestones in our future. The guy has tried to convince me he doesn't need a ring or a wedding. To which I belly laugh and ask if he even knows anything about me.

Brad Rhodes is far too much of a social butterfly to pass up the opportunity for cake, a first dance, and the chance to make a speech to leave everyone in tears at his own wedding.

There's also the whole twang of guilt I'm still trying to make up for when I think back to the day we sat his parents down and told them a slightly condensed version of events about how we first met. I'll never forget how wide his mom's eyes went and how his dad suddenly needed to go mow the lawn for an hour before coming back and shaking my hand and silently passing me a beer.

Turns out, they're more than fine with us being together; it just caught them by surprise.

Can't say I blame them for needing a minute to adjust.

"I feel kinda bad we only gave your dad a book and some socks," Flinn mutters. "That feels like the ultimate 'old man' type of gift. We might as well have added a multipack of new underwear while we were at it."

My grin broadens. "Dad *tolerates* Christmas at best. I bet you anything he'll be asleep on the couch by seven p.m. and will think it's the best gift of his life that we're fucking off so that he's got the ranch to himself for the next few days."

Flinn gives me a lopsided grin. "You really did inherit the Rhodes holiday spirit genes for both of you."

"And don't you forget it."

"Impossible when we've had our tree up since the first of November." He pockets his phone before bringing those big hands of his to cup my jaw.

"Want me to leave the decorations up all year? I can. Just watch me."

He shuts me up with a kiss, and I slide my hands around his back, sighing with contentment and happiness into his mouth.

"I love you, my future husband and sexiest cowboy alive, who will forever indulge my sushi obsession when we travel beyond the bounds of Crimson Ridge." My smirk grows wider at his weary nod in reply. I've been planning my sushi feast with meticulous precision for the past week, knowing that we'll be passing through bigger towns with more options than just black coffee and horse feed.

Flinn grunts and fishes his phone out of his pocket, letting me go for a brief second. He taps the screen, then smiles at me, satisfaction flashing across his hazel eyes. "That's what I needed to do."

He turns the phone and shows me the screen. My exact order, down to the last piece of inari, has already been placed. A little green bubble says my order is being prepared for pickup by the time we'd be driving through.

"Okay, well I was gonna surprise you with dick cookies as our road trip snack . . ." I grab the front of his jacket in both fists. "But I think I might have to sample the real thing while you focus on the road."

My cowboy kisses me again, half-heartedly scolding me under his breath in the process of leaning into me, but I feel his lips curve into a tiny, naughty smile at the prospect.

As he pulls back, before I can turn our sweet and romantic kiss into something more X-rated, he wets his lips and hits me with the kind of gaze I'll never get tired of seeing every day. "I love you, my sunshine boy. *Merry Christmas.*"

I couldn't agree more. My beaming, goofy, cowboy, head-over-heels in love smile says it all.

Merry fucking Christmas to us, indeed.

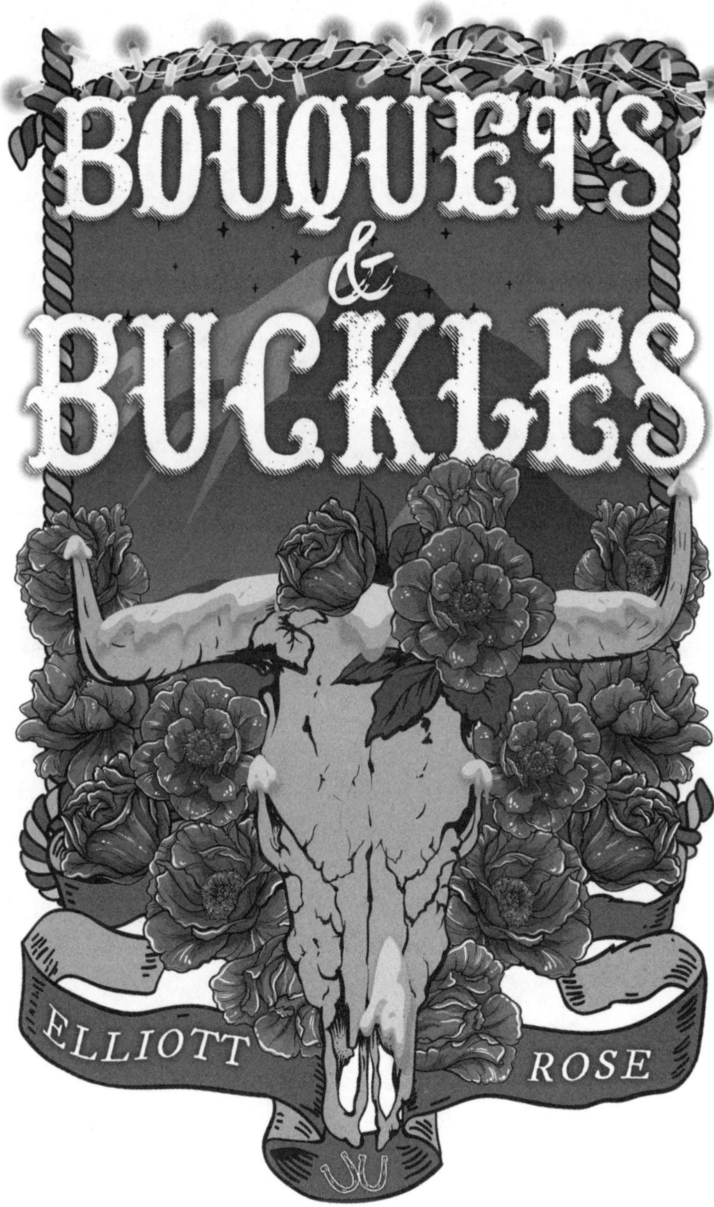
BOUQUETS
&
BUCKLES
ELLIOTT
ROSE

CHAPTER 1

Skylar

It's the most wonderful time of the year.

Yeah . . . when you don't work in retail, events, or hospitality, it's fucking peachy. However, when you've been run off your feet for the past few weeks making sure that everyone else has a magical, glittering Christmas, your own plans of doing nothing more than curling up in front of the fire and spending most of the time naked with nowhere to go and no one to talk to sound mighty appealing.

So that's why I currently have my go-to nineties grunge playlist on blast and my very special hot-as-fuck outfit on after hightailing it out of town at the first opportunity to escape.

I locked the door to my cute-as-a-button florist shop the second my final customers for the year headed out that door.

Bless their sweet little mulled-wine offerings—nope very much—and desire to chitchat about my plans, which are eating and sleeping. But I practically stuffed their last-minute Christmas Eve order into their hands—lord help me not to have to see a single sprig of holly or mistletoe, let alone another festive wreath, for the next eleven months—and damn near sprinted to my car.

Checking my hair in the rearview, I cruise along the empty main boulevard of Crimson Ridge. The place is all twinkling lights and small-town charm, with a giant outdoor Christmas tree erected in the square. Festive cheer of grandiose proportions proudly greets me as I make my return for the first time in twelve months.

My hometown.

The sweetest little Middle of Nowhere, Montana, winter destination, where nothing much happens and the population is pretty much exclusively ranchers and cowboys.

Which is why I made the decision to move to the next town over after college, where my teeny tiny little florist business actually had a hope in hell of surviving her first year of being open.

As much as I would love to still live here, with the gorgeous Victorian-style buildings, trees lining the middle of the wide main street, and an everyone-knows-everyone kind of vibe . . . there isn't much foot traffic in a place like this. Certainly not enough to sustain luxuries like bouquets and floral arrangements.

I'd be better off selling horse feed and leather polish if I was in it solely for the money.

It feels strangely familiar, driving past all the shops and locations ingrained in me from my younger years. Places that haven't changed, yet the years have rolled on by.

Even stranger is the realization that I don't have a reason to come back here anymore now that my parents have left town after selling up everything to buy an RV and begin living the snowbird life.

Love that for them; it's utterly stinking adorable.

They're currently sending me daily photos and awkward but cute selfies from the other end of the country, chasing the sunshine and warmth of a nonwinter in California while the rest of us here are buried up to our necks in snow.

Which is pretty much the standard backdrop for Crimson Ridge at this time of year. I wasn't even sure I'd be able to make it over here on Christmas Eve, but the weather gods have played nice and given me the perfect window of opportunity to surprise Jeremy. He's here house-sitting for his parents, and the drive to the Smith family home is as familiar as the back of my hand.

The cul-de-sac his folks' house is located on is lined with plenty of trees, and I use that to disguise my arrival . . . I mean, my boyfriend thinks I'm currently picking up Christmas Eve takeout before heading back to my apartment, where I told him I'd be getting ready to face mask and video chat once I've curled up on my couch with a glass of wine in hand.

Not that I'm actually here in town, about to surprise him.

I pull off to the side of the road a couple of houses up the block, parking my car where it can't be seen. Out here in this neighborhood, it's all cute festive decor, with lawn ornaments and garland lights festooned over the houses, making the dark Christmas Eve night a whole lot brighter.

While grinning to myself, I pull out my favorite magenta lipstick, and twist the rearview mirror in order to paint my lips. The shade goes perfectly with the waves of my pastel-pink bob framing my face. The thought of turning up to surprise Jere when we didn't think either of us would be able to see the other for the holiday season—with how busy I had been at the shop, not to mention the snow often being too heavy to get to Crimson Ridge—sends a curl of excitement through my stomach.

This will be our first proper Christmas as a couple, after dating for the past three months, and to be able to burst through that door and hug him has been the only fucking thing getting me through all the insanely long hours I've worked this past week.

Grabbing my coat, I bundle myself up and figure I'll do the *surprise* part with his gift first. I can come back, get my bag, and move my car into the driveway later.

As I slide out of the door, the air has that weird energy to it. Too calm, too still. Experience tells me is the sky is on the verge of starting to snow prolifically and turning everything into a real-life snow globe. So I cradle the jar of his favorite peanut butter cookies against my chest, duck my chin into my collar, and scuttle my ass and cute boots down the sidewalk.

Jere's house has the curtains shut out front, but I can see lights on. As I slip around the side towards the back door, there's music playing, and the closer I get, the more the anticipation builds.

I've always been the "single one" over the holidays, and this year, it settles something inside me to know that for the first time, I won't be alone.

The back door has a glass panel built in, which looks into the open-plan kitchen area, all aglow with lights switched on over the kitchen island. I roll my lips together with eager excitement when I see Jere standing on the far side of the room.

He's looking down, his gaze fixed on something I can't see. Light brown hair flops over his forehead, those metal-rim glasses giving him that scholarly hottie vibe, but there is an unusualness in his expression. Enough so that it makes me pause before I reach out to grab the door handle.

I see the way his hand moves, partially obscured by the countertop.

Something about this scene isn't right. The fine hairs on the back of my neck stand on end, not because of the winter's air, but because if I didn't know any better, I'd say he's mouthing words.

If I didn't know any better . . .

Oh god.

That's when the entire damn script flips right before my disbelieving eyes.

The reason his hand is doing something becomes apparent. Dumping realization on me, cold and brutally sudden, like a slab of snow falling off the roof.

It's fisted in some bitch's hair.

Her glossy blonde head comes into view as he drags her to stand up.

She's been down there on her knees.

Jesus. This fucking asshole has got some other girl blowing him in the kitchen.

On Christmas Eve, no less.

My chest goes numb, and I stumble backward, still not wanting to believe the cock-sucking evidence right in front of me.

And that's when he shoves his tongue in her mouth.

CHAPTER 2

Skylar

My toes and the balls of my feet don't have any sensation left in them. Neither do my fingers.

Neither does the cavity left hollowed out inside my chest.

Fumbling in my jacket pocket for my keys, I'm like a shadow in the night, disappearing back toward my car as fast as I can fucking move.

Humiliation has kicked my heart out into the snow, leaving it to freeze amongst the rows of illuminated reindeer and gaudy candy canes.

The backs of my eyes sting, and I'm about two seconds from bursting into a torrent of ugly, snotty tears.

What a piece of shit.

Is there a worse way to spend your Christmas than discovering by accident that your boyfriend has been fucking around behind your back?

As I dash across the curb to reach the driver's door and get myself the hell out of here, I nearly collapse at the sight before me.

Oh my fucking god. Not right now. No, please, no.

The front tire on my car is as deflated as my stomped-on little heart, sitting flaccid and drooped. The array of red flashing Christmas lights on the fence of the house I'm parked in front of helpfully lights up the tire enough for me to see that I cannot possibly drive away from here.

That's the moment the waterworks erupt.

Fuck this. Fuck it all. Fuck Jere and whatever slut he's been secretly banging down here in Crimson Ridge every time he needed to come and "house-sit" . . . which, now that I think about it, was a lot.

Ugh. I'm so tired and can't even process what the hell I've done to deserve a night like this.

With fat tears rolling down my cheeks, I slide into the driver's seat and grab my cell. Stabbing at my contacts list, I know Brad will save my ass. He'll come rescue me, cuddle me, and let me watch a rom-com marathon while bundled under a blanket on his sofa. If there is any man I can count on to have enough booze and ice cream to drown my every last sorrow through the duration of the holidays, it's him.

Bradford Rhodes will also know how to change a tire because he was raised on a ranch, and as much as I'd love to claim to be Miss Independent, I simply am not.

My knee bounces. The phone rings several times. Just when I think he's not going to pick up, to my relief, the line connects.

I don't even wait, launching straight into full meltdown mode, blurting out everything through sniffles and hiccups. "Brad . . . he's such a douchebag . . . Cheated on me . . . You were right all along . . . I can't believe I was so fucking blind . . . And now, I'm stuck on the side of the road with a flat tire, and it's about to snow like crazy, leaving me stuck here on Christmas Eve, and god help me, I will die if he realizes I'm out here . . . Please, please say you can rescue me from this living hell?" I sniff loudly, wiping tears away with the heel of my palm.

"Skylar?" The gritty-sounding voice in my ear makes me do a double take.

"Brad?"

"Skylar, is everything okay?" The voice on the other end of

the line is most definitely *not* Brad. It doesn't sound like Flinn, his boyfriend, either.

My eyes are blurry with tears when I pull the phone away, and my hand flies to my mouth when I see the name lit up on screen.

Brad's dad.

Oh shit. Oh shit.

I just accidentally sobbing-dialed my cannot-ever-stop-swooning-over, hottest-man-in-existence, lifelong cowboy crush.

My best friend's father.

"Skylar, what's going on?" His voice echoes through the quiet of my car.

"I'm so sorry, Mr. Rhodes. I didn't mean to disturb you. I meant to call Brad."

"You're upset." He ignores my feeble words.

"Uhhh, it's nothing. Don't worry. I'm hanging up now. Hope you have a lovely Christmas." My heart is in my throat. I want to bury myself in a shallow grave alongside Rudolph.

"Don't even think about it. Where are you?" His voice sounds a little rough, like he'd maybe been sleeping, and that makes me wince harder. My damp cheeks grow hot with the embarrassment of everything colliding together in the worst possible sequence of events.

"I'm over on Jones Avenue, but honestly, please erase this from your memory. Forget this call even happened. I'm so sorry, my thumb must have slipped and hit your contact."

Fuck my life. My eyes squeeze shut, and I lean my head forward against the steering wheel. I can already taste the sweet burn of whiskey and salted caramel ice cream that I know Brad cannot survive without. That boy always has a gallon of the good stuff stashed in his freezer.

"Are you inside your car?"

"Yes. Honestly, I'll be fine. I—"

The line scuffles a little and he cuts me off. "Turn your ignition on and keep the heating running; otherwise you'll freeze. Give me ten minutes."

That makes my eyes pop open. What?

"Oh, no . . . no, you really don't have to—"

The man doesn't allow me to finish speaking. "Skylar, I'm already in my truck and on my way. Stay put."

With that, he hangs up on me.

CHAPTER 3

Lucas

What the hell am I doing?

It's nine at night on Christmas Eve, and I'm driving through empty streets to offer a helping hand to my son's best friend—to assist with whatever emergency situation she's gotten herself into.

A girl who I haven't seen in a year.

Not since she was back in Crimson Ridge last holiday season, and certainly the last person on this planet who I expected would be calling me.

Adding to all that, she's in tears.

I didn't catch most of what she rattled off over the phone—I must have dropped off to sleep on the couch after I finished up with the horses for the night—and I was only half awake when I answered her call.

Doesn't matter. I don't need the hows or whys; the girl is clearly in some kind of distress and sitting on the side of the road when snow's about to roll through at any moment and cut off the town . . . Well, she couldn't have picked a worse time to have a flat.

Worst timing? Or best timing?

Holy fuck. No. I scrub one hand over my mouth. Don't even fucking think like that for one second. She's Brad's best friend, his same age, and she spent half her teenage years round the ranch while the two of them grew up together.

That puts her in the "don't even goddamn think about it, you old perv" category.

The only problem is that Skylar is very much now a *woman,* and Jesus, if I didn't see that far too easily this time last year. It was impossible not to notice how much she'd matured and grown into herself. How animated she was talking about her new business. Brad had invited her, after taking it upon himself to organize a New Year's Eve party. Which, to no one's surprise, he's doing again these holidays.

Supposedly, he tells me with that smile of his that asks for forgiveness rather than permission, it's great promotion for the ranch.

What do I know? I'm good for training horses and that's about the only thing I've ever known.

Brad's the one who understands crap like networking and marketing and *branding.* All the parts of modern-day ranching I'm terrible at. Whereas my son and his boyfriend are goddamn naturals at those kinds of things, and I'm fucking grateful they're here to handle that side of the business.

Then again, my kid is a social fucking butterfly, so he lives for that kind of shit. He certainly didn't inherit those genes from me.

Thinking back to almost a year ago, I wish I could blame liquor for the fact that I noticed her when I shouldn't have, but I'd offered to be a sober driver for folks coming along that night. There wasn't a drop of drink in me, so I couldn't put it down to anything other than being out of my damn mind. As if being twice her age wasn't reason enough to stop seeking her out wherever she floated around the room, the stone-cold reality is I should know better than to stare at my son's best friend.

Skylar caught my eye and threw my whole world off center, and then to top it all off, I even drove her home just after midnight.

We barely exchanged two words, and all I remember is

white-knuckling the steering wheel the entire way in an effort to prevent me from making a goddamn fool of myself.

When we pulled up outside her parents' old house on Oakwood, however, I coulda sworn she hovered in the truck, painted fingernails resting on the handle.

Maybe it was all in my head, but it seemed like she opened her mouth as if to say something but then thought better of it and bolted out the door into the darkness and back out of my life.

At the time, I rationalized that it was absolutely one hundred percent for the best that I was most likely not going to see her again for a very long time, outside of her and Brad getting together for something or other that might make our paths cross momentarily.

Now here I am, twelve months later, and the young woman, who a man like me has no business thinking about, is the reason I'm driving across town.

It dawns on me as I pull into the cul-de-sac where she's stranded that her folks don't live in town anymore. Last I heard, they sold up everything and went traveling.

Fuck.

Annnnd I'm guessing she doesn't know, or has forgotten maybe, that Brad isn't here either. He's gone to spend Christmas with Flinn's family.

Double fuck.

As I pull into the street, I see her car straight away. The same little silver hatchback she's had since she turned eighteen and headed off to college with my son.

Now I've gotta figure out what I'm going to do with a girl who won't be able to go anywhere until I help her change that tire this late at night on Christmas Eve. Not to mention that the snow has already started piling up in the time it has taken me to drive over here.

Or, more to the point, I've got to figure out how to stop my dick from being ready to leap to attention at the mere thought of this girl nearly twenty years younger than me.

CHAPTER 4

Skylar

Headlights sweep over my vehicle from behind, lighting up the fluffy, white evidence of snowfall that has started coming down thick and fast in the time I've sat here waiting for Lucas Rhodes to arrive.

Nearly crawling out of my skin the entire time.

About ten times, I've seen something out of the corner of my eye and nearly had a heart attack, thinking that it was Jeremy or his side bitch appearing at my window and catching me in the act of lurking down the street.

My pulse thuds a frantic, unsteady beat in my neck. In the rearview, I see a big truck pull up and the headlights cut off. The driver's door swings open and boots hit the gathered snow, revealing my cowboy fantasy and teenage-girl obsession striding through the elements toward me.

Jeans fitted to perfection. High-collar weatherproof jacket. Of course, he's got his requisite Lucas Rhodes felt cowboy hat on his head.

The man is cut straight from a romance novel and yet somehow has remained single in all the years I've known his son.

He even has his own ranch, runs horses, and does *cowboy things* when the other larger properties around here need help.

I quickly brush my hands over my hair to smooth down any strays. Have I got eyeliner running all down my face? God. This is humiliating.

My best friend's dad has had to come rescue me on Christmas Eve. Would the ground kindly do a gal a solid and swallow me up? Better yet, can I just fast-forward out of this nightmare and wake up in my own bed so this can all be over?

As he draws level with the passenger side, I do a painfully awkward wave and grimace.

He gestures for me to roll the window down, then leans a forearm on the door as he bends to look in on my misery.

"Stay there. Don't want you catching a cold." He cuts straight to the point. No smiles, giving me only a display of cheekbones and a short beard to make a girl weep. "Pop your trunk; I'll get the spare."

Shiiiiit.

"Um. You're standing right beside it." If I hadn't already cried my eyes out before, I would be tempted now. How could I forget? I had been meaning to replace it since getting a flat just as winter started, only to wind up endlessly run off my feet with the shop. I never got around to it, and now I want to smack myself in the jaw for sounding like the dumbest bitch alive.

"You ain't carrying a spare?"

I wilt as fast as a dehydrated petal under his dark gaze. His eyes like night study me from beneath the brim of his hat, no doubt chewing silently on my stupidity.

"No. I'm so sorry, Mr. Rhodes. I tried calling Brad after you, and he's not answering, and I'm . . ." This is the moment. The moment I run out of words. What am I actually going to do? This town shuts up shop for the holidays, nothing is open, and I'll bet that all of the options for accommodation are displaying "No Vacancy" signs, thanks to the festive season.

He pokes his tongue against the inside of his cheek for a moment. No doubt thinking I'm the human equivalent of a dumpster fire. Meanwhile I'm sitting in the front seat, wearing an outfit that is definitely not appropriate for spending time with a man old enough to be my father.

Hell, he's friendly with my parents. A little younger than them, but they know each other all the same.

"This your stuff?" He jerks his chin toward the weekender sitting on the back seat.

I nod. Feeling numb and helpless.

"Lock up. Get in the truck."

Without elaborating, he opens the door, grabs hold of my bag, and then steps back, waiting for me to rediscover how to use my brain. He stands there, filling the sidewalk with snow dusting his broad shoulders, white flecks settle against the dark rim of his hat, and doesn't move.

Meanwhile, I'm stuck in place, not processing what is happening here.

So when the rugged cowboy of my silly little dreams stoops to peer at me through the open window for a second time, my heart zooms around inside my chest at his next words.

"You're coming home with me."

CHAPTER 5

Lucas

What am I supposed to do in a situation like this? If I attempted to offload my son's best friend to some random motel in Crimson Ridge—right on Christmas—what kind of person would that make me? That's the kind of shit reserved for heartless fucking bastards.

Skylar doesn't have anywhere to go, and I'm sure as hell not going to abandon her all alone.

However, is the prospect of bringing her back to my house, my ranch, with the way the snow is sticking on the ground, going to be the greatest test of my sanity . . . Most likely, yes.

I've yet to grill her about what I'm sure I heard her say over the phone just before. Even though I might have been still foggy with sleep, I know what she said down the line between her tears.

He's such a douchebag . . . Cheated on me.

Exactly like the last time we sat in this truck together, the drive has been silent. She doesn't seem keen to talk, and I'm shit with words on a good day. Too many years on my own and too much time with only horses for company, as Brad likes to remind me.

Except, everything changes the moment we pull into the long drive winding toward the house. Out of the corner of my eye, I see her sit up a little straighter and take in the snow-covered trees and the sloping track leading to the stables. In front of us stands my simple property—nothing fancy but it's home all the same, with a wooden porch wrapped around the outside. Steps run along one side that I can remember her and a group of their friends from high school spending hours sitting on while playing music and being kids together during the summers.

"I'd forgotten how this place always looks so pretty," she breathes, taking in the swirling snowflakes reflected in the headlights and the glow of the house from where I'd left the lights on.

Yeah, I'll agree with her on that. The only problem is that I'm certainly not looking at any of the sights outside this truck.

I don't run a big property. Enough for my own horses and ones that I stable here on the behalf of others. During the warmer months of the year, I'll offer training clinics and riding lessons, and some of the local rodeo guys and girls come use the place for their offseason practices. Brad and Flinn have their own cabin by the barn and yards situated beyond the house.

While having my son here working the ranch is great and all, he's an adult, and I'm happiest in my own company. Our living arrangement gives all of us enough distance so that we're not on top of each other.

That boy sure as hell loves to tease me that I wouldn't survive without him, which is bullshit, but it's easier having the two of them live on the ranch, I'll grant him that. Even if they do love to steal my beer and help themselves to my fridge while they're at it.

I pull up out front of the porch and cut the engine as Skylar keeps looking around with wide eyes like I've driven us into some sort of fairy tale or some shit. "Winter looks gorgeous out here."

God, I can't fucking get my head on straight. She sounds so relieved, so happy to be here, and that's screwing with my already very messed-up thoughts.

Something bucks around inside my chest and tries to crow about how good she looks here, too. With that pastel-pink hair skimming her jaw, shorter than when she was in that passenger seat a year ago, but it suits her even more at this length. It highlights that pixie, heart-shaped face, perfectly framing those baby blue eyes of hers.

"Let's get inside, get you warm. This snow is gonna keep piling up." Coughing into my fist, I keep my eyes firmly on the house, the porch, anywhere but the gorgeous girl whose feminine scent is filling the cab of my truck.

"Thank you so much again, Mr. Rhodes."

Jesus. I both love and loathe the fact she's calling me that. It collides inside my head with the force of two bulls charging one another. The fucked-up part of my brain enjoys it more than I want to dare examine. The other part of me wants her to call me by my first name, because at this stage, I'd do damn near anything to erase any lingering evidence of boundaries.

"Don't mention it." My jaw is almost frozen in place.

Do I dare admit the truth to myself? That I'd be tempted to discard my morals real quick if it meant being able to eliminate those infuriating invisible lines stretching between us. You know, the ones that relate to our difference in ages or the plain and simple fact that she's my kid's best friend.

Staying in my seat is a bad idea.

I make the move to hop out and grab her bag from the back, but she beats me to it and our gazes lock from where we're standing in the open doors facing one another from opposite sides of the vehicle.

From here I get my first proper look at Skylar. I get to really look at her, and there might as well be a bronc's hoofprint on my chest judging by the way air struggles to reach my lungs.

Her cheeks are a little flushed, plump lips painted a stunning shade of pink that, on someone else, might look ridiculous, but on Skylar, it's perfectly balanced with the sweetness of her pastel hair and hot-as-fuck silver ring in the center of her nose. A *septum piercing*, as I was informed by Brad, mid–eye roll, when

I fumbled around completely tongue tied seeing her with it for the first time last year.

He thought I didn't know what kids these days call that kind of thing, when really all I knew was that she caught me off guard turning up at the house looking like a dream I hadn't dared to believe existed.

Now, here she is. Catching me unprepared to navigate the way my attraction to her hasn't faded in the slightest.

Clusters of puffy white settle on top of her wavy curls as delicate snowflakes, making her look like some sort of winter fairy that I've been gifted as a Christmas miracle.

Goddamn, why does this girl have to be so insanely attractive?

It might be snowing, the air swirling thick around us, but neither of us seems to be able to move, and that's when her eyes waver. They dip behind those thick lashes, and if I wasn't already aware of the thundering rhythm caged inside my ribs, that beat becomes erratic as all hell.

Her blue eyes drop to my mouth.

My fist grips the door to the truck so hard I'm sure the frame is going to buckle.

I'm not imagining this.

I'm not hallucinating.

Skylar's tongue pokes out to wet her lips, and we both stand there like statues. Neither wanting to make the first move to break whatever unspoken connection this is.

Only, the outside world decides to choose that moment to invade our privacy.

Her cell phone bursts to life in her coat pocket.

CHAPTER 6

Skylar

"Oh my god, Sky . . . Are you okay? I've got like fifty missed calls and you didn't leave a single message. Way to freak me out." Brad's voice booms down the phone when I answer.

Across from me, the cowboy who I'd just been locked in the most intense moment of . . . *I don't even know what that was* . . . slams his door and strides toward the front porch.

Whitewashed boards, worn down in places where countless boots have stepped on them over time, a particular spot that holds a thousand memories from when I would hang out here as a teenager.

A teenager with a big, fat, secret crush.

"Hey, B, I'm okay now." With one shoulder, I clamp my phone against my ear, carrying my bags as I follow his boot-prints left in the soft powder coating the gravel.

"Do I need to send out a search party, or call a lawyer, or post bail, or what?"

"Nah, you can stand down. Crisis averted for the moment." My eyes drift up to the open doorway and the broad shoulders waiting just inside. To the man holding the door for me because that's the kind of thing he does without question. The cowboy who ended up being my knight in shining armor, after all.

"Did you make it to Crimson Ridge okay? The weather turned to shit over here real quick tonight."

"Over here? Where are you?" Walking into the Rhodes home feels as natural as anything. I know every nook and cranny in this house, and there's something comforting in the fact it hasn't changed hardly at all that I can see at first glance.

"We're spending Christmas with Flinn's family this year, remember?"

Oh, shit.

"Sorry, crown me world's crappiest friend right now. Totally forgot you guys were heading out of town for the holidays."

"I'll forgive you. Can't blame you for forgetting, considering the fact you didn't sleep and made like five thousand Christmas wreaths in two weeks, Sky. Crazy bitch workaholic that you most certainly are." He chuckles in that deep voice that reminds me of weekends spent teasing each other and driving back roads with the windows rolled down, blasting Nirvana, and daydreaming of the bright futures that our lives might bring.

I'm standing in the entrance hall, knowing exactly how many steps it takes to reach the guest room at the top of the staircase to my left. A room that I've stayed in too many times to count over the years. Yet, I don't make a move. Something about *this* particular visit, when Brad isn't here, changes things.

"So why were you blowing up my phone, bestie? Do I need to egg a certain wank face's house when I get back?"

Scrunching my eyes, I brace myself for the inevitable. "Yeah . . . so . . . you were right about him. The guy was cheating on me." I say that last part as hushed as possible, because I don't know where Brad's father has disappeared off to inside the house after shutting the door behind me, and I also feel insanely embarrassed at the prospect of having to discuss the truth behind my roadside rescue.

"Bitch, I knew it." The phone rustles as Brad does something on the other end of the line. "Flinn, babe, I told you," he hollers in the background.

"Okay, okay, you don't have to alert the entire village," I hiss.

There's a pause while he mutters something under his breath and hums in agreement. "Flinn says he wants you to know that he knew it too, by the way."

"Well, aren't you both just a pair of clair-fucking-voyants."

"Our powers extend beyond bi panic and having excellent style, you know." He clicks his tongue at me. "Wait . . . so, if you're in Crimson Ridge . . . but you've ditched Jere Prick Face . . ."

Shit. Here it comes.

"Um, so I might be standing in your house."

"Huh?"

Words tumble out as I give Brad the rundown of my shitty night while shifting in place awkwardly in the entrance. It's set back a little from the open-plan farmhouse kitchen, and as I fidget on the spot, I still don't know where the man of the house has vanished to.

"God, Sky, I'm so sorry . . ." he groans. "But I'm warning you now, Dad's probably gonna insist on his incredibly lame, old-man Christmas routine. Where he plonks his ass in a chair reading by the fire and alternates that with going to sleep, snoring, and just being super boring in general."

A smirk threatens to escape onto my lips because Brad should know by now that that is one hundred percent the perfect-sounding day for me. My best friend is the social butterfly extrovert out of the two of us, and right now, curling up in front of the fire with a book sounds like my kinda heaven, Christmas or otherwise.

That quite possibly might be the perfect solution to soothe my bruised ego as I wait for the snow to clear, thanks to Jeremy and his kitchen blow job, and recharge my drained social battery after the craziness of the shop.

"I fucking heard that." A gruff voice cuts across my head spin moment. Lucas Rhodes appears in front of me.

"Actually, maybe it's kinda perfect. You two can both hate Christmas together." Brad lets out a hearty laugh down the line. "Take good care of my girl, won't ya, Dad?" he says loud enough for him to hear.

I'm internally dying at this entire situation.

Why yes, I would very much like to be taken care of by this slab of cowboy.

"Merry Christmas, guys." It's impossible to miss the way those dark eyes lock on mine as he replies to Brad.

"Yeah, you too. I'll give you a call tomorrow, and we'll aim to be back once the snow has cleared in a couple of days."

We say our goodbyes, and by the time I hang the phone up, I'm squirming beneath the weight of this man's stare.

He's stripped out of his outdoor gear to reveal a faded denim shirt pushed to his elbows. Those jeans he wears the hell out of are far too easy to appreciate up close.

Lucas Rhodes has reached his forties but is the epitome of a man who could easily pass for much younger than that. It's only the dusting of gray at his temples, the salt-and-pepper beard, matched with a sexy white streak that has always curled through the front of his disheveled hair that belies his age.

I've swooned over that rogue lock of white amongst the longer dark strands falling across his forehead for more years than I can remember.

"Let me take your coat." His voice comes out husky, and I swear to god my knees buckle a little.

He steps around to stand behind me, and our height difference is marked at this proximity. I barely reach the man's chest, even in my heeled boots.

I'm a curvy girl with thick thighs, a soft stomach, and tits I wish were bigger to give me more of an hourglass shape. I know how to dress in order to feel myself, yet no matter what, there's no disguising the fact that I'm short.

Standing with this man at my back, I feel dwarfed by his size. He's thick chested. Broad and muscled. The kind of steadiness to him that is a constant reminder of how strong and sturdy he is, with absolutely no interest in being cut or showing off.

This is a man who has a body capable of hard graft and days on end working with his horses and the land.

God, I've got to get my ovaries under control and stop drooling over this cowboy.

Only, he keeps making it nearly impossible to do so. Strong fingers hook beneath my coat collar as I undo the buttons. And that's when I remember.

The outfit I've got on underneath.

CHAPTER 7

Lucas

Holy shit.

The soft wool of Skylar's black coat gives way, allowing me to peel it off her shoulders.

I mean, this girl has a figure to fucking crawl across hot coals for, and I don't know how the fuck we've ended up here, but I say a silent curse.

She's fucking stunning, and what she's wearing . . . Well, if I wasn't already battling an erection, I damn well am now.

My gaze should *not* be roaming everywhere at once like I've never laid eyes on a woman before, but I can't fucking help it. Her black leather skirt barely covers her lush ass, with sheer black tights skimming down those thighs I want to squeeze until she whimpers for me. Her top is also black, but you wouldn't know it because the damn thing is entirely see-through, and from here, I can already see the thin strap and clasp reaching across her spine that tells me she's only wearing a bra underneath.

I'm not sure I'm gonna survive the moment this girl turns around, and I see how her tits are showcased beneath that tempting layer of sheer fabric.

Beneath the long sleeve of her cropped top—if you could even call it a top—are the colorful designs I've only ever dared to sneak small glimpses of in the times I've been in the same room as her. The adult version of my son's best friend.

After Skylar went off to art college with Brad, she started sporting more and more ink each time she returned to Crimson Ridge during the holidays.

Like everything with this girl, the tattoos are hot, she's hot, and now that I can glimpse them up close, I see there's a mix of florals and colors and patterns tracking from the curve of her shoulders down to her wrists. I want to ask her about what kind of meaning they hold for this dichotomy of a girl. Who wears her hair the color of sweet fairy floss and favors chunky black boots.

Skylar has grown into a woman who is a whole lot of gorgeous and a mystery at the same time.

"Help yourself to a drink. You know where everything is." I practically choke out the words. *Do not keep staring at her ass.* "I'll hang your coat up and drop your bags upstairs . . . Same room as always, yeah?"

She turns her chin to peek back at me over one shoulder, all heavy lashes and pretty pink lips. "Thanks, Mr. Rhodes."

My cock fucking leaps to life. "Just Luke is fine. Probably should have pulled you up on that years ago."

"Okay." There's that same breathiness in her voice again. "Can I get you a drink, too?"

Yup. Just hand me the entire goddamn bottle at this point.

"Sure. Whiskey's good for me," I say, taking the opportunity to busy myself with mundane things like hanging her coat and depositing her bag upstairs and trying my best to avoid thinking about the fact I'm going to be stuck in this house with Skylar, alone.

CHAPTER 8

Skylar

My tits and ass are literally hanging out, and I'm pouring my best friend's dad a whiskey.

Meanwhile, I've already knocked back a generous pour, the burn sliding a long trail straight down to my belly.

I don't know what the fuck to think or feel. Right now, I'm entirely messed up because I could have sworn Lucas Rhodes—Luke—stared at me while I was on the phone to his son with something dangerously similar to desire in his eyes.

Then he offered to take my coat for me, and there was no denying the heat twisting and turning between us when he hovered at my back.

Am I reading into every little detail? Maybe.

Am I feeling reckless enough to see what this outfit might strike a match and set fire to? Absolutely.

Why not allow myself the chance to reach out and sample a taste of the forbidden? It is Christmas, after all. We're snowed in together here. As soon as I can get a new tire fitted, as soon as the roads clear, I'm going back home and really have no reason to come back to Crimson Ridge again for the foreseeable future.

Brad doesn't need to know.

I'm in the mood to be a whole lot irresponsible, and the

cowboy I'm stuck in this house with is the kind of temptation a girl like me has thought about too many times over the years.

He's never once been inappropriate or ever acted in a way with me that might have blurred lines. Always being the perfect gentleman, driving any of us home late at night if we ever needed a ride. Always making sure we had his cell number in case of an emergency.

Lucas Rhodes is one heck of a good man, an excellent father, and has always supported Brad.

The cowboy I've swooned over in secret for *years* has always been a kind of distant daydream. The fantasy riding in on horseback I've only ever laid in bed at night and drifted off thinking wicked thoughts about. The forbidden temptation dressed in jeans that should be illegal and with a charcoal-colored hat that makes my knees go weak.

And hell, if it doesn't make it even hotter that now we're both here in a moment when life has turned on its head, and I'm here in this house as a fully consenting adult who most definitely would like to loosen his buckle and worship this man's dick if he'd let me.

Bracing myself against the wooden top of the central island, I look down at my tits. The girls are fully on display, rounded, and threatening to spill over the top of the black harness bra I treated myself to as an early Christmas lingerie purchase. My sheer cropped top is nothing but a flashing neon sign directing attention towards my cleavage.

Little did I know the first man who would see the magical powers of silky fabric and lace would be nearly twice my age. A rugged cowboy who shouldn't know how fabulous my tits look in this outfit, but holy fuck, do I want him to.

I've never been this person.

I've never dared to act like this before.

So maybe the snow and the chaos of emotions running rampant through my veins, along with that shot of whiskey, are what gives me the courage to do the thing I would never normally think of doing in a million years.

As I hear heavy footsteps coming down the steps, I grab the bottle and two glasses, scooting around to the side of the extremely manly, chunky dining table facing the entranceway. Pushing one of the chairs slightly aside, I hoist myself up and plonk my ass on the wooden slab.

My stomach fills with butterflies as his heavy footfall reaches the last stair.

Something has been hanging in the air tonight, like the snowflakes drifting outside the kitchen windows. Something a teeny bit magical that sizzles with potential. And if I didn't know any better, it might just be the once-in-a-lifetime opportunity I'll be able to dream about for years to come.

If there's one thing I'm going to do to get over the turmoil of tonight, it's shooting my shot.

CHAPTER 9

Lucas

I didn't really know what to expect walking back into the kitchen. Maybe to be offering Skylar some dinner, or to have a discussion about whatever upset her earlier, or to make fucking small talk about the fact we're going to be stuck here together on my ranch until the snow melts.

You know, to be filling the role of *Brad's father* that I've filled for as long as I've known her.

What I didn't expect was to find her perched on my dining table, looking like a goddamn wet dream.

Well, fuck.

The sight I'd been steeling myself for while pacing upstairs comes into sharp focus as I walk into the soft glow thrown across the room by the overhead lights. My kitchen has turned into an illicit stage show. Where there used to be innocent hanging pendant lighting has now become a warm spotlight caressing her every curve—highlighting the fact I can see straight through her shirt.

It stops me in my tracks, and I have to scrub a hand over my face. There's no way to disguise my reaction. This girl is so fucking gorgeous, and there's only one reason she's perched herself like that.

Her skirt is short, hugging her thighs, barely covering her from the waist down, and it takes everything to not look at the spot where the material ends and her tights disappear beneath the hem.

But looking up in the direction of her face is no better because this girl's tits are enough to break me. The way they're wrapped up and perfectly presented . . . She was obviously dressing for *someone* tonight, and I'm guessing it's whichever jerk off left her crying and stranded on the side of the road.

"Skylar, what are you doing?" My voice is scratchy. I know exactly what she's doing, but my brain cannot process what my eyes are seeing. A part of me says that I should tell her to get down from there and show her where the leftovers are so she can reheat something.

On one hand, the sensible, boring, fatherly part of me attempts to be *good.*

Then, there's the other guy.

He's the asshole who is beyond tempted to see whether this girl might enjoy a bit of fun. Who is desperate for a taste of the young woman he's been stuck with *unfatherly* thoughts about for the past year.

"You wanted a drink, didn't you?" She bites down on her lower lip and offers me a glass.

Like a magnet, I'm drawn forward. Slowly crossing the last remaining space separating us and stopping just in front of her knees. "A drink, yes. But *this* . . ." I nod at the seductive little perch she's seated on. "This isn't just a drink, is it?" As I take the glass from her, our knuckles brush, and that innocent point of contact feels fucking electrified.

"Do you want it to be just a drink, Luke?" She flutters heavy eyelashes my way and leans back on her palms.

Goddamn, I want to hear how my name sounds on her lips when she's moaning for me and begging to come.

"That's all it *should* be, and you know it." My throat bobs a heavy swallow.

"What if we didn't know each other? Let's say I'd never been here. We'd never met before. We're just two adults who happen to be snowed in together. Would there be any shoulds or should-nots between us then?"

Christ, if the conditions outside weren't a total whiteout, I should be excusing myself to go down to the barn, cool the fuck off, and busy my hands with the horses or shit like that. Instead, I'm locked in this illicit bubble and can't find it within myself to step away.

"I don't know. It's hard to say when you've obviously had other plans for Christmas based on that outfit you've got on."

Pausing to take a sip of whiskey, I let my eyes hold her baby blues.

Something wavers in her energy. "It's okay. I can go change. We can hang out if that's all you want." The way she says those words, it's like she's already preparing herself for rejection, and I hate that this girl immediately assumes she wouldn't be wanted when it's only my own hang-ups and bullshit stopping me from putting my hands all over her.

"Skylar . . ." I run a hand through my hair and blow out a low exhale. "Just give me a second to get my head wrapped around this situation."

That brings the sparkle back to her eyes, and the sight makes my pulse thud even harder. How am I even fucking considering this? But equally, I don't know how I couldn't. Not when it comes to a girl as incredible as her.

"So, that's a *no* to me getting changed?" Her teeth sink back into that plump lower lip, and all I want to do is tug on it. Better yet, I want to see those pink lips around my cock. Jesus, there's no guarantee this girl wants anything other than a bit of flirtation and attention, and here I am already imagining putting her on her knees.

"No." I let my gaze roam across her figure now. Relishing the way she shudders slightly, enjoying this long moment as I sip my whiskey and drink my fill of her at the same time. Allowing myself the act of properly appreciating such a sight. "You look way too fucking gorgeous for my sanity. Whoever all of this was meant for tonight—because I know it wasn't me—they are an idiot and don't deserve you."

Her lips twist into a way too cute and way too irresistible curve. "I'm glad someone got to appreciate it, at least."

She still looks hesitant, but any kind of smile on her, no matter how tiny, is sexy as hell.

"Trust me, I'm more than appreciative." I tip back another sip of my drink and swallow heavily. Unable to take my eyes off her. "Even though I shouldn't be."

I soak up the way her pupils blow out and her lips hang a little parted. That small graze of our fingers might have felt electric before, but now it feels as though the air in my kitchen is crackling like a midwinter bonfire.

"Skylar . . ." I don't want to fucking say anything to disrupt this moment we're plowing toward, but I'd be the world's worst father if I didn't.

"I know." She nibbles on that bottom lip.

"What if he finds out? What then?"

"What if he didn't need to know?"

"But I'll know, and that's entirely the issue." I scratch my beard.

"Couldn't we both pretend? Since it's just this once . . ."

She thinks I only want her this one time. I *should* only want that, but there's a whole minefield of complications that come with admitting out loud how I really feel. That when it comes to this girl, I've had a lot of time to think about what I would do if I ever had the opportunity to have her.

None of which involved a fucking *one-time only* situation.

However, she's right. As I take a long draw of my drink, mulling over what to say next, the writing is already on the wall.

"That snow isn't going to clear for a couple of days." My throat bobs, swallowing down the part of me demanding I find a way to stretch whatever this is beyond something as simple as being snowed in together. "Probably a good idea if it doesn't go any further than that."

"I think that's for the best."

"If we do this . . . we stick to the boundaries. As soon as this has to stop, it stops. Your friendship is more important and I'd fucking hate myself if . . ."

"You don't have to explain." Skylar dips her chin. "We're adults, right? We can play by some *rules*."

Oh, there are a whole lot of fucking games I'd like to play with this girl.

"Then, in that case." I tilt my glass at her. "Until the snow clears."

"Until the snow clears." Her sweet voice echoes mine.

Those bright blue eyes glint at me and my entire world slides sideways with the act of agreeing to this, even though there is no way in hell I should even be entertaining the idea.

"Thank you . . . for being so kind to me tonight," she breathes. "You've always made me feel so welcome here . . . You've always been a good friend."

That makes a gritty noise come out of me, and I place my glass down on the counter.

"Let's make one thing real clear, right fucking now." Leaning both hands on either side of her hips, leaves me looming over her, so close I'm immediately wrapped up in her floral scent. "I don't want to be your *friend*, Skylar."

CHAPTER 10

Skylar

“*I don’t want to be your* friend, *Skylar.*”

Holy fuck.

I’m almost panting as the heat and masculinity of this man fills my senses. Lucas Rhodes is a solid wall consuming my vision and invading my space—along with my last remaining shred of sanity.

“I don’t want to be your friend, or your friend’s father, or anything else that makes it seem like I’m not over here fighting every urge to kiss the fuck outta you.”

My eyes widen . . . entire body flushing . . . pulse fluttering madly in my throat like it’s trying to grow wings.

“You want that . . .” Suddenly, I feel so nervous. My big plan of seduction was all well and good until now we’ve reached that threshold and I’m instantly aware of how much older and more experienced this man is.

If this carries on, I don’t want him to feel disappointed.

“I want a lot of things,” he murmurs. Dark, hungry eyes fix on my mouth. “A lot of things I’m not supposed to wish for.”

“It’s Christmas . . . Don’t they say wishes come true?”

His lips twitch, and he reaches for the glass he set down just before. “I’d say this is more like a fantasy wrapped up in a pretty pink bow.”

God. This man is so hot. My cheeks feel like they might be on fire with his flirty words and roaming gaze.

"One you'd like to unwrap, I hope."

Luke lifts his drink, gives me a heated look, and then slides a thigh forward to part my knees. "You want to be unwrapped, sweetheart?"

Oh, god. I nearly whimper out loud.

Somehow, I manage a nod. Maybe I fumble out a "yes" but I'm not sure.

"Then tilt that pretty little head back for me and open your mouth."

My pussy clenches. The commanding tone in his voice is doing things to me I've only ever dreamed about.

So, of course, I do as he says, lifting my chin and dutifully opening.

Luke leans over me and very carefully pours a little whiskey from his glass onto my tongue. It's just enough to run slowly across my tastebuds, allowing me a taste, and that trickle of warmth feels like it floods everywhere, igniting my veins with desire.

"More?" His husky voice is so close.

I've never agreed to something more enthusiastically. Nodding quickly, I open my mouth again.

This time, the liquid doesn't hit my tongue like I'm expecting. It drips over my lower lip and runs a trickle down my chin and neck.

"Fuck. I'm going to hell for this," I hear him groan, and then his mouth is on me. He fastens over my collarbone. Plush wet lips pair with scratches from his stubble as he sucks up the alcohol gathered there, followed by a moment that will remain forever ingrained in my memory, when he licks a scalding trail, tracing the line of whiskey up the column of my throat.

Up, up, up until he reaches my mouth.

Luke hovers there, our lips only a frantic breath apart. Every inch of my skin feels like it's tingling with anticipation, and if I wasn't already hot for this man, with that one sinfully sexy move, he just turned me into a complete slut, only for him.

"More?" That one word is so gravelly, so alluring. It makes heat pool low in my belly.

All I want to do is lose myself in this man. There's no guarantee Luke will even kiss me, yet right now I'm so lost in the moment, I'm not exactly sure that I care.

Somehow, I muster up the strength to nod. In all honesty, he can have whatever he wants, and I'll happily thank him for the opportunity. Multiple times over.

This time, his eyes roam all over me as he brings that glass up to his mouth. Lucas Rhodes studies me like he's got all the time in the goddamn world, and I feel like I'm about to dissolve right here on the kitchen table.

"*Please.*" That single word gusts past my lips, shaky. I'm so unbelievably turned on. Unwrap me, unravel me—whatever he wants, it's his.

He makes a rough noise, then takes a sip, all the while keeping my eyes entangled in his hooded gaze. Only, instead of swallowing, he leans over to cup the back of my head.

Those calloused fingers slide into my hair, and I gasp at the sensation of his heated touch.

That moment right there is all it takes. He looms over me, so commanding and utterly handsome I feel like I'm living out every single fantasy moment I've ever created in my mind's eye.

And he spits into my mouth.

CHAPTER 11

Lucas

We should probably be talking about why this girl has ended up in my house, on my kitchen table, with my tongue running up her slender throat.

But right now, I get the impression that Skylar doesn't have any interest in talking.

Maybe that makes me an even worse person, but the fact that this beautiful girl was left all alone on Christmas Eve makes me determined to show her just how much she is wanted.

Fuck talking. That can come later.

I spit the whiskey into her mouth, letting the liquid trickle down, and watch, captivated, as her blue eyes go wide and she gulps everything down. The quick swipe of her tongue to wet those damn plush lips of hers has me going damn feral in an instant.

I fall on her with a noise that comes up from somewhere deep in my chest.

Sealing our lips together, it's hot and wet, and she tastes like I've completely lost my damn mind. Except, it's the single most incredible thing, feeling her softness and eagerness and the perfect way that she seems to fit against me.

We kiss like we've done this a thousand times before and this is just one of many, many nights where I've been given the gift of the beautiful girl who hums into my mouth and makes the sweetest little whimpering noises.

"Want more?" I growl against her, meeting those panting breaths of hers in an effort to disguise my own.

Skylar whimpers, and I suck down on her tongue. Each second that our mouths keep searching and exploring while my grip tightens in her hair, well, I'm ever closer to losing my damn mind.

"If that's what you want, I'm starting here." Reluctantly, I draw back, leaving her hastily wetting her lips, no doubt tasting the lingering hint of whiskey from both our mouths. This girl is something else entirely, looking gorgeous, flushed as all hell, and turned the fuck on. My fingers find the flimsy hem of her top, where the translucent material skims the high waistband on her skirt. "First, I'm starting with this slutty little tease of a thing. You think you can walk in here dressed like that without consequences?"

Seeing her little smile and flash of desire lighting her eyes feels like winning a goddamn buckle.

"Did I do something naughty?"

Oh, this girl wants to play *those* kinds of games.

"Extremely. Did you know I can see your bra?"

She feigns innocence, biting her cheek and shaking her head. As those pastel-pink locks swing around her face, my dick is a steel bar inside my jeans.

I click my tongue, and she shivers. "You're not even sorry, are you? Parading around in here with your tits hanging out," I scold, hooking the fabric and sliding it up to sit over the swell of her breasts.

"I didn't mean to."

"I'm curious what you thought was going to happen. Did you think you wouldn't get caught being a little cock tease? Wandering around my ranch in those tiny cutoffs all summer? Creeping into the kitchen at this time of night wearing next to nothing."

"Sorry, I know I shouldn't have." Her chest rises and falls

quicker as the backs of my fingers graze the softness of her cleavage.

Christ, it's taking everything in me to play this game and not tear each item of clothing off her in a frenzy.

"Well, you've landed yourself in big trouble now." Lowering my head, I take the top of her bra in my mouth and tug it down. Her breast pops free, pale, plump flesh and rosy-pink budded nipple right there, ready for the taking. "So much trouble." I quickly repeat the process on the other side.

"God, please." She lets out a soft moan as I run my nose and lips up the soft curve until I reach the tightly furled bud.

"Bad girls don't get to ask for anything." I take the opportunity to blow gently on her nipple, and she squirms beautifully. Once again, I draw back, and it almost fucking kills me. Both her tits are squeezed and framed by the sexy, crisscrossed fucking black straps covering the front. Pressing her flesh and putting it on the most erotic display. Even though it pains me not to take her breast into my mouth—to suck down and hear her soft noises of pleasure like I goddamn want to—my next move is going to make it worth the fraction of extra time till I do so. To make this teasing and taunting worth it when I finally get to taste her nipples like I'm damn well salivating for.

Picking up the whiskey, I press the rim against the line where one of the black straps curves across her cleavage. Skylar quivers, breathing fast, as I let my eyes rake over the pair of breasts I should never have been given permission to see, let alone play with like this.

"Slutty little teases sit there quietly and take their punishment." Tipping the glass, I let a tiny trickle roll down her flesh, letting it run in a delicious track down the curve to cover her nipple, where it beads and hangs full and glistening.

Skylar lets out a soft, porny fucking noise. One that shoots straight to my balls and makes my cock jerk inside my jeans.

I repeat the process on the other side, coating her other nipple, before taking a moment to admire the sight. Both are glossy and have deepened to a more flushed shade. The vision of her, leaning back on her hands, tits bound up in that harness, with knees spread wide . . . that snaps my leash.

My mouth fastens over her breast. I'm swirling my tongue and sucking on her tight nipple, tasting the hit of whiskey and her scent while my hands wrap around and squeeze the outside of her soft thighs.

She tastes like everything fucking sweet and good and forbidden.

Because this girl is not meant for me, and yet I want to spend all night exploring all the ways I can make my son's best friend since they were both teenagers scream my name.

CHAPTER 12

Lucas

"Oh my god . . . *Luke* . . ."

I've officially lost my damn mind.

Skylar Addams is laid out like a feast before me, a girl who is far too young for an old cowboy like me, and I'm probably gonna have to renovate this fucking kitchen in the new year because there's no way I'll be able to do anything in here without getting hard at this memory.

I allow my teeth to graze her nipple and tug gently, drawing another moan and sultry cry of my name from Skylar's lips. A sound that I'm in danger of becoming addicted to.

"No, sweetheart. You've been very bad, wearing next to nothing covering your cunt. I don't think this even counts as a skirt, does it?" My palms push below the hem, sliding the leather up until I discover exactly what she's got hidden beneath that tiny piece of clothing.

If there was any chance this girl might just be my Christmas fantasy, that quick glance just confirmed everything. She's got sexy fucking garters on. Her lush thighs reveal where they're wrapped up in soft black tights ending at the swell just below the hidden apex, and as I push the skirt all the way up, my brain short-circuits.

"Fuck. You've been very, very bad, haven't you?"

Skylar whimpers, and her hips lift for me like the perfect goddamn dream she is so I can really look . . . so I can absolutely devour the sight that absolutely should not be for a man like me.

Yet we're here, and I'm staring at her almost exposed, perfect cunt.

"I think you forgot your panties, sweetheart," I say, my voice low and husky. My eyes tip up to meet hers, and fuck me, she's going to be my utter ruin.

Skylar stares back at me with lust filling her expression, and just a hint of the way she bites her lip lets me know she's wondering what I'm thinking.

If it takes all fucking night, I'm going to show this girl just how magical she is. That she shouldn't be wasting her time with boys who can't appreciate every single stunning inch of her.

I allow my gaze to drop back down, and there's only the tiniest hint of ribbon and lace covering this girl's pussy, to match her bra. It's virtually nothing—my teeth could tear that fragile fabric in a second—and yet it's a thousand times sexier than if she had nothing on at all.

"We're going to have to do something about this, too."

"Luke . . ." She sounds nervous. Hesitant.

"Sweetheart, this pussy is meant to be fucking worshipped . . . and I'm gonna ask you to trust me when I say that even if this is as far as we take things tonight, I need to eat your cunt till you fall apart. Preferably more than once."

She gasps and stammers as I lean closer. "It's—it's been a while."

"Then you obviously haven't had a real cowboy between these thighs, so let me show you what you've been missing out on."

I'm beyond being able to resist anymore. Pulling up a chair, my eyes take in every detail, committing to memory this insanely perfect moment. Lowering my head, I grab her by the hips and tug. Skylar gasps as everything happens in quick succession.

With one palm, I press down on her sternum, firmly guiding

her to lie back. Using the other, I hook her leg over my shoulder and sink forward, allowing my mouth to close over her.

The lace is so thin and fragile, it barely covers her pussy lips, and she tastes like a fucking dream come inexplicably to life right here amongst the snow and the approaching midnight hour.

Skylar's back bows off the table, and she lets out a soft, sweet moan to match the flavor of her filling my senses.

Goddamn. It's addictive hearing how responsive her little noises are and feeling the way she trembles with every sweep of my tongue, nudging the material aside and exploring every delicate inch beneath my mouth.

Drawing back, I reach for my glass once more. This time, pouring a little over the scrap of barely there translucent thread.

Feeling the contrast, the way the cool of the whiskey caresses her skin, she shudders and whines. It's a series of delicious fucking sounds, and they morph and merge with the deep groan coming out of me when I dip my head, chasing the wetness. I can't get enough of this fucking goddess lying spread out for me as I suck and lick and attentively clean up every trace of the alcohol coating her pussy.

Stiffening my tongue, I massage over her clit and feel the trembling start to roll through her body. She's close, so close, and I'm obsessed with the idea that this girl is going to shatter for me.

Somehow, unbelievably, I get to keep her for as long as this snow sticks around.

"That's it, beautiful . . ." I hover just over her, speaking against her drenched core. "Show me how bad you can be."

With that, I suck down on her clit through the soaked lace, and Skylar dissolves into her climax. The most addictive moans burst out of her, and she clamps her thighs around my head.

I didn't think tonight of all my lonely nights this year was going to be anything special, but goddamn, I think this girl might just be my own private miracle wrapped up in pastel pink and sexy-as-fuck lingerie.

CHAPTER 13

Skylar

My brain and body are strung out like a row of festoon lights, dangling somewhere between two different dimensions.

The cowboy between my thighs has a wicked tongue, and not just when it comes to his powers of dirty talk. He knows exactly how to unravel me and have my pussy crying out for him within seconds.

"Look at you, sweetheart. Dripping wet and a filthy little temptation lying here with these thighs wrapped round my head."

Luke's words are spoken right above my clit, and as he blows on the tiniest pair of panties I've ever dared to wear, my core clenches. I want him so badly. I want to know what it's like to be fucked by this man, even if it's only one time. I mean, I might cry if it's only tonight, but at least I've already had a sinful preview of how hard Lucas Rhodes can make me come.

Tonight feels like we've been able to suspend time and all the normal rules. So maybe, just maybe, this can go beyond the moment when this night officially ends.

"Please . . ." I murmur, gazing at him from beneath my eyelashes. Hoping with bated breath that he's still invested in seeing this game through to the end.

"Still hungry for more?" As he runs his teeth across the fabric, they graze my pussy lips, and I swear there's so much heat and possessiveness coming off him, it sends sparks straight to my swollen clit.

I push myself up so that I'm sitting and nod my agreement. Did he just lick me so masterfully that I've forgotten how to talk? Luke straightens but remains seated between my knees, watching me closely. There's a sheen of *me* coating his stubbled beard and mouth that looks almost feral and makes my core clench. Eyes bouncing between my lips, my exposed tits, down to my skirt bunched around my waist, he's sinfully gorgeous.

"If you're hungry, then you can taste yourself first." He stands and swipes up the previously discarded glass of whiskey, swirling a sip around, as his gaze feasts on me splayed out and panting.

Oh god. I know what's coming next, and I'm such a slut for him. My mouth is already watering at the prospect.

Luke's eyes glimmer in the soft lighting, and he leans over me with a silent command in that dark stare.

Open.

My lips part on a soft, whimpering noise, and this time I stick out my tongue. He lets the mix of saliva, whiskey, and my arousal all fall onto my mouth, and it sets my body alight. Cover me in fairy lights, and I'd make the perfect slutty Christmas decoration for this cowboy to use all night long.

I don't know how far this thing extends between us beyond physical desire and sex, but right now, I'm such a goner for him I don't give a shit. All I want is this cowboy's cock. I want him inside me, and I can't think straight about anything beyond letting him do whatever he wants.

Somehow, I just know this is going to be the best damn sex of my entire life.

"Still not satisfied, are you?" He nibbles and sucks on my bottom lip, letting our mouths slide together, with a heady concoction of the scent and taste of *me* intermingling with the alcohol. "Is the taste of your cum on my tongue not enough to tame that hunger?"

"Just a little bit more, please . . . Can I have that?" As he draws back, I flutter my eyelashes—entirely out of my depth and probably drunk on this man's cowboy pheromones alone—and reach out to rest my fingers over his belt. I'm hoping it comes across as sensual and confident, not like I'm so much younger and less experienced than him.

Luke makes a rough noise of approval in the back of his throat. "You're playing a dangerous game."

"If tonight is about wishes, then surely a little *game* wouldn't hurt?" He doesn't tell me no or shrug me off, and that's all I need. It's enough permission. I fumble with his buckle, then make quick work of his jeans. At least he's not stopping me from this next part, and that makes my stomach swoop in anticipation.

Luke's strong hands grip my thighs so hard I'm sure he's going to leave me with bruises to show where he's been. "Look at you. Making a mess all over my dining table, trying to tempt me into giving you what you came here looking for."

Biting down on my lower lip, I make sure to stare up at him as I shove his briefs down and allow the weight of his cock to bob freely.

"Just a little fun? No one has to find out." I'm nearly climbing out of my skin with how hot this is, waiting for him to give me the opportunity to take this further. The power dynamic between us is so heady, and even though he's in command, he's letting me be the one to take the lead with how far we go from here.

"Our little secret." He stares back at me with dark, glittering eyes before allowing his gaze to fall to the space between us.

I follow his silent command as he instructs me to look my fill, and I suck in a hum of pleasure at the sight I've been waiting for. Holy shit, my best friend's father has a cock worthy of worshipping twenty-four seven. His thick length bobs between us. Veined and long and with a glistening bead at the head that makes my mouth water.

"I just want to show you . . . to let you know how good you made me feel." I wrap my fingers around him and stroke from root to tip. Loving the velvety feel and the way his dick swells in response to my touch. "Let me show you what you do to me."

He's so big, and we're already locked together here on the edge of the counter, so I guide him toward my slit easily. With one hand, I hook the lace to one side, and with the other, I stroke his tip through my slickness.

"*Mmmmfuck*, you're drenched. Who's all this for?" His chin dips, and our foreheads almost touch as we both watch the sight of where I repeat the motion over and over, dragging him through my pussy lips and up to circle over my clit.

"All for you."

A rumbling, sexy-as-hell sound fills the air, leaving me shuddering with desire.

"So fucking wet. You're gonna have to be very careful . . . Keep on doing that, and it might just slip in."

God. My entire core clenches. It's so naughty, so wrong, and the fact he's willingly playing this game with me is so hot I can hardly breathe.

"It's okay if it's only a little bit, isn't it? Especially if it's just our secret." My pulse thuds harder as I push the fat head of him down and notch him at my entrance. "No one needs to know. Just the tip."

"Sweetheart, you're going to get us in so much trouble," Luke grunts, spreading my thighs as wide as they can go. Allowing us to both see the evidence of this forbidden moment. Him coated in the sheen of my arousal and pressed up against the spot where it would take next to nothing for him to shove all the way inside.

"It's only this much. We can just play like this." I moan as I hold him tight against me, and he pushes forward just a fraction, fitting the broad head against my entrance.

"This pussy is so fucking greedy. You say you only want the tip, but really you're being a little tease, trying to tempt me deeper already." Luke's hips pulse, allowing his head to pulse in and out, thrusting agonizingly slow so that barely an inch dips inside before he pulls back. I wedge my fingers there in a V shape to help guide him in place, to encourage just a fraction more of him to press inside my channel. The whole thing becomes even more erotic as each tiny movement is accompanied by a slick sound. One that proves exactly how soaking wet I am.

"It doesn't count if it's just this." My breathing picks up pace because, holy fuck, this man's cock is so insanely good. The feel of him stretching me is wiping my brain of any thoughts.

All I want is to lose myself in this man.

Luke shifts forward and then holds steady. His dick pushes inside, edging a little further, and I'm so close to begging him to slam all the way home. My pussy walls flutter and clench around him, and a dark noise leaves his chest.

My cowboy lifts one hand and pinches my chin, forcing me to look up at him. "You let me inside this pussy raw, and I'm going to have you stretched around my cock and leaking cum for as long as that snow sticks to the ground." He searches my gaze, eyes flickering between mine. "All games aside, better decide right now if that's what you want."

"Oh, god, I want that . . . more than you know." Yes, please, and thank you very fucking much. The picture he just painted makes my blood heat and sing. "I'm on birth control; I've been tested recently, and I always normally use protection," I add hastily, feeling a little out of breath. Silently praying that if this man has any lingering doubts about going all the way through with this . . . well . . . hopefully that might convince him to shove all the way in deep.

He studies me. Something unreadable in his expression, and his jaw flexes. "Well, I haven't been with anyone without using a condom in . . . let's just say a long time. If that's enough for you to take me at my word, but I understand if it isn't."

God, he's so fucking hot. Brooding and powerful, not to mention the fact that he's still fully clothed, while I'm in the sluttiest position where it feels even filthier that I've got *almost* nothing on.

"Please, I need to feel you. I need you inside me." My Christmas wish is coming wrapped up in a big ol' bow of begging, it would seem.

"You're going to watch." Luke guides my chin down, then hooks my thighs with both hands. All I can do is brace myself on my hands behind me as he manipulates my body into the exact position to sink deep. It's the hottest and filthiest sight, us joined in the most carnal way.

"Look at your pretty little pussy taking every inch. See how well you take me."

We both stare, fixated on the place where his cock disappears into me. Where my body wraps and fits perfectly to stretch around all of him. With every mind-scrambling moment, he pushes forward on a long, wet glide.

"Luke . . ." I gasp. It's so full. He's everywhere, invading my body and mind on a level I'm not sure I'll recover from.

I've spent so many years of my life admiring this rugged man from afar, never wanting to let on just how much I've adored him for as long as I can remember knowing him.

"Goddamn, you're so fucking wet. So slippery. It's too good." Luke grits his teeth before he bottoms out, and we both let out a groan of pleasure.

He holds there for a second. The darkness in his eyes is completely hypnotic. They're black as the starless night outside, and as he pulls back, I bite down on my bottom lip.

Luke thrusts forward again, so commanding, so powerful,

the force of him makes my breasts bounce, and the look on his face is entirely wild.

This man is going to turn my entire life on its head with this singular moment, I can feel it.

Sliding out again, I'm so slick and turned on, he draws back to just the tip. With a rough noise, his fingers grip my flesh and he thrusts home. Again and again.

"Holy fuck." His voice is so gritty and sexy. I'm immediately lost in how insanely pleasurable it feels to be with him.

Not to mention how every single detail of this moment is unfathomably hot.

My best friend's father pounds into me while I'm spread out on the dining table we've sat at for countless meals together. A place so familiar it might as well be my own kitchen.

Nothing will ever be the same after this, but I have no fucking regrets. This is everything I've wanted for so long and never thought could ever be a possibility.

"Oh god. Oh god." As Luke keeps thrusting forward, tension starts to whirl and build, and pleasure starts to build from my toes like a whirlwind intent on sweeping me away.

"Jesus. You're gripping me so tight. It's too fucking good."

"I'm so close." The moan I let out is loud and desperate.

"You're gonna let me inside you all night." Strong fingers sink into my softness, holding me exactly where he wants me to keep hitting a spot that makes my eyes roll back in my head.

"Please. *Please.*"

"Where do you want me to come?" He grits his teeth. We're both dangling on the edge as his thrusts start to get jerkier and sloppier. Just how fucking good this feels consumes the two of us all at once.

"Inside," I gasp, barely holding on.

"You want me to fill this pretty little cunt up?" Luke grinds out the words with each punishing thrust.

"Yes. Come inside me." My words are hardly more than a whimper. "Oh god. I want to feel it."

Letting out a dark noise, that's when he seeks out my clit.

I simply dissolve. My pussy clamps down so hard I think I see stars and blank spots behind my eyelids as a powerful climax tears through me.

"Jesus. Fuck. *Fuck.* I'm gonna fill you over and over."

Luke's hips jerk in an unsteady rhythm, and as my orgasm is still rolling through, my pussy still rippling and gripping him, I feel it. The length of him swells, and he makes a rough noise, burying himself deep.

His cock throbs and spills inside me, and I'm pretty sure there are moans coming out of me at how good it feels.

Holy shit, the feeling of him unloading, pulsing inside is like nothing else.

Nothing is going to compare to this.

As we both remain there, joined together, panting and attempting to catch our breath, I suspect that I've just allowed part of my foolish little heart to stay right here when I leave this place.

CHAPTER 14

Lucas

"Don't act like it's the end of the world, Tessie girl."

She nudges my shoulder and nibbles the collar of my jacket with a snort as I give her breakfast.

We're all creatures of routine, and the horses have all looked at me with big, dewy eyes as if I have three heads for being out here so early this morning.

It's still dark out, the freezing air crisp, and I've left a gorgeous girl sleeping in my bed after the hottest night of my life.

However, a ranch doesn't wait, or give a shit, about my sex life—or lack thereof, the majority of the time—so I'm rushing around with a flashlight in the dark and trudging through snow.

All so I can get back to her at the earliest opportunity.

Munching noises and gentle huffing sounds follow me as I check on all the stalls and make sure everyone is warm and comfortable after last night's storm.

The familiar scent of wood, leather, and hay surrounds me. Smells that feel embedded in my very bones after so many years running this ranch. There are plenty of jobs I'll have to get to later today, but mucking out stalls can wait.

I've got somewhere else I need to be.

My phone vibrates in my coat pocket, and I scrunch my brows

as I dig it out. It doesn't matter that it's Christmas morning; I don't know anyone who would be messaging me at this time of the day.

Brad:
Merry Christmas, old man.

Guilt immediately floods me at the sight of Brad's name. Does my son have fucking sixth sense or what?

You're up early.

Oh, good. You're as pleasant over text as you are in person at this time of day.

Repeat after me . . . "Merry Christmas, my son, the light of my life. I hope you and Flinn have a wonderful day and enjoy the thousands of dollars I just deposited in your bank account."

Go on. Try it.

Fuck off.

Merry Christmas.

There we go.

Not so hard, was it?

Doesn't answer my question. Why are you texting me at this time of the morning?

Jesus. I'll warn Sky you're in particularly good spirits for Christmas Day.

In case it's escaped your notice, ranch life has ruined mornings for both me and Flinn.

Even when it's a day off, we can't enjoy sleeping in anymore.

More dots bounce on the screen.

Please, can you at least not be all "grumpy asshole" today?

Treat my best friend nicely . . . You know, be good to her when she gets up.

Oh. I've got plans to treat her extremely well, but my son doesn't need to know any of that.

I readjust my hat with my free hand, staring at my phone glowing in the dark, contemplating what to write in reply. God, I feel like no matter what I say, it'll sound suspiciously like I know exactly how Skylar Addams feels when she grips my cock so hard I nearly lose my goddamn mind. If I try to say anything, it'll reveal that I know the exact way her eyes roll back and how her little moans sound as she falls apart.

I figure saying less is always going to be the best option.

Of course.

Love you, Dad.

Give the horses a big hug for me.

I'm about to tuck my phone away when I see more dots bouncing.

Keep an eye on Sky, would you?

She might say she's doing okay, but she found out her piece-of-shit boyfriend was cheating on her last night.

My hand scrubs over my jaw as I see my son's next messages arrive. Texts that leave me with a hundred conflicting emotions about who my son thinks I am as a good father and who I am underneath as the man who wants to savor every second I have left in secret with this girl.

Not to mention the extreme need I'm battling . . . the urge to go beat the hell out of whoever this asshole is. The mere sight of those words on screen has me seeing red.

Except, Brad's next message arrives and reminds me that I don't need to go over there and acquaint my fist with the fucker's jaw. Because I have her.

I have her.

Even if it's just temporarily.

Thanks for being there when I couldn't be.

I'm just glad she's safe with you.

CHAPTER 15

Skylar

My body runs white hot, with a cascade of liquid pleasure flowing through my heavy limbs.

There's a weight draped over my body, pinning me hard to the mattress, and as I stir, the scents of *Lucas Rhodes* and the soft cocoon of his sheets gradually come into sharper focus.

Followed by the glide of his tongue.

His hot mouth is on my pussy, working me, guiding me into yet another climax.

I don't know when we finally drifted to sleep, but after a marathon of sex, he's still not satisfied. Taking his time to lick and suck and drive me into a bank of rainbow clouds, flying somewhere high out of my body.

My fingers reach down and sink into his hair, holding him in place against my pussy, and a sigh of pleasure escapes into the darkness of his bedroom.

Fuck, this cowboy is my every fantasy and dirty fascination come to life. He's so skilled with his tongue, building my coiled desire up before easing back and letting me sink even deeper into how fucking incredible this feels.

Luke isn't doing this to try to get me off in a hurry like some guys I've been with in the past might have done; he's nestled himself between my thighs and seems like he's intent on staying there.

"You're gonna have me addicted, Mr. Rhodes." My voice is raspy with sleep, and possibly from screaming his name over and over, as I roll my hips and tighten my fingers in his hair.

He grunts. A delicious, hungry noise, sucking and nibbling on my pussy lips. "Fuck . . . Christmas or not, today can fuck right off . . . neither of us is leaving this bed for the rest of the day."

A moan gets dragged out of me when he doubles down and pushes his tongue inside. "Mmm. Oh god," I whimper. Yes, please, I'll gladly dissolve into orgasm after orgasm without coming up for air. If his mouth, fingers, or cock is involved, that's more than enough to satisfy my needs.

"So pretty when your legs shake for me," he speaks against my sensitive bundle of nerves, and I want him to keep circling with that perfect rhythm. I'm a swollen, slick mess after everything we've done since last night.

"Luke . . . I can't . . . not again," I moan, but the man is relentless.

"Be my perfect little slut and soak my face." Those wicked words are followed by him sucking down on my clit, making my back bow up off the bed as my orgasm rushes in from where it has been hovering in the wings, waiting for my mind to wake up.

The intensity and suddenness surprises me, showcasing just how long he's been playing with my body while I've been asleep. With how insanely hot that is, how naughty, well, the sensation roars through my blood, and I'm making all sorts of wanton noises while chanting his name over and over.

If I wasn't already dangerously close to falling head over heels for this man, I think he might have just sealed my fate.

How will I ever top this? How will I ever find anything to compare to how good it feels, inexplicably so, with a cowboy twice my age?

Luke doesn't stop, expertly flipping my body so that he can drive into me from behind. This time he fucks me fast, our bodies line up perfectly at this angle and he hits a spot deep inside that makes me feel delirious with pleasure. I'm spun out of my head entirely by his forceful thrusts and powerful body braced over the top of me.

"Fuck, you're the sweetest thing. Moaning my name and coming for me. You're gonna have me addicted to your cunt." His voice is hot at my ear, and it makes my climax drag out or keep building—I'm not sure which anymore. But all I know is that I'm tightening around him again, and he curses, feeling the way I can't help but respond. To him, to his words, to the way he spears into me, to the dragging sensation of his thickness gliding in and out of my channel.

"God . . . Luke . . ."

"You want me to fuck you full, sweetheart? Have my cum dripping out of you?"

"Yes. *Yes.*" I dissolve under the weight of his filthiness.

His hand snakes around to find my clit, and it only takes a couple of firm circles; that deft touch picks me up and washes me over the edge. Luke follows me. His hips falter, and his cock throbs and jerks deep inside my pussy as he grunts out his release.

It's so fucking sexy hearing the way he falls apart above me, and even though my pulse races blindly with desire, I feel my heart melt more than a little.

His mouth roams across my shoulders in a sanity-stealing glide of wet kisses.

"Hell, you squeeze my cock like a dream," Luke rumbles at my ear, not making any attempt to move. God, I can't get over how incredible it feels to be filled by this man.

"How does a bath sound?"

Holy shit, did I just squeak out loud?

"So, that's a yes?"

Reluctantly, we untangle ourselves, and I squirm around to face my cowboy, who leans over my body, caging me in with his impossibly broad arms.

"I forgot you have a bathtub. I miss having one since I moved out of home." I peek up at him, still floating around somewhere on blissed-out waves. "Yes. A *very* enthusiastic yes, but on one condition."

He brushes strands of hair away from my face and raises one eyebrow. A silent question.

"You have to join me, cowboy."

Luke blows out a chuckle and drops his head against my chest. "I'm trying my damnedest to be giving you some rest, Skylar. Not trying to get inside you at every opportunity."

"Can I be honest, and you promise not to laugh?" I just want to hold him here, pressed against me, weighing me down against the mattress.

His lips brush my collarbone as he speaks against my skin. "Anytime. You know me."

I bite my lip, trying to find the courage to ask for what I want, when eventually, I just blurt it out. "I'm a cuddler . . . after sex . . . and since we've, well, you know *a lot* . . . it's feeling extra intense for me right now."

Luke nuzzles my neck and runs his nose down to my cleavage. "Sounds like a dream. A hot-as-fuck girl who can't keep her hands off me. What's not to get excited about in that scenario?"

I try not to give away, with the look on my face or the immediate tension that fills my limbs, the number of guys—my asshole ex included—who would never give me that kind of simple affection afterward.

The man pinning me to the bed senses it all the same. "Don't even answer that question because I don't need to spend the next hour talking myself out of going over there and sorting that piece of shit out."

I can't help but laugh. Luke picks me up off the bed, sets me on my feet, then herds me toward the bathroom, as if I've got any intention or interest in going anywhere else. Before long, we're both soaking in divine, steaming water, with him at my back and his big palms running soap leisurely over my arms, my stomach, and my breasts.

He's not trying to start anything, but he treats me to a constant stream of touches that make my bones dissolve with bliss.

At this point, I'm willfully ignoring the fact my heart has formed a little puddle of besotted happiness, too.

CHAPTER 16

Lucas

I could die a contented man if I never have to leave this damn bathtub.

The sweetest, most gorgeous woman I've ever met is wrapped against my chest, and time feels like it has gone into hibernation while we've been soaking in here together.

"Don't you need to go take care of the horses this morning?" Skylar plays her fingers over my forearm, sending tiny sparks swirling beneath my skin as she does so.

"Already done."

"What? When?" She tries to tilt her head around to look at me.

"Earlier . . . I didn't want to wake you."

"Oh my god. I could have at least come and helped out, you know."

I shake my head ruefully, quietly laughing to myself at how pouty she sounds. "Sweetheart, it's freezing outside, and everything is buried under three feet of snow. I've done that routine what feels like a million times. It's easy for me. The fact that I could climb back into bed and have you soft and warm and moaning my name . . . now that's the best gift you could give me."

Skylar makes a little noise, part protest and part embarrassment. Fuck, she's so cute, the way she starts to squirm.

"I still can't believe this is real." Her voice is quiet.

How much do I tell her?

How much do I dare admit?

"Why wouldn't it be?" My hands roam freely because there's every chance I'm more than addicted to the way her delicate skin feels beneath my rough palms.

"I didn't think *Lucas Rhodes* would ever notice someone like me."

Fucking hell. If only this girl knew . . .

"I've always noticed you," I speak against her hair. Sitting like this, it's impossible to ignore the way she fits so perfectly, nestled into my chest.

"Really?"

"Look . . . not when you were younger, of course. Not in *that* kind of way back then," I'm quick to add, while painfully aware of the fact I now have my son's best friend naked in my bath.

She can't help but giggle a little. "It would be way too easy to tease you about that right now."

Pinching her thigh makes her jump and let out another laugh. The kind of sound that roams straight through my chest, breaking through years of self-imposed guards and walls that have existed there for too damn long along the way.

"Joke all you like, sweetheart, but let's just make it abundantly clear. I never looked at you that way when you were younger. The reason I always noticed *you* was because Brad was able to be himself around you."

I rest my lips against her pink hair, inhaling deep lungfuls of her scent. Shampoo and soap and sweetness that are so undeniably Skylar.

"You know, Brad came out to me when he was about twelve, I think . . . He asked me if I liked boys as much as I liked girls. If I ever had trouble choosing between the two. Which at the time he asked was outta left field, but we were right in the middle of grooming the horses together, so all we did was chat about it while we worked, and he was just so certain. As a parent, there wasn't ever a doubt in my mind that he was bisexual. It's just who Brad is. But I know not every person in the world can see past their own prejudices and bullshit. So I always worried about him. I always worried about who he was hanging out with . . . and yet, I always knew if the two of you were together, he would be okay."

A wistful sigh comes out of her. "I don't want to hurt him, and I don't want to do anything to mess up your relationship with him either."

"I know you never would." This is also why I know this girl will never jeopardize their closeness or friendship, no matter how good it might feel to temporarily indulge in whatever this is together. "It made me sleep better at night knowing he had you as a friend, Skylar."

"You're a good dad, you know. The best."

I groan. "Can you maybe not remind me about that while I've got you naked?" Right now, I definitely don't feel particularly responsible in the father-figure department.

Her silent laughter rolls through her body, making her shake a little against my chest.

"Okay, funny girl, laugh all you like. I told you when I first noticed you." Dropping my head down, I brush my lips up the side of her neck. "Now you have to confess . . . When did you first notice me?"

She makes a sinful little noise as my lips explore the side of her throat, and even though Skylar arches her neck to give me more access, her hands fly up to cover her face.

"Ohhhh . . . it's like that, is it?" I tease.

Skylar continues to squirm.

I'm enjoying this much more than I should. My dick is, too.

"You can't torture me on Christmas. That's not fair," she whines.

"I think I can. Maybe denying you any more orgasms might

work?" My fingers play over her inner thighs, taunting as I dip close to her pussy without making any contact.

Skylar's hips try to chase my touch, and I have to stifle a groan. All I want to do is lift her up and settle her back down over my cock, but we both need to actually leave this bathroom and eat something, considering we've done nothing but fuck since last night.

"I can't remember a time when I didn't have hearts in my eyes whenever I saw you." She twists so that she can meet my gaze, tilting her chin to look up at me. "How you didn't see that, I'll never know."

"You must have been pretty good at hiding these baby blues," I murmur. Wondering how, in all those years, I never noticed her looking at me like that.

"I would have been nothing more than a silly little girl to your eyes."

Bringing one hand up out of the water, I tuck her hair behind her ear and brush wet fingers along the softness of her cheek. Once again, I take my time to study her, to look my fill and really, truly savor looking. To commit to memory the swirling, endless orbs filled with azure blue and tiny flecks of silver.

"Sweetheart, even if I had noticed back then, it wasn't my place to look at you . . ." I brush my thumb along her bottom lip. "But now? I'm selfish and greedy, and I'm gonna want you naked until that snow clears so I can look at you all I like. How does that sound?"

Her teeth catch her bottom lip, and she looks like a goddamn dream.

"As long as I get to do the same with you, cowboy."

Skylar

Is there anything better than spending Christmas without wearing a single item of clothing, at the request of the hottest cowboy to ever stroll into my life?

After the unfathomable turn of events my life has taken in the past twenty-four hours, I can't quite believe that this time yesterday, I was busy secretly planning to spend today of all days with the asshole who is firmly now in the trash. My *ex*.

Even worse, if I had stayed at home, like originally had been my plan all along, I would have never discovered the truth about what his cheating ass was up to.

All things considered, the fantasies I might have had—revolving around Lucas Rhodes and possibilities of getting snowed in with my best friend's dad—could never quite have lived up to the reality of how things have transpired since last night.

One thing's for certain: I'll never look at a bottle of whiskey the same, ever again.

My grin is a permanent landmark on my face as I snuggle further below the blanket I've got wrapped around my blissfully naked, and ever so slightly sore, body. While I might have my Kindle in hand, my mind is mighty distracted by a replay of a thousand tiny moments of all things *Luke*.

His hands and mouth on my body. His gruff words in my ear. God, I don't know how I'm supposed to function, let alone concentrate on anything, when I now intimately know how it feels for him to slip into me from behind. When I've been treated to what it's like to hear Lucas Rhodes whisper filthy things while his hips thrust lazily against my ass.

Holy shit, my body must be on high alert to every single thought of him, because all it takes is my mind wandering back to the early hours of this morning for my nipples to become hardened, sensitive points rubbing against my blanket.

Maybe it was a good thing that he had to go back out for the afternoon to take care of the horses.

At the rate I'm going, I'd be mauling the poor man if he were here.

I'm feeling more than warm, but I'm well aware my "indoor task" for today is to keep the fire stoked up and the house toasty; I wriggle around, get to my knees, and lean over to carefully pluck a piece of wood from the stack beside the fireplace.

Just as I toss it into the flames, my phone starts ringing. I'm flailing, a clumsy, completely off-balance mess, while trying to keep myself partially covered up, and despite my best efforts to the contrary, I somehow manage to hit the green button by accident.

To my utter mortification, the screen immediately fills with the beaming smile of my mother.

I watch on in horror as she juggles the phone and puts on her reading glasses. All while my tits are hanging out and I've got a blanket pooled around my waist.

I am oh so very naked.

And I'm very obviously seated on the living room floor of my best friend's father's house.

This is a situation I absolutely *cannot* explain, in any universe.

I do some sort of part-screech, part-commando roll and dive away from the camera on my phone.

"Sky? Do you have service? Is the call connecting?" I hear my mom mutter, and I swear to god I'm about to combust like the flames beside me.

Crawling on my belly, I slither across the carpet until I can reach out very carefully from my hidden position of shame and tap the "end call" button. As soon as the call disconnects, I promptly flop onto my back with relief.

That does it. No more phone for the rest of Christmas Day. Not while I've got Lucas Rhodes to myself for such a short window of time—and plans to spend the day without a stitch of clothing and at his mercy.

I very efficiently and briefly text my confused mother, informing her that I'm just getting in the shower and I'll call her back later, then turn my phone on Do Not Disturb.

I'll deal with her much, much later.

Wrapping the blanket around me, I get to my feet and proceed to waddle like the world's most embarrassed penguin in the direction of the kitchen.

Other than tossing my phone straight into the freezer, I'm not quite sure how to prevent a repeat of my full-frontal, nipple-shaped Christmas Day greeting. So I plug it into my charger on the counter and back away like the entire device is liable to explode.

My plans for today involve nothing more than the cowboy I've fantasized about for years.

If there was ever a convenient time to forget about the outside world beyond the snow piled up beyond those windows, today would be that day.

CHAPTER 17

Lucas

A sultry moan drops out of Skylar. "Oh my god."

She squeezes her eyes closed, and I have to fight the urge to toss our plates aside and give in to the perpetual need to have my mouth on her again.

"This . . . hands down . . . is the best Christmas lunch I've ever had," she says through a mouthful.

Taking another big bite of the grilled cheese, she's a gorgeous sight, bundled up in a blanket in front of my fireplace in the lounge. Hair damp and skin glowing after the bath. I got my wish to keep her naked, but Skylar reluctantly agreed to let me throw on some sweats while I made us a meal.

"I don't believe that for a second." Biting into my own, the savory hit of melted cheese and caramelized edges of the bread do taste damn good. "But I will say, there's an art to grilled cheese. I don't give a shit what anyone thinks. You gotta do it properly. Crisp that motherfucker a little, ya know?"

Skylar chews quietly, then gestures at the sight beside us where we've camped out on the floor for this impromptu picnic.

"The tree looks so pretty. I didn't think I'd want to see a single bauble or scrap of tinsel after the past few weeks of being neck deep in making everyone else's Christmas look gorgeous, but I'm kinda glad to get to see some cute decorations and lights."

I clear my throat because, if anything, the sight I'm looking at right here before me with her pink hair and gorgeous smile is a thousand times better than that goddamn tree. "It's all Brad's doing. Can't say I've contributed anything really."

"Bet you still chopped the tree down for him, though, just like you do every year?"

Giving her a wry smile, I reach forward to brush a crumb off the corner of her lips with my thumb. "Shh, sweetheart. Don't give away all my secrets. If I had it my way, I'd have nothing at all . . . I've never been much into Christmas, to be honest. Brad, however . . ."

The prettiest girl in the entire fucking world tips her head back and laughs, earning her a glare.

"What?" I huff.

Skylar rolls her lips together, shaking her head. "I'm not really sure I can be bothered with it either . . . All the day usually does is remind me of being single, and it's just another day where everything seems to be about buying shit they don't need and spending time with people they don't want to be around."

Ain't that the fucking truth.

"So my stupid little grilled cheese and a tree that my son insisted on inserting in my house and decorating—that's enough Christmas spirit for you?"

She hums while breaking off a corner, letting the melted cheese stretch out between the pieces with a smile that I don't deserve to be enjoying so much. "Look, I'm nothing but a hazard in the kitchen. Anyone who can make me a meal that tastes *this* good is a saint in my eyes."

"Do you not cook for yourself?" My brows crease.

"No, either I'm too tired or too busy, or I find it easier to get takeout." She mulls over a mouthful, and then her blue eyes roll at me. "Don't give me the *dad* look of judgment either."

"Well, what do you expect me to say? You're not taking care of yourself."

"I've never been any good at cooking, and it's just so hard when your business is new." Skylar brushes some additional crumbs from the corner of her mouth with a thumb.

I get it. I really do. There have been plenty of times on this ranch when work or the horses have come first, and my own needs a distant second. Even so, it chafes me to know this girl has been potentially working herself to the bone with no one there to take care of her.

"No one's been there to help you?" I want to fucking punch whoever she's been allowing in her life. Clearly, the asshole she was with didn't know shit about how to keep such a perfect girl.

His loss.

My gain.

She takes another mouthful, avoiding my eyes as she chews. The fireplace pops and hisses to fill the silence. "Turns out I let the wrong kind of asshole into my life, and I should have listened to Brad a long time ago," she eventually admits. "But, is it okay if we don't talk about that?"

"Fine by me. I probably shouldn't be threatening to break anyone's jaw, seeing as it's Christmas and all."

Skylar gives me a small smile. "Cooking for me and defending my honor. Where have you been all my life, cowboy?"

I know she's teasing, but hell, if it doesn't make me wonder the same thing. How the fuck has this girl been in my life all these years, yet only now are we discovering this spark between us?

Especially when I know there's only a matter of time until that snow is cleared and she's gone again.

"You're letting me help with the horses tomorrow. End of story." Skylar drops her Kindle into her lap and pouts at me when I walk back into the lounge.

I've been out getting all the basic shit done down in the stables but insisted that Skylar didn't need to help me.

Besides, I'd never have gotten anything done anywhere near as quickly if she'd been there alongside me. Not because she's incapable, but because I wouldn't have been able to keep my hands off her.

I tug my hat off my head and run my fingers through my hair. "Ahh, but that means putting clothes on, and I much prefer the idea of coming back in from the cold to find you naked on my couch, sweetheart." I lean a shoulder against the wall and touch my tongue to the front of my teeth, eating up the way she flushes perfectly under my words.

"I'm serious." She tugs the blanket tighter around her shoulders, and I fucking love that she's stayed right here, without anything on, settled in front of my fire all afternoon.

"Okay, fine, you can come scoop horse shit to your heart's content tomorrow. Does that make you happy?"

"Very. Thank you." She gives me a satisfied little smirk and then picks up what she was reading. Only, as I go about stripping out of my jacket and boots, I feel her eyes straying my way.

"Good book?" Once I've hung everything up, I cross the room and bank the fire with more wood. Purposely taking my time.

"Mhmm." She sinks her teeth into the plump curve of her lower lip, trying extremely hard to keep her eyes focused on the screen.

"Not too boring for you, I hope? Being stuck in here all day with only a book to keep you occupied."

I've got plans to make this much more interesting.

"Nope, it's kinda perfect." Her tongue darts out to wet her

lips. Pink spots deepen, high on her cheeks, and fuck, she looks so sexy.

"You're welcome to put a movie on . . . if you prefer?"

"I don't mind. It's your house. What do you want?"

"Me? I like the idea of getting cozy right there beside you with a book. As long as that doesn't sound too *old and boring* to you?" Crossing to the couch, I'm shit-stirring after what I heard Brad say to her on the phone last night. Except if I'm truthful, beneath the teasing, there is a tiny part of me who is still a little unsure what this girl even sees, or wants, with someone like me.

Skylar shifts over, making room for me to wedge myself in the corner of the L-shaped couch as I swipe up a book I've had sitting on the side table here for months, yet my eyes are usually too heavy to manage reading more than a couple of pages at a time.

"Honestly . . . after how crazy the last few weeks have been at my shop, it actually feels amazing to have the luxury of time and quiet and to not have to talk to anyone."

Oh, I can definitely do *not talking*.

"Come here." My dream girl, whom I cannot keep, nestles herself against my side, with her head on my chest and hand holding her Kindle braced against my stomach. I prop my own book up on my chest, but in all honesty, I'm not focusing on a single fucking word.

My other arm snakes over her waist, palm covering her hip. It's too tempting to see just how silky and wet she might be between those thighs.

As we lie there together, I feel her shift a little beneath my fingers. That's the moment her breathing shallows, and I can't help myself. Slipping my hand between the layers of blanket, I trace the lush curve of her stomach down, down, down until I find the exact place where I want to explore.

Skylar's breath sucks in with a quiet gasp as my fingers dip into her pussy and find exactly what I'm looking for.

Discovering how absolutely drenched she is.

"Luke . . ." She makes a tiny moaning sound that makes my rapidly hardening cock kick inside my jeans. Turning her head into my chest, teeth graze the front of my shirt.

"Are you sore?" I stroke gently, running my fingers through the velvety feel of her. The slippery evidence of how turned on the girl in my arms is coats my fingers.

"No." Her hips lift and adjust, giving me easier access. "I can't stop thinking about you being inside me again."

That makes me more feral for her than I have any right to be.

"Keep reading. If you can be a good girl and let me play with you, without coming, I'll give you exactly what you want."

CHAPTER 18

Skylar

"Can you be good and do that for me?"

The glide of Luke's fingers against my clit, rubbing through my soaking wet pussy is all I can focus on.

"I don't know." My whimper catches in my throat as he strokes and fondles me so damn leisurely, almost like this is completely normal. As if we lie here on this couch wrapped together like this every night while he teases my pussy until my thighs shake.

How much I want that . . . how much every detail of that scenario swirls in my mind as something I dearly wish could be true, shocks me.

I mean, I know how deeply besotted I've always been with this man. Except all of those years he was simply a fantasy, a young girl's infatuated desire with a much older and sinfully attractive cowboy.

This feeling right here catches me by surprise, that I might want this to be something more than just sex and being able to finally live out the longing I'd had in my head for so many years.

"*Hmm*. I think you can. Especially if you want to have me inside you all night." Luke's deep voice vibrates through his thick chest and into me, along with the ripples of pleasure each time he lingers over my clit, before easing away, continuing to torture me the whole time.

I'm panting within minutes. Quivering for him. Tiny, slutty, begging noises burst out of me. The climax threatening to take over, which I so desperately want to chase, hovers close and then ebbs time and time again. Somewhere along the way, my Kindle slipped from my fingers, and all I'm capable of is clutching onto his soft shirt.

"Please. Luke, I can't take any more." A shudder rolls through me, and white sparks dance behind my eyelids as I get lost in how insanely good it feels to allow him command over my body.

"This might just be my favorite way to spend the holidays," he murmurs wickedly. Using two fingers to curl inside me, he presses forward to gather up more of my slickness, then spreads it up and over my clit with a slide of his touch that is just enough to wind me tighter, but nowhere near enough to get me off. "Feel how goddamn drenched you are for this."

There is every chance I'm flying out of my head by this point. I've never had anyone treat me like this before, and my entire body feels like a sparking livewire.

My skin is overheated, and my breasts ache, and it takes everything not to start damn well humping his hand.

"Oh god. Please." Begging is my only currency.

"You want to come, sweetheart?"

"Yes," I whimper, digging my fingernails into his shirt. I want him naked, too, like he promised me.

"Get up here." His fingers drag out of my pussy, leaving an obscenely slick trail across my stomach. Slipping out from under the warmth of the blanket, I allow him to guide me up over his chest.

I'm not even sure I can support my own body weight; every limb feels so heavy with pleasure.

A gasp slips out of me as he makes his intentions clear.

I was expecting us to be fucking, but it seems Luke has other ideas. His big hands wrap around my waist, strong fingers digging into the softness of my curves, and he firmly holds me still while sinking lower down the couch.

Holy shit.

There's a hunger in his eyes that turns me upside down and inside out as I realize he's positioning me over his mouth. That look, right there, makes my blood sizzle with anticipation, but it feels so insane. We're doing this, right here, out in the open, and even though I know that no one could possibly see anything, there's enough risk that it turns up the intensity of this moment to scalding proportions.

"No hovering. Full weight. Sit your pretty little pussy right where I want." He licks up the swell of my inner thigh. The exact place where I know I'm coated in wetness from being so turned on and so out of control when it comes to this man.

"But—" I can't help it. I want this, and I want him, yet I'm also so easily stuck inside my own head with doubt.

"Full." *Nip.* "Body." *Lick.* "Weight." *Suck.*

"Oh fuck. Oh fuck." My hands fly to his hair. Sinking into the unruly dark strands, threading through the flashes of silver, tangling with that insanely hot white streak I've longed to reach out for.

Luke forces me to sink down onto him, and his mouth closes over my pussy, leaving me moaning out loud. I'm grinding down on him immediately because it feels so incredible. After all his teasing and torturing, I'm strung tight and know I'll hurtle over the edge of this cliff almost straight away.

He doesn't waver this time. This man is on a mission to make me shatter, and as his tongue pushes into my pussy, I'm moaning, cursing, chanting his name. I tug his hair so hard it must be painful, but that sting against his scalp only seems to spur him on.

That's when he shifts me slightly, fingers digging into my hips so hard they might surely bruise, and he locks me in a dangerously dark stare. He sucks down on my clit so hard my back bows, and the wave breaks right on top of me. Leaving me shaking and crying out.

Hopefully *not* telling him that I'm in love with him, or something equally ridiculous.

With each subsequent moment he makes me shatter, I'm only falling deeper into whatever this is. The sensations keep growing more and more intense, and I don't know how I'm going to cope when it all has to stop.

"Oh my god. I need you inside." My heart thunders in my throat. Blood tingling and sparks flying through each limb form a pulsating rhythm.

"You want my cock?" he speaks against my pussy, and I nearly jerk away with how overstimulated I am.

"I do. Please. I've been so horny for you all day." The desperate words burst out of me.

"Well, I'm nowhere near done here. So, if you want my dick in your mouth, you better turn around for me."

"Holy shit."

There's a devious look in his eyes and glistening evidence of my wetness all over his mouth and beard.

"Problem?" He steals my breath as he holds my gaze and runs his tongue in a long line to lap at my pussy.

"Right here?" My eyes flicker around the room. I'm intensely aware of how naked I am, perched over his face.

"My house. My rules. If I want the sweetest damn pussy I've ever had soaking me right here, that's how it's going to be."

A tiny smile tugs at my lips. "You're naughty, Mr. Rhodes."

CHAPTER 19

Skylar

"*I'm naughty?* Says the girl who walked in here wearing nothing but a bra and a pathetic excuse for panties last night. Now suck my dick while I eat your cunt till you can't argue with me anymore."

Luke tumbles me down, and in my post-orgasm haze, I'm entirely boneless, allowing him to position me in the sluttiest way possible. Completely naked, on hands and knees over the top of him, with his bulging erection pressing against the front of his jeans right there in my face.

God. How I want to show this man exactly how much I enjoy having his dick in my mouth.

In between all our midnight fucking, I had a few opportunities to run my tongue over his length, to lick, to wrap my lips around him briefly. This moment right here is the first time I'll properly get to suck his cock, and I'm practically salivating for him.

Luke lets me kneel over his chest while I work his jeans and briefs in order to take him out. As soon as his cock bobs free, the second my hungry fingers have succeeded in their quest, he strikes. Dragging me back up over his mouth, he tips me forward in order to begin running his tongue all over me again.

Building me back up in a way that I didn't know was even possible for my body twenty-four hours ago.

My mind goes blank, pleasure washes through me, and my toes curl.

"Oh fuck." I'm the horniest girl alive for this man. "How are you so good? Everything feels so good with you." My words are part moan, part sob, as I allow my tongue to run the length of him, from root to tip, sloppy and desperate licks that feel incredible against his thickening shaft.

Beneath me, I feel him groan against my pussy, and I take that as my invitation to do it again and again. Drawing as many of those delicious noises as possible out of the cowboy with his head between my thighs.

I'm getting close, the wave starts to build, and the intensity of pleasure winding a path straight through me sends me to a place where nothing exists except trying to please Lucas Rhodes.

I allow a long trail of spit to fall from my lips and watch on in fascination as his dick jerks in response.

Luke makes a muffled noise against my pussy, tightening his hold on my hips. "*Ffffuck.*"

"Do you like that, Mr. Rhodes?" I'm not sure what has come over me, but there's a reckless devil at the helm now, and she wants to see this man lose control.

"Christ." He grunts and drags his teeth across my sensitive flesh. I don't miss the way his tip glistens and length throbs in response to me calling him that. "If you can still talk, that's a problem. Be a good girl and give me one more, then I'm going to fill you with my cock all night."

Luke shoves his tongue inside me and I nearly fall apart right then and there. He's relentless, devouring me, and I do my best to match his pace, mirroring his actions. Swirling my tongue over the fat head of him before sucking down.

His dick tastes masculine and feels velvety, filling my mouth. That slight saltiness of precum slides across my tongue, and everything about him is perfect. I can take him so much deeper at this angle, letting him in with ease. It's so fucking hot, like this, on his couch. The fact he's been so desperate to have me, that he's still fully clothed and I'm naked . . . well, that feels powerful somehow.

Like this man would gladly worship me and tend to my needs and my needs alone.

As I start to tremble and feel that rush of pleasure building higher and higher, I'm moaning around his length. His heat and scent fill my senses, and when he works me with two fingers along with his tongue, that does me in. My orgasm hits with a rolling force. I'm a mess of drool, bobbing up and down, making all sorts of desperate, panting noises.

"Fuck, you're so perfect." In between the buzzing in my ears and the thundering pulse in my neck, I'm being manhandled once more.

Luke flips us so that he's sitting up and has me in his lap. I'm dimly aware that my arms hook to drape around his neck while letting him maneuver my body, and I don't fucking care.

He can have whatever he wants.

"*Mmmmfuck.* Don't tempt me with wanting to keep you, sweetheart." He sinks our mouths together at the same time as impaling me on his fat cock. I'm such a wet and swollen mess after having him eat me until I can't even think straight that he slides in so fucking deep, stretching me perfectly around him.

All I can do is cling to his neck and whimper into his mouth. Everything turns to bright sparks and unfathomable pleasure. The material of his shirt drags against my hard nipples, and my clit brushes up against his lower stomach.

"God. You're so tight. So fucking perfect." He pinches my bottom lip between his teeth, fucking up into me, while my body burns hot and blazing for him. "Give me those tits."

With calloused, big palms, he cups my breasts. Pinching and squeezing my nipples while dipping his head to suck and swirl his tongue everywhere.

My fingers dig into his unruly hair, and I keep clinging to him. Holding him there with my head dropped back and eyes squeezed shut.

"Oh god. Oh god." I can feel it. The liquid feeling starts to flow up from my toes, and it's so good but so much, and I don't know how much more of this I can take.

"Milk my cock. That's it. Just like that," Luke grunts against my breasts, still lavishing them with attention in a way that feels like he knows every single key to unraveling my body.

"I'm gonna have you wrapped around me until morning. I don't wanna stop fucking you. It feels too good to stop."

"I can't, Luke. It's too much." Already, the wave rushes in, preparing to carry me off somewhere into the deepest waters.

"You can. Look at you. Taking me like a fucking dream." He slides his hand between us, and his thrusts grow more erratic.

My clit is so sensitive. I feel like there's no way. Not again. Not so soon. It's impossible . . .

"God, you squeeze me so tight. That's it, beautiful, come for me. Steal every last drop out of me. It's all fucking yours." His teeth tug on my nipple, just as his thumb finds my clit, and I dissolve. This time, I go blank. The roaring sensation curls through me and sweeps me up in a darkened cloak, where I lose touch with my senses for a moment.

When I come back into my body, our mouths are desperate and hungry, locked in an intense fusion. The taste of myself on Luke as he slides our tongues together is so damn hot I can hardly breathe. He's buried deep inside me, unloading, pulsing. Holding me so tight against him, it feels like we're both coming for an eternity.

"Jesus. Fuck." Panting against my mouth, Luke's groan is so primal it reaches into my chest and plants itself there.

It's the kind of noise that makes me never want to stop this with him. That tempts me to forget everything about who this man is to me, the complexities of how our lives are intertwined, and to throw caution to the wind.

How could anything else ever be this good?

"You make me crazy, you know that? This pussy . . ." He's so strong, lifting us easily and tumbling me onto my back.

With a hiss, he pulls out, but he has a look on his face that tells me he's still not satisfied.

"Oh my god, Luke . . . No. I can't." My hands push at his head as he falls over me. Kissing and licking a trail down my body. There's no way in hell. I'm so out of my head with too much pleasure, too soon. A thundering torrent of emotion and overstimulation pours through me, unrelenting, beating frantically through my veins.

"Lie still." He stares up at me with hooded, darkened eyes from just above my pussy.

I'm still trying to push him away. Trying to inch up the couch, close my legs, and escape whatever he's got planned for me next.

"No more. I can't take any more."

His palms are scalding hot against my knees. Pinning me in place.

"You were begging for my cock not long ago." He hovers over my pussy with his mouth, trapping me with those dark eyes, and spreads my legs wide for his inspection.

"This is too much," I whine, although even as I say the words, my fingers clench in his hair. Maybe I'm tugging him closer. Maybe I'm pushing him away. Maybe I'm just a total slut for this cowboy.

"Look at you. Leaking my cum." His gaze drifts down, and I can feel the slickness of him at my entrance. It's almost unbearable, having him so close, watching in rapt fascination at the evidence of both of us gathering there. Of the fact he's made a complete mess of me and yet can't seem to get enough of being wedged between my thighs.

"Let me look after you." It's a quiet, gravelly murmur. Words that in such a voice, rumble right through me and drop deep into my chest. Latching onto something that had been floating around untethered for so long.

Luke doesn't wait for me to say anything in reply.

I can't.

It's too intimate. It feels like more than just sex when he looks at me like that with those words and traces of my pussy on his lips. I'm a fool if I'm reading more into it than the afterglow of orgasms.

However, he's not interested in waiting for my response. Luke takes care of me all the same; his mouth fastens over my entrance, and my back bows up off the couch, feeling the scrape of his beard and the insane pleasure he keeps giving me just when I truly think I can't take anymore.

He gathers up our cum and pushes it back inside me with two fingers, followed by wicked swirls of his tongue, pressing into me until I'm whining his name.

With every single second he treats me so perfectly, this man steals my heart and drives me out of my damn mind.

Before carrying me to bed and continuing to do just as he promised.

Taking care of me for the rest of the night.

Lucas

"Okay, Mr. Rhodes . . ." The sweetest thing I've ever seen gives me a look of pure trouble from her spot lying in front of the fireplace. "This morning, while we were in the bath, you said you never noticed me in *that way* . . . but you didn't actually say *when* it was that you first noticed me."

I tilt my glass of whiskey back and let the burn slide down as I contemplate Skylar's question.

All around us, the world seems still. Silent snowflakes drift down through the darkened sky, and the glow of the Christmas tree combined with the fire are the only lights surrounding us.

"You wanna know, sweetheart?" I raise an eyebrow her way.

She's drowsy, lying with her head cradled on both hands and ankles crossed in the air. I'm still getting my head around the fact I've been able to have her here like this, secretly, all to myself.

I'm still wrestling with the guilt I feel for lying to my son, but I'm also enough of a selfish prick that I'm not quite guilty *enough* to stop this thing we've agreed to.

"Mhmm. I told you . . . about my crush . . . It's only fair." Her blue eyes are so damn pretty, reflecting the lights decorating the tree.

"A year ago." I swirl my whiskey, keeping my gaze fixed on hers. "Do you remember last New Year's Eve?"

Skylar nods and bites down on her bottom lip.

"I drove a lot of people home that night." I take another sip, then reach out to stroke her hair, relishing the feel of the silky soft strands. Caught, as always, by the way this girl is so vibrant, so full of color, as the pastel-pink curl slips over my fingertips.

"It was very kind of you," she murmurs.

"What I can tell you is that out of all the people I offered to drive home, there was only one who I really *didn't* want to say goodnight to."

"You didn't?"

"Not in that way." I let my hand slide down to trace over her lip, tugging it out from the hold under her teeth.

"What did you want instead?" She leans into my touch, and that tiny act of seeking out my attention makes my pulse kick.

"I certainly had a very different type of goodnight I wanted to say than the one I settled for, which was letting you disappear off into the darkness."

Skylar shifts her weight and then gets up onto her knees. That blanket she's spent the day curled up in comes apart and gives me a perfect view of her body. Goddamn, this girl is so unbelievable. Her softness, her pale skin, and those tattoos. Jesus.

She clambers into my lap, straddling me, and tugs the ends of the blanket to enclose both of us as she wraps her arms around the back of my neck, toying with the short hairs at my nape.

My hands are drawn straight to her hips, squeezing gently as she settles herself there like this is the most natural thing in the world. As if it's the thing we do all the time.

As if it's how every night might look. To dream of having this beautiful girl pressed up against me in the dim lights and seclusion of the time of evening when it's just the two of us talking and spending hours in each other's company amid the firelight.

"I was so nervous." She smiles at me softly. "I thought my

heart was going to burst out of my chest the whole way home that night. I kept thinking to myself, 'Oh my god, Lucas Rhodes is taking me home.'"

My lips quirk. "Funny how things turned out. I'm not sure whether I should admit how many times I thought about that drive. How I regretted not having the freedom to say what was going through my mind. How I should've walked you to your front door."

Skylar tilts her head and lets her eyes flicker around my face. As she does, I wonder what she sees when she looks my way. Frown lines, gray hairs, and all the weathered planes a cowboy like me has accumulated over the years.

"I had this little fantasy that you might kiss me at midnight . . . or just after . . . since that was when you drove me home," she murmurs.

Tilting my head, I glance at the clock on the stove over in the kitchen.

"Would you look at that?" My eyes fixate on her mouth. "It's just gone midnight."

Her mouth tips into a coy little grin. "It isn't New Year's Eve, Mr. Rhodes."

"And yet here we are."

"Here we are," she breathes.

"How about since I'm almost a year late, I make it up to you?" I slide my palm around to the front of her thighs and dip my thumb between her soft pussy lips. A place where I've spent more time than I should by all rights have done today. But hell, if it isn't a Christmas miracle to have unending access to Skylar's perfect cunt.

Goddamn, she's the sweetest thing. As I lean forward to speak over her lips, I hum the words I shouldn't have any right to say, yet I'm powerless to stop myself where this girl is concerned. "What do you say I take my time and show you exactly the type of kiss you deserved that night?"

CHAPTER 20

Lucas

There are a dozen curious creatures in this part of the stables. All angling their long necks and letting out impatient snorts in order to get a glimpse at the girl out here helping with the chores this morning.

Skylar croons and chats away to each of them as she works her way through the stalls. She's taken over mucking out and shooed me off as soon as I showed her the ropes.

I've busied myself elsewhere . . . because I'm unable to keep off her. Every part of me wants to reach out and touch her in some way.

Not just sexually—I mean, that's undeniably part of my addiction to this girl—but in the way we seem to be able to spend time together so easily. It's effortless to be with her.

She's smart and quick to tease, and for someone like me who has enjoyed his own company for a very long fucking time, Skylar fits with that in a way I wasn't expecting.

We haven't even talked about Brad all that much, which I thought might be where things faltered between us. Once the fucking and tension were out of our system, I had worried that maybe we would have nothing to talk about beyond her being my son's best friend. That our worlds would be too distant from one another.

Instead, we've spent the past day and night together. *Talking.*

She showed me her store's Instagram, photos and videos of her floristry work—which is stunning—plans she's got for events and clients who have already booked her for the new year. Skylar's smile only grew brighter when she sheepishly told me about the dream she's had of growing different varieties of peonies, of having a farm-gate style "pick your own" operation while building a team to handle the shop front for her.

This girl has got budgets and spreadsheets and she absolutely has her shit together. When I think back to being young and dumb and her age, I'm embarrassed to admit all I was doing was roping, riding, and chasing skirts.

Everything is done with such an eye for aesthetic detail, it's no surprise Skylar's busy as all hell.

In between phone calls with her parents and some other friends, she told me about her folks' travels and how they want her to fly to meet them somewhere during the summer.

I mean, admittedly, a lot of those conversations have been while naked or in between another round of sinfully hot sex, but there's a familiarity there between us.

In all honesty, I hadn't expected to find that sort of connection with anyone, let alone a girl half my age who I shouldn't even be looking at.

Something that was put into sharp perspective when Brad video called, and it made for a very awkward twenty minutes when both of us tried to pretend like we didn't spend all of Christmas with my tongue in her cunt.

"He's so glossy." Her voice glides in and interrupts my thoughts. I've been busy grooming my bay gelding, Fizz, lost in my own mind and didn't even hear her approaching.

"That he is. Fizzy loves a compliment, too." Sure enough he's nuzzling Skylar, looking for a bit of extra attention. "How's it going down there?"

"I think I'm all done. You might have to check my work, though, Mr. Rhodes." Her lips roll together, and lashes flutter. Baby blues bounce between my eyes, down to my mouth, then up to my hat. She settles her gaze there, lingering, and her tongue darts out to wet her lips.

Tossing the brush into the bucket next to my boots, I tuck my hands in my jacket pockets and close the distance between us. Advancing slowly, watching eagerly as Skylar retreats with a teasing little smile playing on her lips until her back makes contact with the wooden wall.

"Did you get distracted on the job, sweetheart?" I selfishly eat up the way her pupils dilate and lips part on a shallow exhale.

"Maybe." Small white puffs leave her lips with the heat of her breath on the crisp air.

It's way too goddamn cold out here to be sinking into her, even though that's a particular fantasy I've played out in my mind's eye one too many times over the past couple of days.

"Can I tell you a secret?" Skylar hums.

"You can tell me anything." I lean one arm over her, high on the wall, brushing our bodies together.

She bites her bottom lip, and the glassy look in her eyes spells my impending doom. Because I know it—I know whatever comes out of this girl's mouth next, I'll agree to.

Her tiny fingers curl into the front of my jacket, and she goes up on tiptoes. I have to duck my head lower so that she can reach my ear and it sends a shudder roaming through me.

Illicit thoughts drift in of having days, months, years on end when this could be a reality between us.

"I'm sorry, Mr. Rhodes, but I forgot to put any panties on." Skylar's voice is a sultry whisper. "And I can feel you running down my thighs."

"Jesus." I swallow thickly. My pulse starts thudding as hard as hoofbeats in my neck.

"Then you had to go and stroll around in that hat and those jeans . . . and . . ." She peeks up at me through a heavy curtain of lashes.

"Are you telling me that your needy little pussy is out here bare and slutty and dripping with my cum?" With my other hand that's not leaning on the wall, I rub my thumb back and forth across her bottom lip before tugging it down.

I'm fucking addicted to the way her pupils blow out when I treat her this way. A little bit stern but mostly just teasing her and telling her how perfect she is.

Goddamn, if it doesn't make everything insanely hot knowing that my cum is still inside her from when I had her bent over the bathroom counter this morning.

"Do you want to see?" Her words are soft. Delicate. Just like her.

Fuck. I might just forget my damn mind and propose to this girl.

"I didn't think I could find a way to fuck you out here, but I might have to change that plan." I press my thumb into her mouth, and the good girl she is, Skylar swirls her tongue around and laps at the pad.

Pushing off the wall, I grasp my hat and lift it off, placing it over her pastel-pink waves.

As I sink down to my knees in front of her, those blue eyes widen, and her lips hang parted as she watches me.

I give her a wink as my fingers hook into her waistband. "Suits you, sweetheart."

"Does it?" Her fingers seek out my hair in the way I'm absolutely addicted to. I want those nails digging into my scalp and tugging hard as often as possible.

"*Mmmm.* You're gonna have to let me see you wear it from

another angle, just so I can really get a good look at you." I flick the button on her jeans. "I think you're gonna have to ride me with *only* that on. Right now, there are too many clothes on this perfect body for me to be certain."

She laughs, a light tinkling feminine sound, the kind of playful noise that is so foreign in this barn but that feels so fucking right. Her stomach caves as my fingers press against the softness of her skin.

Just as I work her jeans down, just as I lean forward to lick a long line over her pouty clit—plump and begging for my attention—and suck it into my mouth, there's the sound of a vehicle outside.

Tires crunch over the snow, muffled music plays as the two people I certainly have no interest in seeing pull up next to the barn.

"Oh my god." The fingers that should be guiding me to exactly where Skylar wants my long, slow kisses are now tugging me off her. "Is it Brad?"

I hastily wipe my mouth on the back of my hand. Fucking fuck.

"Christ. Do you want me to get rid of him?" I get to my feet, helping pull her jeans back up. I'd gladly give anything, find any excuse under the sun, to tell my son to fuck right off right now.

She bats my hands away. Eyes gone round as the moon. "Just go stall him," she hisses.

I hate everything about what this means . . . that our time has ended in an abrupt halt. If I'd known this morning was our last chance to be alone together, I wouldn't have come to the stables at all.

"It's okay. Go." She jerks her head and fastens her jeans, then turns. Only, she falters for a second and quickly pulls my hat off and thrusts it back into my hands before she vanishes out of the stall.

Slipping away from me without an opportunity for a proper goodbye.

CHAPTER 21

Skylar

"You can't leave town. Stay." Brad crosses his arms. "What the fuck are you gonna do, Sky? Have the world's most miserable New Year pity party all by yourself?"

I'm being stared down by my best friend and his boyfriend, who are determined to keep me here stuck in torturous longing for the man sleeping in the room across the hall.

Because even though Brad and Flinn have their own home on this ranch, they've been my own personal shadows since arriving back.

Under normal circumstances, this is exactly how things would be between us if I ever came to stay. We'd be in each other's back pockets from dawn until long after midnight.

Except now, I'm painfully aware of the other Rhodes man in this house, who I haven't seen since our near miss at the stables yesterday morning.

"Look, it's only three more sleeps until New Year's Eve."

"And you know he's going to be fucking insufferable if you don't stay, so do me a solid, would you, please, love?" Flinn looks up from his phone where we're all sitting around the farmhouse kitchen table.

The one I was splayed out on, covered in whiskey and Lucas Rhodes's wicked mouth, only a few nights ago.

"Fine. Fine. I'll stay for your silly little party," I tease. "But in return, you gotta help me get my tire and stealth rescue my car."

"You sure you don't want to just claim it got stolen? We could torch it and dump it out on a back road somewhere?"

"Oh my god. Are you insane? I don't need Sheriff Hayes on my ass, thank you."

Brad chuckles. "He's hot. I wouldn't mind that man being all up in my business."

From across the other side of the table, Flinn gives him an eye roll. "I'm literally *right here*."

"Oh, don't pretend like you haven't checked that man's ass out in a pair of jeans before."

"Either way," I say, interrupting the man crush going on over our local sheriff, "we're not disposing of my car. Don't be ridiculous, Bradford Rhodes."

"What? It's an ugly fucking ride." He shrugs, gets up, and starts rummaging in the fridge.

"It's served me well, I'll have you know," I huff.

"Okay, so let's make a plan to get your tire sorted and grab your car." Flinn ignores his idiotic boyfriend and taps on his phone screen. "The garage is open today but closes again until after the new year. So today's our chance to get this shit done."

"Thank you, Flinny. At least one of you assholes is helpful."

"Hey, Dad . . . you need anything from town? We're going in to sort out Sky's car," Brad calls out, and that's when I feel his presence.

My cheeks immediately heat, and I have to fight every urge in my blood to turn around in my chair. I want to throw myself into his arms so goddamn badly it hurts. Which is why I can't let myself even glance his way, because if I do, it'll be too obvious. There isn't a chance in hell I could keep my head on straight or emotions in check when it comes to that man.

The familiar deep, rich sound of him clearing his throat sends goosebumps flying over my skin. "I'll text you a list."

"Sweet. Anything you want us to pick you up for dinner?" Brad heads over to collect our jackets, and yet I keep myself rooted firmly in place. Pretending to read something on my phone.

"No, I'm good. You kids do your own thing for dinner." That's all he says, and then as quickly as he appeared, he's gone.

I hear Brad and Flinn chatting animatedly as I trail after them out of the house, and we all pile into their truck, but I'm only half paying attention to anything in my surroundings. My mind is stuck in a loop of memories of Luke's touch, his kisses, his lips tipping up into a small smile.

The guys occupy the front seats, and as I buckle myself in, my phone vibrates in my pocket.

Brad's Dad:
I wish I could be the one to help you today.

I hate that I can't.

My eyes shoot up to my friend, who is driving and playing rock, paper, scissors with his boyfriend to decide what to have for dinner.

Oh my god. I have to bite the inside of my cheek because I might just swoon right out of this vehicle.

I wish you could, too.

God, there are so many other things I want to say to him. *I miss you already. I want to feel your arms around me. I think I'm in love with you.*

Except it's not possible. Nothing between us was ever going to be more than a temporary bit of fun. To work through the sexual chemistry we have, but both knew it was going to end as soon as Brad came home.

Probably for the best.

Really?

With how beautiful you look today . . .

Let's just say that tire might have been the last thing on my mind.

I'm blushing so damn hard right now. I have to sink into my coat collar to avoid giving away the goofy look on my face.

Mr. Rhodes.

Are you flirting with me?

I shouldn't be.

Do you want to?

Butterflies erupt in my stomach, watching the tiny dots bounce on the screen for what seems like an eternity, stopping and starting before his reply finally comes through.

Sweetheart, I want everything when it comes to you.

CHAPTER 22

Lucas

My son is officially the biggest cock block I've ever met.

After he spent the day yesterday helping Skylar get a new tire, replacing her spare, *and* making sure she was fixed up and able to drive safely to park up here at the ranch, I suppose I should be proud of him.

When in reality, I'm insanely fucking jealous of the fact he and Flinn have been able to take care of her in all the ways I want to be able to.

It's been two nights.

Two nights without her, when she's been in the guest room just across the hall. I've laid in bed restlessly arguing with myself and my moral fiber. Weighing up the possibility of whether I can steal her away to be with me in the midnight hours when no one, except our guilty consciences, could possibly know.

Because Skylar made it clear that she wouldn't do anything to hurt Brad and that she doesn't want this to ruin my relationship with him.

So, who am I to go against her wishes?

The easiest solution has been to stay away. To find a hundred and one jobs to do around the ranch and let them all hang out together, getting things ready for this New Year's Eve party.

This is how everything would *usually* be in the past when Skylar spent time here.

Except, in all those years, all that time she spent around the place, that wasn't when she was on my mind twenty-four fucking seven. Now she is, and I can't erase her from my thoughts.

The three of them have been hanging out here at the house since Brad and Flinn's place is barely more than a single-room cabin. It works perfectly for just the two of them but isn't exactly big enough for having guests over. Right now, the guys are sprawled out side by side on the couch, with some shitty action movie pulled up on the big screen. All I can see is the backs of their heads, while Skylar is curled up in one of the large armchairs over by the window, giving me a perfect view of her side profile. Her Kindle is balanced on her lap, and I'm immediately transported back to Christmas Day, lying with her tucked against my side on the couch . . . and everything that came after.

Fuck.

I have to subtly readjust myself as I linger in the kitchen. Truth be told, I walked in, saw Skylar, and promptly forgot what I meant to come in here for.

She's so much better at this than me, managing to keep a straight face and not look my way every three seconds, which is all I seem to be able to do whenever we're in the same room.

Thank fuck, because if it were up to me, I would have given our entire secret away far too quickly.

After texting her briefly when they went to get her tire replaced and collect her car, I've opened and composed what feels like a hundred new messages. Only, each time I inevitably hit delete, seeing as I shouldn't be saying any of the shit I actually want to say. There's also always too much of a risk my son will pick up her phone or see what's on the screen, which has been enough to have me silently cursing and shoving my phone back in my pocket.

However, right now, I can see that the guys are occupied with whatever they're watching. Brad might even be asleep from what I can tell.

Stop biting your lip so hard.

Crossing my ankles, I lean my ass back against the sink. Partly hidden by the large island in the middle of the kitchen, it's easy to hang back here while still being able to see through to the lounge with the open-plan layout.

I don't hear her phone make a sound; however, as I watch on, she picks it up immediately, which leads my pulse to race a little harder.

Has she been keeping it on silent, just in case I do text her again?

Ever the tease, Skylar quickly types on the screen without looking my way or allowing her expression to change. If anyone were to look at her, she could be texting her goddamn grandmother for all they would know.

My phone buzzes in my palm.

Sweetheart:
Sorry, but it's not easy.

Not when you're making it impossible for a girl to concentrate.

Do I distract you?

No.

I can see you squirming.

You don't "distract" me.

Because it's impossible to be a distraction when I already can't stop thinking about you.

Good.

Then I'm not the only one going insane over here.

I heard you get up during the night.

Kinda hoped it was because you were gonna sneak into my room . . .

Even though I know we can't.

Sweetheart, it took everything in me not to.

I honestly don't know if I can fight it anymore.

We said we wouldn't.

I know.

But I'm a terrible fucking person.

I can't stay away from you.

I see her shift around in her seat, and if I didn't know any better, I'd say she looks incredibly turned on.

"I'm gonna go take a shower." Skylar hops up out of her chair. The other two barely even move, just make a grunting sort of noise in acknowledgement that is more reminiscent of Brad as a teenager rather than a young man in his twenties. "You guys keep watching, and I'll reheat some leftovers for us for dinner once I'm done, yeah?"

She scoops her phone and Kindle up, then crosses toward the stairs.

Our eyes lock.

Those baby blues are almost turned to a deep shade of sapphire, pupils blown out with lust.

My cock is already straining against the front of my jeans.

I let her carry on up to the guest room, hanging impatiently in the kitchen, listening to each footstep, trying to figure out how goddamn long I need to wait before following straight after her. Brad and Flinn seem oblivious to the fact that I'm even here, engrossed in what they're watching or possibly both half asleep anyway.

The sound of water running drifts down from upstairs.

I'm going to hell for even contemplating this.

It takes everything in me not to mount the steps two at a time. I creep up as quietly as possible.

Skylar has left her bedroom door open just a crack, and I slip inside, twisting and lifting the handle in exactly the way I know will allow it to shut on silent hinges.

A trail of clothes leads me straight to the bathroom, and when I step through the doorway, my girl is already naked and wet. Her spine rests against the tiled walk-in shower, with swirling steam filling the room, and a glide of soapy bubbles coats those perfect fucking tits and softness of her stomach.

She hits me with eyes I could goddamn drown in and lifts a finger to her lips.

My eyes drop down to see where her other hand dips in between her thighs. Already working herself, rubbing in small circles over her clit.

I don't need a second fucking invitation.

My clothes hit the floor, and I'm on her, barely stifling a

groan as I hoist her legs around my waist. Holding her tight with her fingers clung around my neck, I shove inside that velvety channel I've been fantasizing about. Having to settle instead for fucking my fist the past couple of nights, choking on her name, desperately missing being wrapped together just like this.

"Oh god." She lets out a soft moan as my cock shoves deep inside. I almost bite my tongue in half with how unbelievably slick she is. This girl is an absolute mess, her pussy is drenched, and it makes me goddamn feral to know this is the state she's in while thinking about me.

Using one arm to band her soft body against mine, I cover her mouth with my free hand. "Shh, sweetheart. You're going to get us caught making slutty little noises like that," I whisper. The water beats down on my back, and I'm sure no one could hear a thing even if they were standing right outside the door, but we both know it's the middle of the afternoon, and we've not got much time.

Her eyes flash, and she laps her tongue against my palm. The curve of her lips forming a smile beneath my touch is everything.

I drive my hips forward.

Skylar's nails dig into my nape, and she tightens around me like a fucking dream.

It's fast and desperate between us; my hips pump into her, keeping her body pressed up against the wall, and I lose any sense of time.

I know it has to be quick. I know I can't linger here. I know we're already crossing that line we said we wouldn't once the snow cleared.

But, holy fuck, this girl is everything.

She keeps squeezing me tighter and tighter, and it's obvious she's as wound up in a frenzy as I am. The headiness of this moment is almost too much. My teeth are gritted against the sounds that want to burst out of me, that want to explode in a series of grunts and guttural roars of pleasure in time with my dick. Tingling builds in my balls and at the base of my spine as I feel my climax racing forward.

Skylar's fingers pull on my hair harder and harder as I feel her body tense up. I drive in deep, thrusting, snapping my hips, chasing the sensation of release we've both been in agony without, because I know it's been the same for her.

I quickly withdraw my hand and replace that point of contact with my mouth. Covering hers with my own in a harsh, desperate kiss. Seeking out her clit, everything is in a race to the finish line, when all I want to do is sink into her over and over. I wish we had hours ahead to indulge in as many orgasms as possible, but this right here, a quick fuck in her shower, is what I'll take if that's all I can have of her.

She gasps against my lips, trying her hardest to stay quiet, and I suck down on her tongue as I rub hard over her swollen, slippery clit.

My gorgeous girl, my ultimate temptation, absolutely shatters like a dream. She can't help the noise she makes into my mouth, and I do my best to swallow it down. As she squeezes the life out of me, like a fist wrapped around my length, my own wave peaks and crashes. My cock throbs as I plunge forward and hold, jerking and pulsing inside her. Cum shoots deep, and it all feels so good; it's always so good with her, feeling like it goes on and on. Like I can't stop coming.

She's still fluttering and rippling around my length. Our mouths are nothing but sloppy kisses as our hearts both thunder in time to the water pounding down.

I just want to keep holding her.

I want to march her to that bed and lick her cunt, to taste both of us there, to hear her moan my name over and over as her thighs clamp down around my head.

Only, we can't fucking do any of those things.

She has to go downstairs, and I have to make myself scarce once more.

CHAPTER 23

Skylar

"You need me to do what, with the what?" I blink at Brad. He should know by now I'm not to be trusted with anything important in this kitchen. *Any* kitchen.

"You'll be fine, Sky. Just keep an eye on the pan, and if anything starts to stick, just turn it." He shrugs into his coat, keys jangling. "I gotta go pick up a few more things from the grocery store for the party tomorrow. I'll be half an hour, tops."

"Don't come for me if these meatballs are all burnt to fuck by the time you get back." I cross my arms and give him a petulant eye roll.

"I have faith in you," he calls over his shoulder.

"No, you don't," I shout after him. "At least bring me back some ice cream, bitch."

The sound of the front door shutting is all I get in reply. I'm tugging out my phone from my back pocket to text him my demands for rich, chocolatey, frozen goodness, when I feel the heat of a broad chest behind me. The proximity and suddenness make the fine hairs stand up on my arms.

"Are these supposed to be charred?" Luke's voice is so close it makes me jump.

"What? No . . ." I spin round in an immediate panic, shoving at his immovable shoulder to get a proper look at the pan. They were fine and sizzling and definitely *not* burnt two minutes ago. "All I did was check my phone; they can't be burnt already."

That's when I realize what's really going on. The mountain of a man beside me has his hand over his mouth, dark eyes twinkling with mirth.

Lucas Rhodes is laughing at me.

"Oh. Not funny. Not funny at all." I pout.

"You're cute. Grab yourself a drink, and I'll keep an eye on all this." Luke nudges my hip with his thigh and I suck in a sharp breath. My eyes immediately fly up to check our surroundings, but the house is quiet. We're the only ones here.

"Flinn's down at their place. I just saw him as I left the stables, and Brad won't be back for a little bit longer." He absently tucks a strand of hair behind my ear, and I just about dissolve into a puddle on the floor, right there, in the middle of the kitchen.

"Do you want something?" My voice is suddenly hoarse. Me? My entire heart and soul, perhaps?

"A beer would be perfect." He sets about fussing with the tongs and the pan, and I think my heart is suddenly about three times too big for my chest.

I grab each of us a drink and hand him one. As I do so, he hooks my pinky finger with his, not letting me step away.

"I was serious yesterday." That rich, gritty voice rumbles through my senses. "I can't stay away from you, sweetheart . . . but you say the word, and I'll respect that. I'll keep my distance, alright?"

"I just wish . . ." I swallow thickly. Not entirely sure what I want to say in this moment.

"Your friendship is more important, I get that. Brad means the world to both of us. I couldn't live with myself if my selfishness ruined any aspect of what you have as friends."

A heavy sigh gusts out of my lungs. I have to fight the urge to sink against his chest and wrap my arms around his broad torso.

Luke holds my chin, sweeping his thumb over my bottom lip. "In another life. In *any* other life, I'd track you down and wouldn't let you go. You're worth that and so much more, Skylar."

I'm gaping up at him. Frozen in place at the sincerity in his words and tenderness in his usually chiseled, gruff exterior.

Goddamn this man for stealing my heart when I know that I can't stay here beyond tomorrow.

Words aren't forming, even though I'm trying, and failing, to find the right thing to say in reply. To articulate the increasingly complicated set of feelings I have for this cowboy.

But the outside world beats me to it. The front door bangs, and I hear Flinn come inside, midway through a conversation on the phone. His boots thud one by one as he kicks them off in the hallway, and that's my cue to put some distance between us.

Luke sets his beer down and turns back to the pan on the stove, but not before sliding me one last look that will stay imprinted on my mind forever.

"Remember all that when the next guy comes along."

Skylar

"Sky, you're gonna give me no choice but to revoke your technology privileges like you're some sort of scowly teenager." Brad nudges me with his elbow, and I almost drop my phone with a start. "You're missing the party, too busy getting lost in your emails. Work can wait till after the holidays," he scolds before turning back to pour drinks for some other friends.

Flames lick my cheeks, and I'm silently hoping it doesn't give away my secrets immediately. There's a reason I've been staring at my phone, zoned out, and it has nothing to do with work, my best friend, or the New Year's Eve party flowing merrily around me.

It has absolutely everything to do with one particular cowboy who has occupied every shred of my attention.

Well . . . more to the point, his *absence* has preoccupied me to the point of distraction.

Luke has been MIA the entire evening as the house has filled up with laughter and music.

Thanks to overhearing Brad and Flinn chatting with some of the other guests here tonight, I've deduced that my cowboy crush is busy with the grill somewhere outside.

Which is possibly for the best. I don't know how successful I might have been at keeping my composure around him tonight. Not when this lounge, the kitchen, even the guest room I'm staying in upstairs—every single room and almost every surface within—reminds me of how badly I want Lucas Rhodes.

We've thoroughly utilized every inch of this house in the time since our agreement began and ended. Now, I can't look around without a replay of illicit memories, recollections of epically heated proportions, no matter where my eyes land.

A cluster of Brad's friends are seated on the couch, swapping rodeo stories, and I have to take a hasty gulp of my soda, thinking back to all the ways Luke and I spent Christmas Day lost in each other on those very same cushions.

God.

I could seriously use some cold night air right now.

Except, I also don't know how I might handle bumping into Luke, especially being in a situation where we'll both be around all these people. Stuck knowing that I can't do anything except smile politely and pretend to only be the girl who spent summers here hanging out with her best friend.

Not like I lost my heart to him years ago when I'm sure the man didn't even know my full name.

My phone buzzes in my hand, and a flutter kicks up in my stomach. Hoping the name I'll see on screen might be that of my best friend's father.

Mom:
Happy ALMOST New Year.

Your dad and I are officially neck deep in crab claws and trying to find our way to the bottom of bottomless mojitos.

How's Brad's party going?

Sigh. This is much less interesting than receiving a secret text from the man who makes my pulse race.

Is he thinking about me at all tonight? Is it killing him to not be reaching out for one another, like it's killing me not to be near him?

No. Skylar. You need to seriously snap out of it. We agreed to this like two very boring, sensible adults.

Boo.

Inwardly I pout at my morals remaining firmly set in place.

Sounds like you guys have got a fun night planned.

We're good here. Brad and Flinn send their love.

Oh, we'll be tucked up in bed long before midnight.

Not like you young'uns partying into the small hours.

I think you've got the right idea.

I'm not sure I'll survive until twelve.

Very boring, blah blah, I know.

Oh, honey. I'm sorry things
didn't work out with Jeremy.

You know I'm only a phone call away
if you need to talk about it.

"Sky . . ." I hear Brad's voice tutting at me, and he swipes my phone out of my hand.

Oh my god. My stomach drops into the soles of my boots. Thank fuck it's my darling mother's beaming smile and words on the screen and not someone else's contact details—that could have led to an extremely awkward moment of discovery.

Brad furrows his brow as he scans the last texts and gives me a look that I can interpret without needing to exchange words.

"I'm doing fine. Promise." I cross my heart.

"You're not just putting on a brave face for the sake of a stupid party?" He drops his voice low and hands me back my phone. Bless him for being so endlessly big hearted.

"I'm totally okay. Go, play host." I shove his shoulder. And the idea pops into my head, with words coming out before I can stop them. "Actually, my folks want to have a cute little family video chat at midnight. You know what they're like when they've had a few drinks and want to talk my ear off." Shrugging, I point at my phone.

Holy shit. I'm about to be so goddamn reckless.

"You don't mind if I disappear while you and Flinn are busy sucking face as the clock strikes midnight?" My lips twist into a grin while my heart kicks inside my chest.

I'm very rapidly forming a plan, one that my parents are about to unknowingly become accomplices in, and if all goes the way I imagine, it could . . . I might just secure my opportunity to welcome in the New Year with the only person I want to be wrapped up in.

Brad rolls his eyes at me, mouthing something rude, and someone calls out his name from the other side of the room.

My stomach swoops, and I check the time. It's still relatively early, but if I plan my next moves just right, I might be able to steal away for one final game with Lucas Rhodes after all.

CHAPTER 24

Lucas

My house is filled with people, music, and laughter.

Brad is in his fucking element, practically buzzing with joy as he makes sure everyone is enjoying themselves and putting on one heck of a night to celebrate the ranch.

I gotta hand it to him—the kid knows the value of networking and being *peopley*. Thank fuck he's got the gift because I certainly don't.

Instead, I've been firmly planted in front of the grill, keeping busy with the night air for company and an excuse to be away from the crowd. There are plenty of people I know here tonight, and most have sought me out for a chance to chat and catch up, shooting the shit before heading back inside into the warm.

Another reason I've kept myself occupied in this spot is to not follow Skylar around like some kind of stray dog. The girl deserves a night with her friends, and I wish it was a different set of circumstances between us, but it's easier this way.

The night is crisp, not below freezing, but cold enough that I've been pleased to have a hot flame to warm myself in front of.

It's getting closer to midnight, and I know I should probably put in an appearance inside. Mingle, or some shit.

Just as I'm steeling myself to enter the house, my phone buzzes in my pocket. That small vibration sends a twitch through my lips and a jerk straight to my cock.

Sweetheart:
Where are you?

Outside, packing up the grill.

Having fun?

Not as much as if you were here.

I know you've been hiding.

I catch myself smirking at my phone like a goddamn teenager.

How much have you had to drink?

Not much, a couple earlier on.

Aren't you enjoying yourself?

I've been waiting for midnight . . .

What happens at midnight?

You meet me at the barn.

A dark groan escapes out of me as I scrub one hand over my mouth at the sight of those six words on screen.

I don't think that's possible.

There are too many people. How are you gonna slip away?

I've already told Brad my parents want to video call me at twelve, so I'll need to disappear off somewhere quiet to chat with them.

Don't you think it's too risky?

Well, either you meet me there and fuck me at midnight, or you can watch me ride my fingers until I make myself come when I send you the video.

Your choice.

Holy crap. This girl. She knows I've already lost this battle. I don't even need to see her face to know the way her lips will be quirking, the way her blue eyes will be sparkling.

You've got two minutes to get your ass out of that party.

The only way you're gonna be falling apart is if my cock is filling your perfect cunt.

Yes, Daddy.

Jesus.

You're trying to kill me.

Well, I'm wet and need you inside me.

Clock's ticking. One minute.

This time, instead of text in reply, an image comes through. It's of her hand holding a bottle of whiskey, and even though the background is dark, I can see that she's already two steps ahead of me.

Skylar is already inside the barn.

My pulse hammers in my neck as I slide the wooden door closed behind me.

It's dark in here, and the horses make little huffing noises, asking me what the fuck is going on and why we're intruding on them at this time of night.

There's a faint glow from the far end, inside the tack room, and I head straight there.

Sure enough, that's where I find my girl.

Except, I stop in my tracks in the doorway when I see her. She's wrapped up in her coat, but her makeup is bolder than usual, her hair styled into loose curls. She's got the same boots and tights on as the first night she hurtled back into my life when I picked her up amongst the snow.

Stunning doesn't even do Skylar Addams justice.

She's perched on a saddle stand and wiggles the neck of the bottle in my direction, eyes bouncing over me.

"You look hot as fuck." She beams my way, and I don't know what the hell I've done to deserve a single moment with this girl.

My tongue pokes against the side of my mouth, and I allow the weight of my gaze to linger on every inch of her in return.

"It's a good thing I didn't see you earlier, or we might not have made it to midnight without me trying to steal you away."

Skylar blushes and it's cute as hell. "You want to have a drink with me?"

"No." My boots thud as I cross the space between us.

The sweetest little laugh erupts from her as she lets me steal the whiskey and set it on the shelf before cupping her face, tasting those lips, sinking our mouths together in a deep fucking kiss. One that I've been dreaming of in a constant loop of memories since our desperately quick moment in the shower.

"How long do we have?" Drawing back, I already know it won't ever be goddamn long enough.

Skylar makes a seductive little noise against my lips. "How fast can you get inside me?"

Reaching up, I grab my hat and set it over her hair, brushing a few loose strands behind her ear as I do so.

"You see, that's where we've got a problem, sweetheart." My palms find her thighs, and I lower myself onto my knees in between her parted legs. The place I will happily always occupy for this girl. "I don't want to do anything *fast*. I want to take my time, and I want to spend hours lost inside this perfect cunt of yours."

She lets out a little moan as I hitch her coat higher and hook the soft jersey material of her dress at the same time. My good girl braces herself so I can separate her thighs even wider.

"Then, give me your phone." Skylar runs her fingers through my hair, tugging a little to tilt my head up toward her.

My heart stalls.

"Are you serious?"

"I want to watch. You want to take your time. Sounds like a good compromise if you can spend as much time replaying this moment as you want." Her teeth catch that pouty bottom lip, and I damn near groan.

"How the fuck are you so perfect?" I dig my phone out of my pocket, unlock the screen, and hand it to her.

"Better save this somewhere safe." Skylar's voice is a little husky as she hits me with the most tempting of looks, pink hair framing her gorgeous heart-shaped face, my hat perched on top of her head. It's a sight I'm already imprinting and committing to memory, with or without a video on my phone.

Her fingers sink into my hair once again with a soft hum of pleasure, and that's when I realize she's already recording. The light of the camera flash plays over the place where my palms wrap her thighs, and she pans up to where she holds onto my hair, threading her grip in the spot where I know my streak of white stands out.

"Are you gonna keep quiet for me? Or do you want to be loud? Do you want all your sweet little moans recorded on camera?"

I don't give her time to answer, maybe because part of me isn't sure it's a good idea to have her say anything. Just in case someone ever did watch this when they shouldn't, I selfishly don't want anyone to know it's her.

Working the coat and dress all the way up to sit above her hips, that's when I have to pause. Skylar holds on to my head a little tighter, keeping the camera trained on my face, and I run my tongue across the swell of her inner thigh, giving her a stern glare as I do so.

"We've talked about this, sweetheart." My teeth nip her delicate flesh, and she yanks harder on my hair in response. "It looks like you've forgotten your panties . . . again."

A soft little noise gusts past her lips, like she's as relieved as I am we've somehow found a way to be in this position once more.

This time, my girl is completely bare.

Garters hold her tights up, hooked to a belt around her waist, and holy fuck, I swear my heart nearly stops at how sexy this girl is. Her hips shift as my mouth roams closer and closer. The whole time, I'm keeping my eyes fixed on her. Looking straight into that camera lens because I don't know if she'll ever keep a copy of this video for herself, but goddamn, do I want her to know exactly how obsessed I am with every little thing.

"Look at your pretty little cunt. Already dripping wet, and I haven't even touched you yet."

Above me, she angles the camera so that her pussy and my mouth is the main show. My hands come up to push her thighs wide, and using each thumb, I part her. It's lewd and filthy, and she's entirely goddamn gorgeous. Swollen and slick, ready to be devoured.

"You know what would happen if I had you to myself all night? I'd lick this pretty little cunt until you begged me to stop. I'd have you shaking and soaking my face and telling me you couldn't take any more, but we'd both know that's a lie. Because you want this all day and all night long, don't you, sweetheart?"

I'm not interested in waiting for a reply; my mouth fastens down on her clit, and Skylar bucks as my tongue slides over her. She makes the most gorgeous noises above me, keeping the camera fixed on where I'm lapping and sucking and working her hard. We don't have the luxury of time, and I need at least a couple of orgasms out of her.

If this is the last moment, truly the *last*, then I need to taste her falling apart on my tongue.

Which doesn't take long.

Skylar is a goddamn dream, shaking and whimpering as I feel her get close to the edge. Sucking down on her clit, my girl dissolves. Her fingers pull on my hair so hard it stings, but I couldn't care less.

Pushing to my feet, my cock is a steel bar, ready to shove into the tight, velvety heat of her.

"This is how perfect you are. The reason I could get lost between your thighs all fucking night long." With one hand, I wrap hers and guide the camera up to make sure she captures this moment. Kissing her, sliding our tongues together, and letting her taste herself there.

Skylar moans into my mouth, her fingers clutching the front of my jacket to steady herself.

In the distance, there's a whole lot of noise that floats on the night air from up at the house.

A countdown.

"Goddamn, I need you wrapped around me, right fucking now." Nipping her bottom lip, I angle her hand to make sure she films what comes next.

Freeing my straining cock, I fist myself and give a few long strokes and eat up the way her eyes follow the glide of my fist.

"Happy New Year, sweetheart," I murmur, positioning myself at her entrance and sliding forward to fit the tip just inside. She's already dripping and messy and takes me perfectly. Stretching and welcoming me into that soft, satiny channel.

The sight of us joined like this is so hot, my balls are already tightening up. Pressure and anticipation are already winding together at the base of my spine.

"I'll never fucking get over this. I'll never fucking get over you." My hips steadily work forward until I'm all the way to the hilt, and her pussy ripples around me.

Holy fuck.

Skylar whimpers louder, biting her lip as hard as she can to keep quiet, her eyes still fixed on the carnal image of where our bodies are joined. She holds the camera trained on that part of us as I withdraw right to the tip. Coated in the sheen of her arousal and glistening in the light of the camera.

"Christ. That's so fucking sexy." My voice is a deep rasp.

I slide forward, nearly losing it completely when she clamps down around me. She's fighting it, already lingering close to the edge. Maybe it's the fact that we're filming this moment. Maybe it's the fact we both know this is really it—the last time we can do this. Maybe it's the fact we've only got minutes left before I have to somehow get her back to the house without looking like she's just had her brains fucked out.

Whatever it is, it drags us both to the edge, real fucking fast this time around.

I pump in and out, hooking one of her legs high so I can really open her up to show the camera exactly how insanely good this moment is.

That's when I feel her squeeze harder, tightening around me, her muffled, desperate noises coming out in time with each punch of my hips. Skylar's just as close to falling apart as I am. Using my thumb, I find her clit and add that pressure I know will get her there.

I don't even know what I'm saying. It's a string of filthy fucking words. Telling her how perfect her cunt is. That she's gorgeous when she's leaking my cum. How I'd spend all night owning every single one of her pretty little holes if I could. That she's my perfect little slut, who deserves to be bent over right here next to the saddles while I pump her full.

Skylar detonates on a low moan. Clamping down and gasping. It's all so fucking intense that my own release follows right behind. My balls draw up, my dick jerks, and I bury myself to the hilt. Holding there as my seed spills and coats her channel, hardly able to register anything except for the pounding rush of blood in my ears.

Both her arms wrap around the back of my neck, filming long forgotten, as Skylar seeks out my mouth. I cradle the back of her head, holding my hat so it gives me access to her mouth but doesn't tumble to the dirt. We kiss in a way that reminds me of being so much younger, without the burdens of being a solo parent, without the stresses and pressures that come with running this ranch. Being with her eases so much of that, in a way I can't fucking explain. As she hums and melts against my mouth, lapping at my tongue and kissing me with all the warmth and goodness that is just *her*, I know it just feels right holding her. As if all those things that on the bleakest day feel like such a struggle, I'd easily face them knowing Skylar Addams was mine.

God, I want to tell her, but that would be madness.

She's leaving first thing in the morning, and her life is waiting for her. I'd never ask her to give up that dream she's working on, and I'd never risk her friendship with my son.

This is the type of kiss that lets me tell Skylar I'm in love with her, but it's also the one that tells this beautiful girl that I'm letting her go.

Even though I hate that I have to.

I hate that we'll still be circling each other in that inevitable way people do when there's a connecting point between us—Brad. It kills me to think I'm going to be stuck on the sidelines, seeing her continue to live out her life and thrive.

As we pull back and I study her in the deep shadows, Skylar looks at me with that same expression as a year ago when she sat in the front seat of my truck with her hand resting on the door.

Only this time, she brings my phone back around and angles it so that it takes in the sight of her wearing my hat.

A sight I'm never going to be able to stop replaying in my mind's eye.

I'm still buried deep inside her when she brings our mouths back to touching. Our lips brush together with the warmth and wetness there of our kisses.

This time she positions the camera to record the way we're joined, and she brushes her mouth over mine, nudging our noses together. Skylar's voice is a gentle, feather-like sound playing over my mouth.

"Thank you for taking care of me . . . Happy New Year, Mr. Rhodes."

CHAPTER 25

Skylar

ONE MONTH LATER

"You can drop by anytime after ten a.m. tomorrow and collect the arrangement, Ms. Heartford."

I feel the vibration in my palm, letting me know I have another call incoming. Pulling the phone away from my ear a little, I see "Brad" flash up on the screen.

That second of recognition is immediately followed by the pout in my heart that it's not the name I want to see on my phone. I love my best friend with my whole chest, but fuck if I don't have a whole lot of emotional baggage ready to tumble out of the closet after what happened between me and Luke.

His father.

The cowboy I fell in love with. Agonizingly so.

"Perfect, see you then." I drag my brain back to the job at hand before wrapping up the call. Taking a big, grounding breath, I hit the missed-call notification, redialing the younger of the two Rhodes men.

Brad picks up immediately.

"What are you up to tonight?" He sounds like he's got a mouthful of food.

"I've got a hot date." I pin my phone against my ear with my shoulder and use both hands to start fussing with the gorgeous bouquet being picked up any minute now. A guy called in earlier to order these flowers, all sweaty palms and nerves, because he's proposing to his girlfriend tonight. It was very sweet, and he asked me what I thought about every detail he's got planned for the special moment. Based on how much thought and planning he's put into this, I told him she'll be swept off her feet.

"A date? You do?" Brad sounds stunned.

"Don't be so shocked down to your cute li'l bisexual booties."

"Are you fucking with me?"

That makes me frown. "Since when did I have to report my every single move to you, hmm?"

"Sky . . ." he scolds.

"What? I do. It's this very sexy evening I've got going on. It's called being a small business owner who has to be responsible and do her taxes." I tug on a length of ribbon from the holder, snipping it off, and begin to tie a bow around the gathered stems.

"So, not an actual date?"

"It's as close as I'll get, B." I laugh at how dismally boring my life is. Not bitter about it, at all. "Super romantic, though. Between my laptop . . . my spreadsheet . . . a bit of wine, throw in some cheese, put on a face mask, it's a whole thing."

"Well, let me come crash your incredibly lame night, and I can try to help, or at the very least I'll do face masks with you and feed you ice cream."

"Salted caramel?"

"I've got a pint of that and chocolate fudge. Didn't know what your broken heart would be in the mood for."

I pause. Licking my lips as I try to figure out how to respond.

"You know I'm long over Jeremy. You don't have to mother hen me. I'm honestly fine." Sweeping my palm across the workbench, I gather up the scattered pieces of cut-off stems from the arrangement and toss them in the trash.

After the scene I discovered on Christmas Eve, I cut all contact and blocked his ass everywhere. He can enjoy whoever his kitchen blow-job blondie is. I'll gladly never see the prick ever again.

"I'm not talking about wank-face Jeremy."

My stomach drops.

"I'm talking about whatever jerk you hooked up with on New Year's and have been moping around about ever since."

"I didn't—"

"Look. I'm gonna be on your front porch at six. So you can try to wriggle out of telling me everything then, but spoiler alert, I'm gonna get it out of you."

The door to my shop opens, with the nervous fiancé-to-be arriving right on time to collect his flowers.

"I gotta go, B."

"Face masks and spilling your guts start at six."

"You suck," I hiss.

"I do. Very well, might I add. Just ask Flinn how good my *sucking* is."

I hang up on his hysterical laughter and flash a bright smile while holding out the perfect bouquet to symbolize *love.*

Meanwhile, my heart aches for the loss of my own.

CHAPTER 26

Skylar

There's a half-eaten wedge of brie, two slices of leftover pizza, and a bottle of white wine occupying my otherwise empty fridge.

At least that's dinner sorted for this evening.

Brad knows me well enough that he'll either eat before he comes over or turn up with takeout of some kind.

I've been a fluttering bundle of nerves since his phone call earlier, trying to figure out the best way to sidestep this entire conversation.

There were a few single guys at the New Year party, but Brad is friendly with all of them back in Crimson Ridge, so I can't pretend to shrug it off as if it was some stranger he doesn't know.

I grab everything out of the fridge, which now glares back at me woefully bare, and toss the pizza in the microwave.

The clock tells me I've got five minutes until he's going to arrive, so I go in search of my clay face mask in the bathroom.

Hell, my reflection isn't exactly a sight that will give Brad any confidence that I'm not out here being heartbroken. My hair is gathered up in two messy buns, my oversized hoodie drowns me, and I've got comfy sweats tucked into my even comfier socks.

But, fuck it, I've got my body weight in cheese and chocolate ice cream to consume. Who cares if I'm sporting trash-panda chic? Certainly not the girl who has to figure out a way not to blurt out to her friend that she'd rather be worshipping his dad's cock.

I scoop out a little of the face mask and smear two fingers across my cheek in charcoal gray. Just as I'm about to start layering that bitch on thick, my doorbell rings.

God. Here we fucking go.

With an exaggerated sigh through my nose, I patter my way to the front door, drooping the tub of face mask I'd been carrying on the kitchen counter as I go past.

"Hope you brought food, 'cause I will cut a bitch if you try to steal my piz—"

My throat closes over mid-sentence.

Dark eyes find mine from beneath the brim of a hat I've been dreaming about for weeks on end. A broad chest fills my vision. The scent of leather and the faint hint of soap engulf me.

"Hey."

I blink like a barn owl. Lucas Rhodes is on my doorstep.

"I did bring you something to eat, hopefully that's okay?"

Oh my god. My knees feel like they're going to buckle.

"Luke? What are you doing here?"

"Can I come in?" His lips twitch a little as his eyes sweep over me, leaving a trail of goosebumps in their wake.

"Are you carrying a Crock-Pot?"

"It's called a casserole dish, actually. Do you have mud on your face?" he counters.

I want to die right here. I *do* have mud on my face, and I've got sweats on, and I'm wearing my baggiest, comfiest, least sexy outfit I could possibly have chosen.

Meanwhile, this man looks like the angels plucked him straight from cowboy heaven and delivered him to my door.

"Why are you here?" My knuckles turn white around the door handle.

Luke's brows crease, and he hesitates a moment, sending my pulse into an erratic, thudding mess.

"I told Brad everything. Well, more accurately, he harassed me nonstop after you left, kept on at me until he wore me down, and I told him what was wrong with me."

Oh god. My face pales.

Luke's expression isn't giving me any clues. Is Brad upset? Angry? When I spoke to him earlier, he seemed fine . . .

"He was a bit weirded out at first, but to be honest, Skylar, it's been him convincing me for the past few weeks that I needed to come here and see you."

"Weeks? Brad has known for weeks?" I whisper-screech. Eyes nearly hanging out of my head.

"My kid is a lot of things, but I didn't expect him to be so . . . uhh . . . enthusiastic about me coming over here."

"Luke . . . I . . ."

My heart is doing backflips and somersaults, but I'm so uncertain what this actually means. We haven't spoken since that final night we had together on New Year. No matter how many times I went to text him, I couldn't bring myself to press send because I didn't want to give hope a chance to bloom.

"Skylar, I had to come and see you. I've been battling with myself this past month because all I want is for you to be happy. You've got your life, your business, so much ahead of you, and it would eat away at me if I fucked any of that up by selfishly knocking on your door.

"But you gotta know, I was serious when I said *in another life* . . . and maybe, just maybe, this is our life after all. If there's any chance you might want to let me be part of yours, I gotta have you know my heart is here. It's with you, even if this isn't something you want. I fell harder than I knew could be possible in just a few short days, and I miss you. So fucking much."

I'm not sure I remember how to breathe. It's like I can't process what he's saying because up until five minutes ago, all of this, everything he's laid out that I'd so desperately longed for, didn't seem possible.

My silence causes his shoulders to drop a little.

"I sprung this on you . . . I'm sorry. It was Brad's idea to do some big romantic gesture, but I can go." His voice drops into a soft sigh. "At least let me put this inside for you." Luke gestures at me with the lidded ceramic dish he's still holding in his big hands.

"Just set it down there." I point at the floor.

Luke's jaw clenches, an inner war going on, but he does as I ask, even if I can see the reluctance written all over him.

If only he knew.

There is only one reason I haven't been able to say anything in return . . .

The second his hands are free is when I make my move. I fling myself at him, leaping up to cling to his neck, and he catches me so fucking easily.

The heat of him, the security I feel in his arms, it all washes over me, leaving my blood singing.

"Is this how you invite all your guests inside?" Luke arches an eyebrow at me.

"Just the cowboy I'm in love with." I exhale, bringing our lips together.

Luke walks us through the door, claiming me with a kiss that races straight down to my toes, leaving me a melted puddle in his arms.

I'm a koala, clung to him, and this moment is everything I'd been wishing for since I drove away from his ranch and Crimson Ridge a month ago.

"Don't move." Luke sets me down on the countertop of my tiny kitchenette, places his cowboy hat on my head—at which point I nearly straight-up whimper—then disappears to shut my front door, returning with the dish he'd been carrying and another bag.

I'm an absolute slut for wearing this man's hat.

"Brad wouldn't let me come without bringing ice cream. That boy has got the world's biggest sweet tooth." He shrugs and puts the pints in the freezer while I unashamedly stare at his ass in those jeans.

As he stands there, a gruff noise comes out of him. Crouching down, he opens the fridge door, looking at the array of empty shelves.

"I should've been here sooner." Luke turns around and gives me a long look. "You're gonna let me take care of you." Stepping closer. "You're gonna let me love you the way you deserve." Closer still. "And you're gonna start learning to accept help, sweetheart."

My cowboy comes over to stand between my knees, then tilts my chin up with a crooked finger.

I want all of that . . . but I can't help feeling like I don't deserve it.

"You're serious that Brad's okay with all this?" Searching his eyes, I chew the inside of my cheek. I'm so lost to this man. So in love with him. But at the same time, I feel like such a shitty friend for not being the one to tell him, and it's even worse knowing that Luke has been talking to him about this for weeks.

Luke doesn't answer my question. Instead he sighs and digs out his phone. "By the way, that video . . . I don't even want to admit how many times I've watched it over and over." Hitting me with a look of pure sin, he taps something on the screen, and my body heats, thinking back to the hottest night of my life.

Except, I don't have time to get lost in that memory because Luke holds the phone in front of his face, a video call dialing, as he watches me through dark eyes.

"Put her on, Dad. She's being weird about it, isn't she?"

Oh god. Brad's voice immediately connects at the other end of the line, and I want to dissolve into this kitchen counter.

When he turns the phone around, with a quirk tugging at the corner of his lips, the screen is filled with both Brad's and Flinn's faces, both grinning like fools.

I peek back at them from behind my hands.

"Already *wearing the hat*, I see." He clicks his tongue, and I turn beetroot red. "If I'd known you were aiming to be my stepmother, I might have put in a good word for you with the old man years ago." Brad cackles, his face lit up with mirth.

Groans come from both me and Luke.

"Do you loathe me? You absolutely do, don't you?" I'm bracing myself for the worst.

"Skylar Addams, believe it or not, I want my best friend to be happy . . . Besides, you don't know the *real* story of how Flinn and I got together." The two faces on screen exchange a knowing and entirely-besotted-with-each-other glance before Brad turns his attention back to me. "Anyway, I can't blame you for choosing a Rhodes man; we are superior after all. Even if you got stuck with the second-best option."

"Hey," Luke protests, his voice a deep rumble I've missed so damn much.

My best friend looks far too pleased with himself, like he masterminded this entire situation.

"Okay, so enjoy your date, don't rush back tomorrow, and please for the love of all things holy, do *not* tell me any details." Brad scrunches his face up, and after blowing air kisses and suggestive winks my way, they hang up.

"Tomorrow? What's tomorrow?" I blink at Luke.

"The guys are gonna take care of the ranch, said I wasn't allowed to come home unless you came with me." He sets the phone down and cups my face in two hands, brushing the apple of my cheeks with his thumbs. Giving me a tiny smile when he touches the smear of clay face mask.

"What if I didn't come with you?" I bite my lip, teasing him.

"I'm pretty sure the plan was more or less for me to keep showing up on your doorstep with food every night."

"Trying to lure me like a stray cat?"

Luke brushes over my bottom lip with a thumb, pressing down slightly and sending sparks through my blood with that move he does oh so well.

"Trying to take care of you . . . to show you how much I want to take care of you."

I swallow back the thick wall of emotion threatening to rise.

"Just so you know, *tomorrow* is only because they want to see you. Brad's got this whole plan to cook you dinner and hang out. This isn't about dragging you back to Crimson Ridge. I know your life is here, and your business. I don't have the answers to all that just yet, but I think we're both smart enough to take it one step at a time and make it work."

God. I love this man beyond all reason.

"I've got one question for you . . ." My fingers tentatively roam up the front of his shirt.

"Anything you want, sweetheart." His words are a deep, velvety timbre.

"Would you like to see my bedroom, Mr. Rhodes?"

A wicked glint in his eyes is the only warning I get as he scoops beneath my ass and hauls me against his chest. "If it involves you falling apart while screaming my name, then I want to thoroughly explore every inch of this place. Repeatedly."

His lips seek my own as he walks us the short distance to my bedroom, and I direct him where to go between tugging on his hair and his clothes.

Tumbling us down onto the bed, the weight of him—pinning me down and covering my body—ignites my bloodstream. I'm panting for more, ready to beg if I need to.

"Luke . . ." I thread my fingers into his hair, whimpering his name. "*Please.* I missed you so much. I'm so fucking in love with you. Don't make me wait."

His dark eyes glitter at me in the soft glow of light spilling from the hallway. "You've been my dream for so long. This time I'm not waking up . . . I love you, sweetheart." He drops his mouth to cover mine, letting me drag him down to line our bodies up perfectly, then murmurs softly against my mouth.

"Turns out, wishes really do come true."

EPILOGUE

Skylar

We pull into the long driveway, passing beneath the familiar wooden arch and hanging metal sign to Rhodes Ranch.

Luke has kept my fingers laced with his, tucked on his jean-clad thigh for the entire drive back over to Crimson Ridge as if he's worried I'm going to disappear in a puff of smoke from the front seat.

Little does this cowboy know he's got nothing to fear on that front; however, I might burst into a fiery inferno of embarrassment the second I see Brad and Flinn when we walk through that door hand in hand.

I'm still struggling to come to terms with how unexpected the past day has been, but getting to spend time with my cowboy—no matter how odd it feels to see the man without a horse or ten following him around—has been a gift I certainly am going to cling tight to.

There was also the slightly uncomfortable, but nonetheless important, step of breaking the news to my parents when they threatened to send out a search party after I avoided their first five attempts to video chat with me. My mom looked delighted; meanwhile, my father looked like he needed to go take a long walk to digest the news.

Mom gave me a wink and quietly whispered that she'd have a chat with him over crab claws and a few margaritas at their current favorite beachfront spot for dinner these days.

She also insisted that Luke fly down with me to come and vacation with them during the summer. Considering I'd barely got the words out of my mouth to say that we were together, I wasn't sure if all I'd be left with was the sight of his taillights disappearing over the horizon.

Yet he smiled and hit her with the kind of "yes, ma'am" cowboy charm that had my own damn mother giggling and planning our itinerary before we'd hung up the phone.

I always knew she had a soft spot for the Rhodes men.

Sneaking a glance at his side profile, I can't help but wonder what he's thinking. Luke has been quiet, not awkward or anything like that, but more like he's just *content* as he rubs his thumb absently against my palm, and that makes my heart turn into a sparkling flywheel inside my chest.

However, rather than pulling up to the house straight away like I'm expecting, he stops with the motor running on a sweeping bend that overlooks a part of the ranch that during spring and summer months is used as grazing pasture. I remember all the times younger me used to drive past this very point, seeing the graceful, long necks and sleek coats of the horses glinting in the sunshine as they roamed around.

"Why are we stopping?" I chew my lip.

"Grab your coat." He hops out his door, slips his hat on, and walks around to the hood of the truck.

I do as he asks but am a little bemused.

Luke rests the ass of his perfectly fitted jeans up against the front grill and gestures for me to come stand in front of him. I mean, I'm not gonna ever say no to being tucked in this man's embrace, so I nestle against his front as he wraps his strong arms around me from behind.

"Is this the part where you give me the pep talk about meeting your son?" I tease.

His gruff, rich chuckle tickles my neck as he runs his lips over the sensitive patch of skin below my ear. "You don't need to be nervous." Before I can protest, he adds, "You always make jokes when you're nervous." Intertwining our fingers together, he raises both our right hands, while keeping the other pressed firmly against my stomach. "See that slope over there, sweetheart."

I follow the direction he's pointing in and nod.

"That's south-facing," he says.

My pulse does a little skitter.

"Bet the horses love catching the sun over there." I swallow thickly.

"They do, but it's not the best pasture for them." Luke's deep voice rumbles through me. "What it *would* be perfect for is growing something that needs plenty of sunshine hours . . . something that doesn't mind the ice and the snow."

Hot tears prick the back of my eyes.

"Luke . . ." I exhale.

"You could plant as many varieties as you like there," he murmurs against my neck, and I can feel the emotion bubbling up, ready to overflow with how much I love the man at my back.

"But it's such a long commitment. They take at least a full season to flower. Maybe even longer depending on when they're planted and the age of the plant itself." I don't know why I'm babbling on and making excuses. Because I don't intend on going anywhere, but what this cowboy is already offering is to help make one of my dreams come true, and I don't exactly know what to do with how immense that feels.

"I'm kinda hoping you might stick around long enough to see them bloom, sweetheart."

He spins me around and cups my cheeks in both palms.

All I can do is nod and sniffle and melt under his steady gaze.

"I love you, Skylar. Grow as many peonies as you want here. Let me invest in your dreams."

"You'd seriously do that? Why? I can't let you do that."

He gives me the sexiest smile and brushes his thumbs over my cheeks to swipe away the wetness gathering there. "Because, you're gonna let me look after you, but more than that, you're gonna make those dreams all tucked away in the spreadsheets you've got in that damn phone of yours come to life." He angles his head so he can kiss me, soft, slow, standing here overlooking his ranch, and I feel like I'm floating.

Pulling back, he pushes some strands of hair off my forehead, while I'm busy dissolving into a puddle. "I want to watch you grow your dreams, Skylar, because you're bringing mine to life just by being here with me."

My heart is so full it's about to burst, I swear to god.

"God, I'm so in love with you . . . I didn't think this moment could get any better."

His eyes dance as I say those words. "Sweetheart, it's only just getting started."

THANK YOU FOR READING

I had so much fun writing something sexy, swoony, and fluffy for a holiday-themed trip to Crimson Ridge. Of course, I'm never quite ready to let our favorite cowboys go after typing *The End*. If you're like me and want to stick around to spend a little more time at Rhodes Ranch, grab the extended epilogues:

elliottroseauthor.com/bonuses

Want to be ready to return to Crimson Ridge at the earliest possible moment? Make sure to come and join my reader group—this is where all announcements, behind the scenes exclusive updates, and sneak peeks will be happening:

facebook.com/groups/thecauldronelliottrose

INSTAGRAM: @elliottroseauthor
TIKTOK: @elliottroseauthor

ACKNOWLEDGMENTS

These sweet and steamy holiday love stories arrived in a creative whirlwind, insisting on the addition of Rhodes Ranch to the growing world of Crimson Ridge. As seems to be the pattern with all my best ideas and inspiration moments, the idea for these novellas galloped in during the middle of the night, and now here we are. I'm so excited to share more swoony cowboys and forbidden love stories with you all.

Thank you to Alex Sunshine and the Kensington team for such a beautiful edition: Our cowboys look absolutely stunning!

Of course, these books are as simply jaw-dropping as they are thanks to some immensely talented creatives. Thank yous and the biggest hugs to Sandra from Maldo Designs for this perfect festive cover, and a cowboy-sized thank you to Marta García Navarro for bringing our lovers to life in the most swoon-worthy series of portraits.

To every single reader who has helped share the love for these characters or pressed one of my books into someone's hands, this is for you. Your boundless creativity and excitement for an Elliott Rose character or story simply blows me away, and I am truly grateful to get to share these cowboys with you.

From the bottom of my heart, and from the lovers of Rhodes Ranch . . . thank you for reading.

xo